The Disappearance of Elizabeth Keaton

Table of Contents

Chapter 1

I peered into my rearview mirror. My now eight-year-old daughter was fast asleep. She had been through a lot in the last few weeks with the passing of her mother and then me being moved from our hometown in Miami, Florida to Golden Loch, Michigan for work. It was going to be a good change of pace for the both of us. The pay was decent enough, but that was not the reason I had taken this job. Okay, so maybe I was afraid of admitting that my wife was gone and that I wanted to get out of Miami. However, I was sure my daughter also needed a change of scenery along with the idea that everything could be okay again.

"What are you thinking about?" My Shadow asked me. That's what I called him, my Shadow. He liked it that way. Made it easier to talk about if someone asked, especially being a detective.

"Oh nothing." I could see ghosts and my Shadow was one of them. They call my kind Necromancers, they as in the shadows or ghosts if you will. We also have the ability to raise the dead.

"Don't give me that, Frankie. I know you are thinking about something." His name was Joseph. Crazy thing about it was that he and I were a team. We were inseparable and did everything together. He chose me, or was it the other way around? I'm not entirely sure myself. All I know is that once I pass, he goes on to be with another Necromancer.

"Really, I'm just worried about Jacquelynn." Jacquelynn was my daughter, the girl in the back of the SUV, who was sleeping. She was still a bit young to see ghosts like Joseph. From personal experience, it starts happening at the age of twelve.

"The girl is fierce. She will be fine." Joseph went on to tell me. "Can't wait to meet the ghost that comes to her." Joseph had little to no concept of time, all he knew was that the day passed because we slept. I wasn't sure why he couldn't figure out that the sky was lit up or dark, but I never bothered asking.

We pulled up to a lake home and I got out immediately. Joseph followed. He watched as I walked towards the steps of the house. I examined it, noticing the porch and the steps along with fans in the ceiling right on the porch. How hot did it get around here? I then turned around to face the lake. There was a path that led to the wooden walkway and it ended as it started descending into the river. "It's decent." All around me were trees and off to the side of the house was a long path that led to the road.

"If it has electric and heat, I'm happy." Joseph teased. He was a ghost as I have mentioned, and he had no concept of the weather either. He was also dressed in the clothes that he was buried in.

I rolled my eyes at his comment. "She is four years away from becoming what I am. I want her to have a somewhat normal life between now and then." I opened the car door and picked her up. I carried her to the steps and slowly walked up them as they creaked. I was to fix that at a later date. Right now, I wanted to get inside and put her in her new bed. Once I had, I shut her bedroom door and grabbed our things from the SUV. I walked through the hallways, looking at my own bedroom and back into Jacquelynn's. The bathroom was right outside her bedroom at the end of the hallway while the living area was right across from mine near the front of the house. The kitchen was attached to the living area. The front door was in the living area, right across from the fireplace and the back door was in the kitchen. I went right for the kitchen then made dinner at the new stove.

"How long do you think she'll be out for?" Joseph asked. He had placed himself at the kitchen table, examining me.

I shrugged. "She had a long week with the drive from Miami. I don't want to wake her if I don't need to." I reached for the box of spices and threw together a quick one-person steak and eggs. It was all I had right now.

After dinner, I turned on the TV and watched the newest edition of the news broadcast. I knew I'd eventually drift off into sleep, it really was a long drive and I was tired myself. I also had to go to my job in the morning, although morning was already here. I started to sift through my papers until I found three names. Ashley

Aequitas, Luther Emsworth, and Mathew Reames. Ashley was to be my partner, Luther was my boss, and Mathew was a Lieutenant. We were the crew in this town, so everyone probably already knew them, and I was the outsider in this situation. I had an idea of what I was going to be working on with Ashley, but she had not gone into detail about it over the phone. I looked up when the hallway light came on.

"Daddy?" Jacquelynn called to me, her voice full of sleep.

I smiled looking up towards the hall. "In here, Pumpkin."

Jacquelynn came walking out to me, and I sat her into my lap. "How was your nap?"

"I'm still tired." She grumbled and curled up in my lap. "I miss Mommy."

"I know, I miss her too. She is in a good place though, I promise." I was hoping that was true anyway. Joseph had no word on where she was or what she was doing. It hurt, but I had to trust my gut. I had to live on the idea that she was out there, and she was just fine. I let her fall asleep in my lap and I closed my eyes, drifting off myself.

We both woke on the couch that next morning, I had not realized how late we slept. I had to get her ready for school and then drop her off. "Pumpkin, we need to get going." I hurried her into her bedroom and told her to pick out an outfit. Once she had, I let her get dressed on her own as she had been for the last few years. Though I had to help her with her hair. It was a long golden color just like her mother, while I sported the dark almost blackish hair. She did, however, inherit my green eyes. I pulled her hair back into a ponytail. "Beautiful, just like your mother." We looked into the mirror for a few seconds.

She hugged me and then I sent her outside to wait for me. I grabbed my things from the living area and ushered her into the car. I wasn't really sure where Joseph had gone, but he always came back even when I didn't want him to. He was somewhere, even if I couldn't see him at this very moment. It is like your neighbor taking a walk around the block, you know they are still there you just cannot see them anymore.

I drove Jacquelynn to her new school and parked. "First day of school, you are going to do great."

She beamed and then got out of the car. I watched her make her way up to the school and step inside. I waited until she was gone for a few moments before I was ready to leave. I heard someone knock on my window, so I rolled it down. The man standing there was wearing a green jacket and some slacks. His dark eyes looked bright and happy as he reached out a hand to greet me. "Mr. Dawson, I presume?"

I gave a nod. "Yes, Frankie please. My daughter is Jacquelynn, today is her first day." I pointed towards the school. I wasn't just sitting here; I had my reasons.

"News travels fast in this town. Careful, Detective." He smiled. "And don't you worry, little Jacquelynn will be just fine here. I'm Principal Harry Davids."

I gave a smile and another nod. "Thank you, sir."

Harry made his way back towards the school before I was able to leave. What did he mean by news traveling fast? Why was that such a big deal?

"You shouldn't worry about her so much." Joseph appeared next to me in the car.

"Morning to you too, Joseph." I didn't look at him, keeping my eyes on the road.

"Don't be so crabby." He poked me, but I couldn't feel it. "You are going to be fine and so is she."

I pulled into the police station and got out. The parking lot was just big enough to fit four cars. Joseph was right there, walking with me. I sighed, pretending he wasn't there as I walked up to the glass door. I pulled it open and walked inside. There I was greeted by a young woman with reddish hair and bright grey eyes. She got up out of her chair at the first desk and walked over to greet me.

"You must be Frankie Dawson." She smiled and put her hand out. "Ashley Aequitas."

"Latin." I smiled back, shaking her hand.

"Yeah, my family comes from England originally." She was younger than I was expecting, but that was fine. She must know what she is doing if she is the Detective around here.

"Ash, you can't just not introduce me to the new guy." This man was wearing a police jacket and had a badge on his right breast. He was leaning back in his chair with a cup in his hands. "Names Mathew Reames. Nothing special in my name." he gave a small chuckle and pointed at the back desk. "And that is our Captain, Luther Emsworth."

I saw Luther look up at me. He gave a small smile and motioned for me to come over. I did.

"Welcome to the force, Detective Frankie Dawson. If you need help adjusting from Miami, a large city, to Golden Loch which has just shy of one hundred, let me know. We all tend to know one another." I watched as his blue eyes glistened in the light and that bleached highlighted brown hair waved around on his head. Something about him did not sit right with me.

"Thank you, sir." I said to him, looking away.

"Please, its Luther. Don't be afraid, there's four of us on this team." He gave a nod and sat back down. "There is also no need for formalities."

I looked over at Ashley and Mathew who slowly agreed. Ashley started to sit back down in her chair. This place seemed decent enough and I was sure I was going to adjust easily.

Chapter 2

I sat down, right next to Ashley at the desk that the two of were going to share. She spoke about a girl who was killed recently and that her body was still missing. I looked at the first set of photos that were presented to me. The girl seemed to be happy in the pictures and looked to have a younger sibling. They must have been close because in each photo they were hugging and laughing together. The second set of photos presented were of the girl's murder scene. I noted that there was not a body present in the crime scene photos. "What is her name?"

"Elizabeth and the second girl in the photos are of her grieving sister, Saidie." Ashley pushed the file over to me so I could read up on the sisters. "They were almost inseparable, they did just about everything together."

I felt for Saidie, she was going through a very rough time. While I read the file, I learned that Saidie was only sixteen and their parents were not in the picture due to a freak accident many years ago when Saidie was only a kid. She was now alone in the world; her parents were gone and now her sister was too. I offered to go speak to Saidie, but Ashley refused. She said that they had already done that, and they had to keep moving with the investigation.

"Hey, don't let this get you down." Mathew poked my shoulder; he was standing behind Ashley and I. He handed me a cup of coffee. "Saidie is a good kid and she can handle this; I know that sounds harsh, but her family has had it rough the last couple years. Beth was almost like a mother to her." I understood that after looking over Saidie's own information. I saw that the freak accident was due to a car accident, but not much more was given on the subject. This part of the file was odd to me as a detective. It was as if Ashley, Mathew, and Luther were just suddenly cut off from finishing their investigation.

Ashley watched Mathew as he was getting settled back in his own chair. "Let's not forget that Saidie has ambitions for her own future, she is young still. We aren't going to let her lose sight of that." She gave me a sympathetic smile.

I picked up the photo of Elizabeth to learn what the girl looked like. Saidie and I were both going through a loss. "I understand how Saidie feels."

"Explain." Mathew leaned forward in his chair, his hands clasped together on his desk.

"A few weeks ago, my wife had passed away due to cancer." I didn't want to go into too much detail, it still hurt to think about, and I wasn't ready to face it head on. I know that sounds childish, but my wife and I were friends for a while before we started dating and eventually getting married.

Joseph had just come back from wherever it was he had been. He looked as if he wanted me to talk to him one on one. "I was watching Saidie."

I also wanted to speak to him, and I needed that information that he had just gathered. We were a team after all, that was what we did. We shared information and took care of one another. I guess you could say I became a detective because of Joseph. He was always encouraging, and I knew I could make a change in this world with his help. He made the job easier and I know that sounds like cheating, but he and I see it as taking advantage. I had a gift which made me feel as if I had an obligation to the public. Who else was going to do it? I had never met anyone else with my own gifts and I was sure that no one else did. I gave Joseph a sense of self and in return he helped me with my personal struggles along with my job. "Do you mind if I step outside for a minute?"

Ashley turned to face her computer screen. Our initial conversation about Saidie and Elizabeth were over. It was time to move on to the actual case. "If you must." I was sure that she wasn't exactly happy about me walking out as I had just arrived, but it was going to help the case whether she knew it or not.

"It helps me think." I didn't lie to her. In a way I was going out front to think, even if that meant speaking to my Shadow. I stood and walked towards the front door, dropping my empty cup into the trashcan before I stepped outside.

"Saidie is very upset." Joseph knew I couldn't answer him right now, so it was best to just let him speak. "She thinks that Luther won't do anything to bring justice to her sister. She is hoping Ashley and Mathew will find the one who did this. She was talking to a photo of her sister as if that was going to bring her back." Joseph was born in a time before photography was invented. I was sure that every picture of him was painted but he never talked about himself, so there was no reason to ever try and ask. Maybe he wanted to forget his life, or he thought that it was not important enough to talk about. I would probably never find out.

I looked at my phone. My way of letting him know I understand what he is saying is to look at my cellphone or to check the time on my watch. We had both agreed that when I was unable to answer, I would do either of the following. It worked, especially back in Miami when I would sit at my desk and he would talk to me. I would review the files while he explained what he had found. I would then find a logical way to explain the findings.

"So, you will do something then. Good. Saidie is going to need someone like you and that is all I ask for." Joseph knew I was going to see this out to the end, no matter what.

I put my cell phone back and checked the time on my watch. I gave the slightest nod to him, I hated ignoring him completely as it did feel rude. I could always explain it away as nodding at the time on my watch if anyone ever asked.

"She is hoping to meet you." Joseph made it seem as if Saidie already knew who I was and had been waiting for me.

Ashley stepped outside, patted me on the back, and walked over to her car. "Let's go."

"Where?" I watched her open the door to her red Ferrari.

"To see Saidie. Luther thinks that a visit will help cheer her up." She got in and started the car. Change of plans? That was pretty normal in my line of work, but it felt way too sudden.

I walked down the steps and over to Ashley's car. "Luther changed his mind all of a sudden?" I had got in the front seat next to her.

"He overheard us talking about Saidie, he was also concerned for you." Ashley shrugged, she probably didn't buy that explanation, but Luther was our boss and that meant he was in charge here. We may not always like what the Captain tells us but they usually have good reason.

"So, where does a girl on a detective salary get a nice car such as this?" I was impressed with the car, it smelled brand new.

She smirked. "Hard work and savings."

I looked at the cute little houses as we pulled up to Saidie's home. They were all different from one another. It was as if these homes were built by different families for their own idea of pretty.

"Hey tourist, stop staring." Ashley grabbed my arm and pulled me towards Saidie's house. We stepped onto the front porch, then Ashley knocked on the glass door. There was no answer, so she knocked again. She put her hand to the handle looking unsure as to why Saidie would not be answering. The door pushed open. I figured most people around here didn't lock their front doors. "I'm coming in, Saidie!" Ashley's voice echoed through the tiny kitchen.

"Upstairs, now!" Joseph had appeared in front of me, yelling.

I ran upstairs as fast as I could, Ashley right behind me. I pushed the bedroom door open and felt the sudden breeze of the window. She was right there just about to jump.

"No!" I ran towards the window, wrapping my arms around her body. "No Saidie." I said quietly. "This is not the way to make things better."

Ashley had come in the room behind me. "Shit, Saidie." She mumbled; her voice concerned.

"You guys won't do anything about it!" Saidie cried out, trying to fight me from holding her back. This wouldn't be my first time talking a kid down from the ledge and it never got any easier. Each time was as hard as the first and just as terrifying. I pulled her away from the window.

Ashley closed it behind me, and we sat her on the bed. "Look at me." Ashley leaned against the window; she was standing in the way of Saidie from trying again. Most usually didn't, but there was always someone who had.

Saidie looked up at the two of us. I could see the desperation in her eyes screaming *'help me'*. "*Do something.*" She looked down at her hands, her shoulders started to slink down.

"We are doing everything we can." Ashley tried to assure her. "Please try and be a little more patient until we can bring Elizabeth's killer down."

"And what about *him*?" Saidie's eyes had slid over to me.

"That is Detective Frankie Dawson. My partner." Ashley told her. "He is going to help us find Beth."

Saidie bit her lip, looking around the room. "I am all alone." She was starting to cry.

I glanced up at Joseph as he came into the room to see how I was doing. He knew what that glance meant, *'Go and find some answers.'* Over time we had developed glances and gestures that I would use to get him moving ahead of me while I was consoling the grieving family and friends.

"I'll start looking." He then turned to leave and then disappeared.

"We will find your sister and when we do, you will be the first one to know. Okay?" I knew exactly how she felt, she was grieving just as I was. "I understand what you are feeling right now. I lost my wife a few weeks ago, my daughter Jacquelynn is going through this too. You have to look at the positive." I know that was not always the easiest thing to do, but it was needed to try and move forward.

"She was a good person." Saidie looked my way. "She didn't deserve this."

"No one does." Ashley reassured her.

"She had so much life left and then it was all taken away from her because someone thought it be a good idea to kill her. She was in the wrong place and the wrong time." Saidie's eyes shifted down to her hands. "And they ruined not one but two lives. Please bring my sister back home." We knew that was not possible, but in Saidie's grieving mind it probably made sense to try and get her sister to come back. The first week after my wife had passed, I was sure there was something I could have done as a Necromancer to bring her back. That was obviously not true, but it was something I thought about a whole lot.

I put my hand on her shoulder. "Ashley and I are going to visit some people who knew her." I gave Ashley a look that I hope she understood.

Ashley stood up and moved towards Saidie. "Promise me you won't jump."

Saidie nodded. "I promise."

"Do you want me to get Mat here?" Ashley asked her. "He can keep you company for the time being."

"No, I promise to stay here." Saidie hugged Ashley. "Just get me my sister, that is all I ask for."

When we were leaving, I saw a little blonde girl at the house across the street. She was peeking at us from behind a bush. "Shouldn't she be in school?" I got in the car with Ashley. It *was* the middle of the school year.

"Don't get me started." Ashley waved her hand at me. "Mat and I have been trying to get Scarlet to take her kid to school for years now. She refuses as if the idea is repulsing. The poor kid has a hard time socializing with others and you can see it."

I watched as the little girl ran back inside the house. "Poor kid, she needs an education. Is Scarlet at least homeschooling?"

"I wish I knew; she doesn't like cooperating with Mat and I." Ashley sounded defeated.

I decided to drop the subject.

We pulled up to the diner. The entire parking lot had maybe ten spaces and three were taken. Ashley pulled into one of the spots even if it felt like a squeeze.

"This is where Beth worked." Ashley led me inside where it felt like you were entering the late 80's. Everything was decorated to keep the feeling that you really had stepped back in time. I could see the man in the kitchen window, prepping up some food.

"Morning, Lucius." Ashley led me over to the kitchen window to introduce me.

"Ash! How are you?" Lucius smiled, he seemed to be a pretty happy man.

"Lucius is the chef here." Ashley let me know. "Anything you want is made by him."

I smiled at Lucius. He had dark skin and I could see how well he took care of it. It glowed in the light. His brown eyes locked with mine for a moment before he looked at Ashley. "Who's this?"

"This is Frankie Dawson. My new partner." Ashley smiled. "He is the detective that Mat and I decided to hire for our force."

"And what brings you here? You definitely aren't from Michigan." He walked out into the dining room.

"For my daughter. She needed a change of pace." I answered.

"Lies, he wanted the pay." Ashley teased.

I smiled at her. She and I were going to get along, there was no doubt about that.

"Lucius, do me a favor and tell Frankie about the last time you saw Beth. He is trying to retrace my steps in the case so he can catch himself up." Ashley asked.

"Jee, what? Four weeks ago?" He looked at Ashley then back at me. "She was getting ready to leave; her shift was over, and Delilah was coming in. She seemed irritated, I figured she was just having a bad day, so I let her be."

"Delilah is Malcolm's girlfriend." Ashley informed me. "Malcolm is also the owner of this diner."

"Is she here now?" I was hoping to speak to her, maybe Elizabeth had said something to her that day when she was leaving.

"No, we hired Payton." Lucius pointed to the other room. "She is on her break until we open back up in an hour. She won't know anything though. She had just started last week."

"Do you mind if I spoke to her then?" I wanted to know what she was thinking with everything going on here. If news traveled as quickly as Harry Davids has said, then she ought to have some sort of clue.

Lucius shrugged. "Sure, but like I said she won't know much." He started wiping down the tables in the dining room to get ready for customers.

I walked into the other room, listening to the music. It was Queen. "You like them?" I didn't think young kids would be into old 70's and 80's music. This however was an 80's establishment so it probably wasn't that far out there.

She looked up from her phone, obviously irritated that I was distracting her. "They are catchy, didn't know that was a crime. You are?"

"Frankie Dawson. Believe me it isn't. That is also not why I am here." I slid into the booth across from her. "Payton, right?"

She nodded. "Lucius told you my name, didn't he?" Her head hit her hand, her elbow on the table. "You're that new detective, right? Ash's partner."

"He may have mentioned you and yes that is me. I wanted to ask you something." I sat back, making myself slightly more comfortable in the seat.

"If this is about Saidie and Elizabeth, then I don't know." Payton shrugged. It was not going to be easy to talk to her. "They kept to themselves most of the time. My sister taught them both when they were in elementary. Both good kids but I only really ever see them in passing these days. It is a real shame, what happened to Beth."

"I'm actually more curious about how a body can disappear in a small town such as Golden Loch." I saw the way she glanced at the window. Her interests were somewhere else and not with me, clearly not interested in what I was talking about.

"Hey, Payton." A tall slender dark-haired man walked in. He looked annoyed and I was sure it was because of me.

"Mal." She stood up as quick as she possibly could. "Sorry, I was just getting my break in before the dinner rush."

He shook his head, the anger disappearing from his face. "Mind giving Delilah a hand?" He patted her shoulder.

She nodded and left. Malcolm looked around the room as if he was waiting to see if someone else would come in.

"Look, you and Ash can find Beth, I know you can. You just suck at your job. I also don't need you two sniffing around here." Malcolm grunted, crossing his arms.

"How does one girl disappear like that?" That was the burning question. Where was Elizabeth? Her body had to be somewhere. I know what has to be done, even if I don't like the idea.

19

I had to summon help and that meant working with Joseph personally.

"That is your job to figure out. I am not the detective here." Malcolm leaned both hands on the table and looked me in the eyes. "Now can the two of you please leave? We have work to get done before our dinner rush." His jaw was working, and his annoyance was towards me.

I didn't say anything to him, I just smiled. Getting up I went back to see Ashley in the front of the diner. She was waiting for me to get back from my chat.

"Well?" she raised an eyebrow. She did this dance already and knew where it was going, but I had to be sure for myself.

"Payton has nothing, and Malcolm is asking us to leave." I pushed the door open to get outside.

Back at the office, I sat down in my chair, feeling a bit defeated. The first day was always the hardest. You never know if people are going to resent you or be completely cooperative while talking to them.

"Don't get so down. This is usually how it goes around here." Ashley grabbed her things; she was ready to get out of here. "It takes a while to find people who go missing. It sucks but-"

"Ashley, don't ruin his perception of this town." Mathew shook his head. "Let the man think we are better than that."

Ashley then whispered something to Mathew that I couldn't quite get. She looked back at me and smiled. "See you tomorrow, Detective Dawson." She then walked out the front door.

Mathew nodded to me, grabbing his own jacket. "Careful around here, Frankie." He patted my shoulder and then also walked out the front door.

Luther was already gone that evening, something about a family dinner that he was not able to miss. He told Mathew before Ashley and I had come back from Malcolm's diner. I sat at my desk looking over the paperwork once more before I called it a day. I grabbed my things and went to my SUV.

"Sorry." Joseph said as he appeared in the seat next to me.

I looked at him. "For what?" He made it seem like this was his fault.

"She isn't dead." Joseph looked confusingly at me.

"What?" How? Ashley and Mathew had even said that Elizabeth had been killed.

"I poked around, there is little to no proof that she is gone. It seems that our dead girl may not actually be dead." Joseph reported to me.

"So, they deemed her dead? But why?" That made no sense, Ashley was so sure of Elizabeth's murder.

"They must have found her blood at a crime scene." Joseph was only theorizing. "Then considering that they haven't found a body, assumed it was disposed of somewhere."

"I have an idea." I still hated it but it needed to be done.

"What is that?" He then asked, slightly concerned for what I was about to tell him.

"We summon a ghost." I told Joseph, he seemed to be okay with my idea.

After putting Jacquelynn to bed, I sat outside on the porch with Joseph. We were bouncing ideas back and forth on how we were going to proceed with the summon. He wanted to call a ghost who knew what was happening around town and who had been around long enough to understand how the people here think.

"No, no." I was pacing back and forth on the porch. "I want to, but I just don't think that summoning a ghost who knows too much is a good idea. I will find one, but not one that knows way too much."

"But that is your specialty, you summon people like me. Who cares what they know and don't know? It isn't like you have to live with them."

"I know the routine; it runs in my blood. Blah blah blah, What the heck is another ghost going to tell me that you already haven't?" I hated the idea of bringing in help, especially a know it all. Ghosts always tried to take Joseph's place. They thought if they offered up their services that they could just hang around for a while longer until they got comfy enough, that Joseph would leave, letting them take over. I shuddered at the idea.

"Talk to the one who lived here." He suggested, hoping that would change my mind about who I should summon. "It's the easiest way to solve this case and save Saidie any more grief."

I grunted; I still didn't want to pick the first person that Joseph suggested. "Fine. I'll do it." He knew I couldn't resist helping someone else, so that was where he always won in the end. I always summoned who he wanted, not that it mattered, really. I slowed my breathing and gave out the key words repeatedly to summon the ghost of this house. Suddenly, I felt the temperature drop. A sign that the ghost had been summoned successfully. A young man had made his appearance in front of us.

"Hello." He put his hand out to greet me. He seemed friendly. They always did.

"You know what you are, do you not?" Joseph was already annoyed even if nothing had happened yet. He was the one who wanted me to summon the ghost who lived here, so getting angry was dumb.

He looked at Joseph and chuckled. "You are right. I do. I'm like you, a dead man just trying to find his peace." That was already a sign that he wanted Joseph's place.

Joseph rolled his eyes. He was better at this then I was. Of course, he was also doing this much longer than I ever had been. As I was saying before, he will go on to someone else when I eventually die. "That's an old wives' tale and you know it."

"Name's Sebastian." He ignored Joseph. "I used to live in this house here, so I'm as good as you get." He pointed at the house and I'm sure he wanted to sound like he was important.

"Did you see a girl named Elizabeth get murdered?" I ignored his comment about living in the house. I also didn't care enough about his name. I know that sounds selfish, but I just wanted to get information on Elizabeth.

"I won't talk about that." He shook his head and backed off. "She should have known better then to get into that kind of trouble. No way will I speak on the matter. I do not intend on becoming the next victim." He said it like this person is a cold-blooded killer out to just slaughter everyone.

"You are a ghost; how would our killer even know about you?" I was sure the man who did this was human, just like any other killer I had ever caught.

"That doesn't mean I won't be next." He wanted something from me. I knew what that was, but I still asked him the question anyway. "What do you want?"

"To be someone's Shadow." Sebastian smiled like he was ready to fight and take Joseph's place. I had no idea how any of that worked as I had never seen it happen, and I didn't plan on starting now. I certainly wasn't one to jump from one Shadow to another. I was planning on being loyal to Joseph to the end, whether that is my end or his.

"Go find someone else." Joseph gritted his teeth; he was ready to stand his ground and get rid of Sebastian.

Sebastian started getting closer and closer to Joseph, clenching his fists. "You live in my house."

"Now it's mine. Frankie is mine. Get someone else." He repeated. "I won't tell you again."

"You Englishmen are all the same. Entitled." He looked at me. "Good luck finding that woman." He then disappeared.

"Brat." Joseph grunted.

"This was your idea, you know. They are always like that. Wanting to be my shadow in exchange for information, and you wonder why I don't do this." I then went inside, shutting the front door and locking it behind me.

Joseph followed, walking right through the locked door. "I want to make this easier for you. I am sorry if I screwed up, just don't blame me for what that kid was trying to do."

I sat in my chair by the fire in the living room. "You know what would make things easier? If you found a way to talk to my wife." I tried not to snap at him, but my own patience had been wearing thin.

Joseph sat on the coffee table in front of me. "You know I want nothing more for you. I'm doing everything I can." He was quiet now; he always was when I was getting upset.

I stared at him for a long moment. "Let's just forget about it all, it's been a long day and I'm tired and I'm sure you have things you want to do before I wake." Even when Joseph was not around with me, he was still here. He never leaves, I don't think he can really. He doesn't sleep either, so he usually takes advantage of when I am sleeping to do his own thing, except for when Jacquelynn is running a fever or even a little sick. He stays to make sure that she is okay and informs me of any changes. He did it for me as well when I was young and in denial about so many things in my life.

"I'm going to look for more information on Elizabeth." He disappeared just as he always did.

"Daddy?" Jacquelynn walked into the living room, she rubbed her eyes looking up at me in my chair. "Are you okay?"

I smiled and invited her over to sit with me. "Do you remember when your mother talked of getting a big home and moving out of the city?"

She nodded, climbing up into my lap. "Lots of horses." Her smile got big.

I pulled her closer. "I was just thinking about that." I wanted something nice for her and this was my way of doing that. Jacquelynn had always wanted to see a horse for herself.

"Why?" Her eyes met mine before she looked over into the fire. "Daddy wants to live Mommy's dream?"

"I thought that maybe if she is watching, we could make her smile some more. What if we had some horses?"

"Do you think that the town mayor would allow it?" Her eyes showed concern.

"And who is that?" I knew his name, but I didn't think that my daughter knew, so I was going to challenge her.

She thought long and hard about the question before coming up with her answer. "I think his name is Axel or something."

"It is. It's good that you know that." I kissed her forehead. "I'll talk to him over the weekend and then we will get those horses just like your mother wanted."

She snuggled up against me. "Daddy, you have to sleep too. Your job is very important you know."

"I know, Pumpkin." I felt her drift off into sleep, so I closed my own eyes to get some rest of my own.

Chapter 3

That next morning, I woke with Jacquelynn on my lap. She was sound asleep, and I didn't want to disturb her if I didn't have to, so I slid her off my lap and went to get myself ready before I had to get her up and ready as well. I went right to the kitchen after getting ready, made a cup of coffee for myself, then I went to wake my daughter. I touched her shoulder and shrugged her awake. She mumbled that she didn't want to get up yet. I had to remind her that she could not be late to school. She reached out to me. I picked her up and carried her to her bedroom. I shut the door behind me to let her get herself ready. I moved down the hallway, back into the kitchen, and grabbed the keys to my SUV so I could start the car as it was cold here, compared to the warm days back in Miami.

Jacquelynn came running outside, handing me her hairbrush. I had her sit down on the porch steps, getting her hair pulled back and sending her to the car. I put her brush down on the chair and joined her.

"Let's face the day head on, Pumpkin." I adjusted the rearview mirror and saw her buckle herself in.

"Let's go, Daddy!" Her hands went up in the air, with excitement. It didn't take much for her to wake up in the morning, and once she was up, she was excited to get going. She was like me in that sense, always ready to just keep pushing forward no matter the situation.

After dropping Jacquelynn off at school, I arrived at the office, ready more than ever. I gave a small smile to myself knowing that my daughter was facing a new problem, just as I was, and I knew she was going to be fine handling it. I got out of the SUV and walked to the front door. I pushed it open, stepping inside. "Are we sure that she was killed?"

Ashley looked up at me. "What?" I had caught her off guard, she probably hadn't even had the chance to think about the case yet.

"Well-" I grabbed my chair and pulled it closer to hers. "I think if there wasn't a body, maybe she might be out there somewhere."

"Or the body is missing." Mathew said walking over, giving Ashley her coffee, and then sitting at his desk behind ours.

I glared at Mathew. He and Ashley really believed she was dead, but there wasn't a body to prove so. "Is he always late?" I pointed to Luther's desk, curious as to where our Captain may have been.

Ashley shrugged. "He's the Captain." She spoke as if he was allowed to do whatever he wanted just because he was in charge here. Back in Miami, that wouldn't fly, and the higher-ups would have his job in a heartbeat. Punctuality was important, but I guess with how small this town was, there was no need to be on time every day, especially when you ran the place.

I shook my head, avoiding the argument and headache if I spoke about it. "Anyway, I just think we need to retrace our steps. Nothing crazy, I was hoping to see if maybe we had missed something."

"You mean go to the crime scene." Mathew raised an eyebrow, opposed to the idea.

"Yes. I think that if we reconstruct the scene, we may see something that may have been missed before." I needed Ashley to go along with this so I could see the crime scene myself.

"No." Luther walked in. "You will not go there. That place is off limits. We were lucky to get access the first time."

"Axel is your closest friend." Mathew looked at Luther. "Ash could possibly take Frankie."

"Closest?" Luther asked. "No, he isn't. He is just someone who looks after us as a team and wouldn't do anything like that." He had dropped his things onto the desk and fell into his chair. It was almost as if he didn't care enough to find out what had happened to Elizabeth.

Ashley grunted something under her breath. She was obviously unhappy about the situation as well. I didn't blame her; she was working on this case much longer than I had been. I would be frustrated too if my old Captain told me I couldn't do my job.

"What is it, Ash? Would you like to share with the class?" Luther asked, his tone a bit like he was trying to tease but it came off much harsher than it ever should. Luther seemed like he was going to be a delight to work with, sarcasm intended.

She shot him a glare. "Oh, trust me, you don't want to know." They probably didn't get along very well.

Joseph came into the room, looking around to make sure it was safe before entering. He leaned against the wall, getting my attention without having me look his way. "You and I may have to go there ourselves." He was probably right, whether I wanted to go or listen to Luther and stay here didn't matter.

I checked my watch, that way he knew I understood what he was saying.

"What is the matter?" Mathew raised an eyebrow. "Time going by too slow?" he smiled my way.

I shook my head; I knew that he was messing with me. "Oh, nothing is the matter Mat, however, I don't think we should be sitting here, doing absolutely nothing."

Ashley looked at me. "We aren't doing nothing, Frankie. We are all working as hard as ever to get Beth found. It's not easy, I know." She shot a glance at Luther, annoyed. "We are sitting and doing computer work for now until we can do this right without handing in our badges to Luther."

I looked at Joseph for a moment. I was hoping he would get the message that I wanted him to go there himself and take a second look around, especially since I was going to be stuck here for a while longer.

He sighed understanding what I was trying to tell him without the need of words. "I need someone who can move and touch things. You need to make a choice here, Frankie. Even if Luther gets angry, what is more important to you? Finding Elizabeth or your job? Please do the right thing." He then walked through the wall, leaving.

I knew he was right. I wanted to find this girl. I had to. When I worked in Miami, I was able to get away with it easily. My boss never second questioned my motives, and I normally had a good enough reason. I will never understand how humans do this job alone. It is hard enough doing this with Joseph. I've also had Joseph around since I was twelve. He had always helped me through every situation and had never asked for anything in return. He seemed to enjoy just having someone to talk to and be with. It sounds sad, I know, but I'm sure it is true enough.

At lunch, I told both Ashley and Mathew I was going to go for a drive. After a few questions about where I was going, and I had not budged with an answer, they let me be. I drove with Joseph in the passenger seat as he gave me directions to the scene. I should know where this bridge is, but I don't. I eventually pulled into the gravel parking lot next to the bridge. After getting out, all I could smell was death. "Ugh, that smell."

Joseph smiled. "Don't know what smell you mean, but I will take your word for it." He started to the railing. Of course, he wouldn't know what smell I meant; he was dead after all.

I rolled my eyes, following him over. "They say she jumped here." I peered over the edge and down to the crick below. There were plenty of moss-covered rocks and clear water but no sign that she was there.

"And what evidence leads to that?" He wasn't there for the briefing originally so of course he had to ask. He may not have the badge and twenty-first-century knowledge, but he did understand enough to know that evidence has to lead you to your conclusion.

I pointed to the rail in front of us. "Her fingerprints were found on the rail here. Her hair and some blood, along with DNA, were also found." I know that meant a sign of struggle or she was contemplating her own jump. This fall was too short, less than three stories, for anyone to force themselves over. There was a greater possibility that she had been pushed over, with little time to react. Questions that I needed to ask myself are 'Who pushed her?' and 'Why did they push her?' We already had our where and when, we just needed the why and who.

"But no body." Joseph looked my way. "And there are no fingerprints, DNA, or a sign of struggle." He was already contradicting what I was trying to come up with.

I gave a nod, understanding what he was trying to say to me. "No body." I peered over the side once more. "They found her backpack down there, which is what helped conclude a push. Ashley and Mathew think she was running from someone." If she *was* running from someone, why hadn't Saidie known? Maybe Saidie didn't know anything, and this was another freak accident. I knelt to examine the railing better.

"A push, or was she jumping to get away? Maybe she had slipped." Joseph replied. How could she have slipped? There was no rain that night and according to what Ashley had reported, the ground was also dry.

"She couldn't have slipped; the railing is too high, and the ground was not wet that night either." I stood up, my hands going into my pockets.

"That is good to know, we can scratch that off our list of conclusions." Joseph reached to the railing, looking a bit lost himself on what may have happened.

"There isn't enough evidence for any conclusion at this moment in time, we will have to keep looking and asking questions until we get some answers." I shook my head, walked down the steps, and into the crick below. The water was just shallow enough that only my shoes were covered. I looked at my own reflection in the water.

"You're alive, Frankie." Joseph had followed me down. "Do not think otherwise."

I saw his reflection, but never felt his hand. "Some days I'm not so sure." I was looking at him in the water, I had been feeling lost since I had lost my wife. His smile meant he knew how I was feeling.

"You will find her. I know you will. You are good at what you do, and that is finding people." Joseph reassured me. I may have wanted him to mean Elizabeth, but he and I both knew he was talking about my wife.

"You are also a huge help." I looked at the sky, rain was coming. "There is a cold drift coming in, winter here does not seem to be very pleasant."

"Comparing it to winter back in Miami." He shook his head at me. "Don't do that, Frankie. Weather up north is always worse. It actually reminds me of home." He was referring to his home back in London. "I only do what you ask. If it wasn't for you-" He stopped, his presence was gone.

"Joseph?" I turned and he was not there anymore. "Joseph?!?" Where did he go?

"Quit your screaming."

I turned to a voice that had come from behind me suddenly.

"Calm down." He approached me. His skin, which I pinpointed he was from South America slightly glistened in the sun and his bright blue eyes were brighter than the sunlight. Who the hell was he?

"You must be that new cop." He put his hand out. "Daeron." His smile seemed sincere, but his body language was off.

"Frankie." I said, realizing it slipped before I could catch myself. I wasn't sure how that had happened, but it did.

"Well Frankie, if you came here to find Elizabeth, she isn't here." Daeron told me. He circled around me as if I was prey. "You'll have to look someplace else. You can also tell Luther and Ashley that we don't want their kind around here." Was he responsible for Elizabeth? I made a mental note of his name.

"Kind?" He must've meant cop, that was what the three of us had in common, but he seemed to have purposely excluded Mathew.

"Be nice to the man." A voice of a female. She had approached from behind me, touching my shoulder before also circling me a few times.

"Illyanna." Daeron spoke softly. He had stopped walking and was standing right behind me.

"He is only doing his good cop duty." She smiled softly. Her dark eyes and dark skin tone also shone as she peered into my own. What the heck did I walk into?

"Hey! Frankie!" I looked up to see Ashley was standing there on the bridge. Both Daeron and Illyanna were gone, vanishing into thin air as if they were never here.

Ashley came running down the stairs. "I figured you would have been here." She looked like she wanted to slap me for coming to the place that we were told not to come to.

"Who is Daeron and Illyanna?" I asked her, hoping that changing the subject would get her to forget about this.

"They live here." She grabbed my arm, pulling me out of the water.

"Well I figured that, but they don't seem to like you and Luther very much. I don't know what their thoughts are on Mathew, but-"

"Frankie." She stopped my train of thought. "Look, it is all very complicated. You are better off not knowing, that family and we

32

police have a long-standing history. They aren't people you want to associate yourself with, okay?"

I slowly nodded. I had a bad feeling about all of this, but I wasn't ready to talk to Ashley on it yet. Was Illyanna innocent? How was I sure that it wasn't one of my own either?

At home that night, I started filling out the paperwork to get the horses for my daughter. She was staying late at school for some activities with her classmates. I had to wait for the bus to come home so we could get dinner together. I was hoping to take her to Malcolm's diner as I was sure that their food was good. They were getting ready for their dinner rush when we came by this morning. I figured that they only served breakfast and dinner, skipping lunch time.

"Sorry about that." Joseph apologized to me. I'm sure he had felt bad for leaving, but that still didn't change that I was annoyed with him.

"Bout time you came back." I didn't look up, wanting to make it clear that I was not happy with him.

"They must have thought you were a crazy man." He walked over. "Horses?"

"It's for Jacquelynn." I still didn't look up, who cares if they thought I was crazy, that didn't matter.

"Frankie, I know you are probably mad at me, but I had a very good reason." Sure, you didn't want to be there when Daeron and Illyanna came by.

I glared up at him, slamming my pen on the table. "You abandoned me out there today." I stood up.

He was about to speak when my daughter pushed the front door open and walked into the house. "Daddy!" She came running over and hugged me. "Are you okay? You looked angry."

"Hey, Pumpkin." I glanced up, but Joseph had left us alone. "Everything is just fine. Are you hungry?" I knew she wouldn't keep asking because she had full trust in what I told her.

"Yes!" She nodded fast and pulled out of the hug.

"Good, go get changed, and then we will go get dinner." I went outside and started the SUV up; it was pouring now. I watched as she came running out and then climbed into the back seat.

"Where are we going?" She leaned forward. Her wet hair falling in her face.

I pushed it back out of the way for her. "Malcolm's diner. I think you will like it."

She sat back in her seat and put her seatbelt on. "Safety first!"

We arrived at the diner, and we were sat by who I figured was Delilah by her nametag, immediately. This was Malcolm's girlfriend. I wasn't entirely sure if they were responsible for Elizabeth either. Malcolm didn't seem to like Ashley and me all too much, but that does not mean they committed murder.

"What can I get you two to drink?" She asked, pulling out a pen and a pad book.

"Coffee, black." I nodded to her. I needed some caffeine after today's events.

"Apple juice, please!" Jacquelynn chimed in after me.

"Alright, Payton will be right by to take your food orders and bring you your drinks." She then walked away, going back towards the front of the diner.

"Payton is Ms. Trudell's sister. Alexa is my teacher's kid, and she is in my class." Jacquelynn had informed me.

"Oh yeah?" I looked at her, smiling.

"Yeah, and that is her." She pointed to a table across the room. "They eat here because Payton works here."

I glanced over for a moment then back at my daughter. "Do you like her?" I was hoping she was making some friends at school.

She nodded quickly. "She is nice."

Payton came over with our drinks. We ordered dinner quickly. I got a plate of clams and pasta, while Jacquelynn had got her favorite chicken parmigiana. Payton wrote our orders down on her pad book and stuffed it into her apron. "It will be about twenty minutes."

"That is just fine." I told her, taking a sip of my coffee.

Payton shrugged at me; she probably wasn't sure why I came back today even though Malcolm told me to leave. She was probably going to tell him I was here.

"Ms. Trudell's sister didn't like seeing you." My daughter slid down in her seat. She looked disappointed and confused. "I saw the way she looked at you."

"We spoke yesterday." I watched Malcolm come our way after speaking to Payton. She had slipped into the back, out of sight.

"Detective." He had put his hands on his hips as he approached me.

I nodded to him, wanting him to know that we were only here to eat, and there was no need for any form of hostility. "I figured we would try your food."

"This must be little Jacquelynn." He smiled at her. I wasn't sure if that was out of kindness or because he despised seeing us here.

I raised an eyebrow, curious how he knew my kid. I figured it was Payton and Jacquelynn's teacher who had mentioned her, or maybe it was her classmate, Alexa.

"My friends' son has spoken about you. His name is Emmett." Well, I was wrong, Jacquelynn had another classmate, a boy. I looked to her, but she was too busy cutting and eating her food. She was barely paying attention to Malcolm and me.

"Pumpkin." I reached across the table to her hand. "Do you know Emmett?" I motioned my head to Malcolm.

She then smiled at me. "Yeah I know him." She looked to Malcolm. "We are classmates."

I was then relieved. I wanted to make sure that Malcolm was not making this kid up.

Malcolm shrugged, his hands going into the air. "Enjoy your meal, on the house." He sounded a bit frustrated with me.

"That isn't necessary." I told him; I didn't want Malcolm to get the wrong idea about me. I wasn't here to get a free meal.

"You just keep doing your job, Detective." He walked away. I was sure that Malcolm was not involved with Elizabeth. He was only trying to do his job; this place was his life and he wanted to keep it running.

"Free food?" She asked me, unsure what 'on the house' meant.

"I would seem so, Pumpkin." I patted her arm.

I drove us back home afterward and then carried my daughter into the house. She had fallen asleep in the car on the way back, so I put her into her bed and tucked her in. "Sweet dreams, my little Pumpkin." I shut the door quietly and then shut the light off before I went into the living area. I looked at the paperwork on the coffee table taking a seat, unsure about this town. Something was off and very odd about the people here. Daeron and Illyanna were there and then not, Ashley and Luther are in some sort of quarrel that did not seem to end, Malcolm doesn't like anyone very much, and I am sure one of them is guilty. I went into my bedroom with thoughts still going through my head. I had already chosen to eliminate Malcolm and Delilah. They just were not guilty of murder. I eventually had fallen asleep.

I had a dream that night that I found Elizabeth. She was alive and well, but she wasn't right. Something was very wrong; she couldn't tell me what happened to her as if it had never happened at all. She looked like she had been lying in the river for days, yet she didn't. I couldn't tell where she had been or where I was going to be able to locate her. I tried to reach my hand out to her, but as I did, she disappeared. I called out to her, my voice ringing in my own head, but no words were coming out of my mouth. I kept calling, but she just wasn't there.

I woke up suddenly in a bit of a panic and felt sweat beading down my forehead. I saw Joseph standing there right next to my bed, concerned. My daughter was watching me from the crack of the door, unsure of what just happened. I sat up, calling her over to the bed. "I'm sorry that I scared you."

She shook her head, pushed the door open, and climbed into the bed next to me. She then hugged me. "It's okay, Daddy."

"Do you think you can put yourself back to bed?" I wanted her to be able to take care of herself, especially when I wasn't around.

She crawled out of bed and got to her feet. "I can. Just be nice to yourself, okay?" Her innocence was always comforting.

"Okay." I gave a sympathetic smile. My heart rate was starting to go back down to normal.

"Promise me." She looked me in the eyes, saddened.

"I promise." I kissed her on the forehead. "Now, go on." I turned her to the door. "I will be fine."

She then quietly walked out of the room, looking back at me one last time, and shut the door behind her.

"What happened?" Joseph asked after peeking through the wall and into her bedroom to check to she was back in her bed. He then sat on the bed next to me.

"I saw Elizabeth, and she looked saddened. She then disappeared, and I have no idea where to." I answered. "I've been on this force for two days, and I'm already getting restless."

"Which means she's dead." Joseph said quietly.

"She wouldn't reach out otherwise." I looked up at him. "I have to find her."

Chapter 4

When I walked into the station the next morning, I found Ashley and Mathew standing by Luther's desk. The two of them looked up at me as I put my jacket on my chair and made my way over to his desk.

"What is going on?" Did they come any closer to finding Elizabeth's killer?" I asked concerned.

"Luther is out back with Malcolm and Delilah." Ashley looked my way. I could see the frustration in her face, and it was directed towards me now. "You went back to the diner last night, alone." Her tone had implied that I was in trouble, and maybe her initial instinct about me was wrong. I didn't want her to get the wrong impression.

I pursed my lips and glanced to the back door for a moment. I could see that it was propped open, and I saw the back of Malcom. Luther and Delilah were out of sight. "I was off duty; my daughter was hungry. Is it a crime around here to get some food?" My eyes shifted towards Ashley. "I'm sure you have also had a bite to eat there."

"That is not the point here, Frankie. We cannot jump into something without running it past Luther first. I'm not sure how they ran things in Miami, but here we all work together as a team." I could see she was calming down, even if she was still upset with me.

Mathew sighed, chiming in to add to what Ashley was telling me. "Most people in this town don't really like or care for the police. They would much prefer to police themselves. If we go behind Luther's back, there could be a problem, and Luther would have to deal with it. We could all lose our jobs."

I shoved my hands into my pockets, my eyes shifting back to the rear entrance as Luther came inside with Delilah and Malcolm. "Someone has to keep things in check."

"Just keep your dogs away from my restaurant." Malcolm growled at me and then glanced at Ashley. "And keep your newbie in check." He took Delilah by the hand, and they left before anyone could say a word to them.

"Dogs?" I looked at Luther. I was sure that was supposed to be an insult, especially after what Ashley and Mathew were telling me. Malcolm and Delilah did not want us coming around.

"Just do yourself a favor, Frankie, and don't go to his diner." Luther had sat back in his chair. "You are way better off." His look felt cold and unconcerned with what he was telling us. Did he want Ashley, Mathew, and I to keep going? No, he was the one who told us not to go out there, stopping us from solving this murder.

I sighed. "Yes, sir." I had a bad feeling about all of this again. Something inside was telling me that I needed to go back to Payton and Lucius again. They had to know something. I then figured it would be best to visit them at their own homes. I was sure they would be way more cooperative if I did this.

"What's next?" Ashley looked at Luther.

He handed her paperwork. "You and Mathew need to pay a visit to Ruby." He looked at me. "And I need you to stay here, do some paperwork." I figured Ruby was another resident here in Golden Loch and probably had some information on Elizabeth. I took the paperwork from Luther and went back to my desk. Sitting in the chair, I had a feeling this was punishment for going to the diner.

Ashley leaned towards me on her way to the door. "Research what you can on mental illness." She had a saddened, concerned look on her face.

I looked her in the eyes. "Is this for Ruby?"

Ashley slowly nodded without saying another word before taking Mathew and leaving the building.

I sat at my desk, going over what I had already read. Ruby was diagnosed with a form of schizophrenia and it had stated she would see the same girl all the time. Ruby and this girl have conversations with one another, and she has described this girl as a young South Korean who died in a car accident. She wore clothes from the early 2000's and was her only friend. The file also stated that Ruby named the girl Keiko.

I looked up at the clock after doing some research on schizophrenia. It had been almost two hours since Ashley and Mathew had left for their visit with Ruby. I had barely enough information on our teen to draw any kind of conclusions about her on my own. Luther also just didn't seem interested in talking to me about her.

Joseph sat down next to me in Ashley's chair and smiled. "Guess where I've been." He leaned over to see what I was looking at on the computer screen.

I looked at my phone next to me, so he knew I was listening to what he had to say. I then started typing on the computer again, giving him my ear.

"I had hitched a ride with Ashley and Mathew. This Ruby girl is being held at an institution right outside of town. Thing is, there's nothing wrong with her. She is like you." He informed me.

I stopped typing, glanced at him, and then wrote down the information he had given. Ruby was being given medication for a mental illness that she didn't even have.

"She has been seeing Elizabeth just like you did last night. I think we should go see her." He pointed to the file. "She may have some information on what has happened to her."

I knew that we needed to, I could claim to be a relative and completely get away with it. I also knew that it wasn't a good idea as I was already being punished for last night's dinner. Luther was right, I shouldn't have been there. I only went to see if I could get any kind of answers. I was tempted to speak with Jacquelynn's teacher last night, but after my encounter with Malcolm, I figured it was better left alone.

I heard Ashley's car pull up to the office. She and Mathew were talking to one another before they came inside with a bag of food. From where I was sitting, they seemed to be good friends. She handed me one of the contents from inside the bag. It was wrapped in foil. Joseph got out of Ashley's chair and stood there ready to listen in on our conversation.

"I'm sure you are hungry and considering that we can't eat at the only diner around here, I stopped at the fast-food joint right outside of town." Ashley sat down next to me. I wanted to tell her my plan about seeing both Lucius and Payton in their own homes but decided against it. I was going to go do this on my own, I could not drag her down with me.

Mathew sat at his desk behind us, his feet going up onto his desk. "What have you come up with?" He bit into his burger.

I turned my chair so we would be in a triangle. "Are we sure this girl is crazy?" I wanted to see what they thought about Ruby. Surely, they believed her diagnosis.

"She is seeing things that aren't there." Ashley leaned back in her chair, crossing her arms. "You really think that is considered normal?"

"She has also been talking to people who aren't there." Mathew went on. "You can see everything on her file." He motioned to the it with his chin.

I wasn't entirely convinced that there was anything wrong with her. "Right…." How would they even know what she is going through? They aren't like me, and they certainly are not like her. I learned how to deal with who I was going to become one day; I had my mother to teach me. Ruby doesn't have anyone. Her parents had left her there to fend for herself without help.

"Well it seems that when someone has schizophrenia, they are like that forever. I can't exactly explain it as I'm not a doctor but-" Mathew paused when the phone rang. He sat upright to answer. "Golden Loch police, this is Lieutenant Mathew Reames." He stopped talking, as he was listening to the speaker on the other end, he had picked up his pen and was writing things on the notepad in front of him. "Yes. We will." He then hung up with a very concerned look on his face. "Ruby's escaped."

Ashley and I looked at one another, confused. How had she escaped?

"That isn't possible, she is in a very secure area of the building." Ashley leaned on Mathew's desk. "Unless she had some kind of help."

"No way." Mathew shook his head. "The voices in her head wouldn't know how to get out of there." His sounded like he was slightly upset and wanted Ashley to stop. Joseph had said she was a Necromancer, so it was possible that her Shadow had got her out. I glanced to Joseph, who let out a smile. I had a feeling he had something to do with this.

"Go." We heard Luther. "All of you, before she gets too far." We all jumped up and got into Ashley's car. She had pulled out of the parking lot so fast her tires squealed around the corner. She was driving down the empty roads towards the institution.

As soon as we got to there, we had raced inside to the front desk. The best way to describe this place was dark and somewhat gloomy. I couldn't imagine being here every day, it looked to be really depressing.

The lady there at the front desk looked at us, terrified. She had probably seen Ruby escape, while also talking to someone who she could not see. Working at the front desk meant you never saw patients. I was also sure she was not used to seeing an escape.

"Which way did Ruby run?" Ashley asked the lady as she was sure to know.

The lady pointed to the north, her hand shaking. She didn't speak to Ashley, Mathew, or myself on the matter. I didn't blame her for that either. I would probably be just as afraid if I were her.

Ashley thanked her for her cooperation, grabbed both my arm and Mathew's before leading us back to her car. We then got in, and she drove north.

"How did she accomplish an escape?" Mathew shook his head. "It just isn't plausible."

"But these things can happen, Mat. She has obviously done so." Ashley's hand went into the air. "I wish I had an answer for you."

I knew exactly what she did. Her Shadow told her the easiest way to get out, and Joseph helped. Her Shadow must have been planning this escape, and once they had the chance, they got out. I saw someone run past, and thinking it was our escapee, I leaned forward towards Ashley. "Stop!"

Ashley stopped the car, pulling over to the side of the road. We were just outside of Golden Loch so there was a good chance we were going to run into Ruby.

I got my seatbelt off and pushed my car door open. I stepped onto the sidewalk and started running towards whoever it was that I saw with Ashley and Mathew following behind me. This area looks to have been abandoned for some time so there was no one else around. We should be able to catch Ruby without much trouble.

"What is it?" Ashley had caught up. She was right next to me and keeping pace.

"Did you see that?" I pointed. "I saw a girl. She went down one of these alleyways." I came to a skidded stop when I found the girl who was hiding behind an old dumpster.

"Roxann?" I heard Ashley behind me. Ashley glared at me. I had stopped way to quickly for her, and she almost ran into me.

"I tried to stop her." Roxann stood up. She had natural blonde hair and dark brown eyes. "I was coming to see her and-" She shook her head, tears streaming down her face. "I'm sorry, Ash."

"Don't apologize. Things happen." Ashley put her hand on her shoulder. "Why were you hiding?"

"I saw you coming. I wasn't sure it was *you*, so I was trying to hide. You know how crime is abundant up this way with no one around." Roxann had answered Ashley.

Ashley grumbled something under her breath before agreeing with Roxann. "I understand."

"Which way did Ruby go?" I asked Roxann. Surely, she knew where Ruby had run off to.

She hesitated, not sure if she could trust me. Was it because she didn't know me or because I was a cop? Honestly, it seemed like she and Ashley were cool with one another, maybe it was because I was the newbie here.

"Go on." Ashley tried to encourage Roxann to talk to me. "You can trust him; he is with me."

She looked to me, back to Ashley, then to me again before answering my question. "She went back towards town."

Ashley thanked her. "You should come back with us; it isn't a good idea walking around in this part."

Roxann agreed to Ashley's statement and walked back to the car with us.

"There you two are." Mathew was waiting for us. "I circled back when you two had found Roxann. I didn't think it would have been a good idea to leave your car unattended."

Ashley took her keys out of her jacket pocket and unlocked the doors. After getting in, we made our way back to the office.

After getting back, Ashley, Mathew, and I decided it be best if we split up to look for Ruby.

"Mat and I will go north and east. Frankie, I want you to start heading south. Roxann, would you be a dear and head to the west side of town?"

Roxann nodded slowly. "I sure can, Ash. Anything to find Ruby. I just want to bring her back safely." She was the first to leave the office.

Mathew had left right after her, along with Ashley. I followed right behind them. I decided to leave my car here and make this trip by foot. I didn't want to freak Ruby out by driving, and if I needed to get somewhere that I couldn't have my large SUV, it was better to leave it here.

Joseph had then appeared right next to me. "I know where she is. I have been in contact with her Shadow."

Of course, he had been in contact with her Shadow. He really was part of her escape plan. Ruby must be very confused right now. "Take me to her."

He led me to an abandoned building on the opposite side of town. Walking inside, you could see that this used to be an apartment building. Whatever happened to it, time was not kind to this place. I could only imagine how many ghosts were here waiting for a Necromancer to come along and be their host. "Ruby?!" I called down the empty hallways. There was no answer.

"You." A girl appeared; I knew it was a ghost. I can always tell, and she must have been waiting for me to come here with Joseph.

"Keiko, where is Ruby?" Joseph had asked. So, this was Ruby's Shadow who had been with her locked away in the institution for years.

"Hiding." Keiko's voice echoed through the building. Even if ghosts are not actually here, their voices still carry as if they were. "Come on." She led us down the halls. "So, this is Frankie?" She looked at me.

I gave a nod. "You two know one another?" Of course, they do. Joseph had helped them escape that building. Surely Keiko didn't need him, but having another set of eyes was helpful.

"Barely, we only met earlier today. He helped us out of that terrible place." She pointed to a table in one of the bedrooms on the first floor. "Behind there."

I walked over and knelt to be closer to her. "Ruby?" Her knees were against her body, and her head was buried in them, hiding her face from the world.

She looked up at me, slowly. "Are you real?" she had dark black hair and honey brown eyes. Those eyes looked terrified, and the clothes she was in screamed patient, but I wasn't planning on taking her back. She needed someone like me to help her find her way back into society without making herself seem as if she was crazy.

I gave a sympathetic nod. "I am." It hurt me knowing she really wasn't sure who was real, and who wasn't anymore. I had to lead the way.

She touched my arm. "I don't want to go back there. The medicine makes me sleep all the time, and I still see her when I wake. Please. Don't make me go back."

"Her?" I thought she was talking about Elizabeth.

"Keiko." I was wrong then; she was afraid of Keiko.

"Oh-" I looked back at Joseph and Keiko. "Ruby, can I introduce you to my personal friend?" I wanted to be gentile about this introduction, but there was only one way do this. If I could get Ruby to understand, then it would not be so hard to get Jacquelynn to understand.

"Friend?" She asked, pulling her hand off of my arm and putting it into my own. "Who?"

I helped her stand, leading her over to both Joseph and Keiko. "This here is Joseph."

She swallowed. "But-" she hid behind me. "No. He is like her. Make them go away, please."

"I can see Keiko too." I went on. "It seems we have some things in common." I led her closer. "Don't be afraid, Ruby. They are here to help us, and they have no malicious intent. I can promise you this much."

"No. That isn't possible." She shook her head, closing her eyes. "There is no way you can see what I see that is not there. They told me that I see people and I shouldn't."

"I can tell you with certainty that I see both Keiko and Joseph." I propped her forward to be standing in front of me. "If I couldn't, then how do I know she has brown hair and brown eyes?" I asked.

"It's on file." Ruby muttered.

"Ruby…" Keiko said. "Frankie is here to help you. He is telling you the truth, at least try and listen to what he has to say."

"Frankie?" She looked at me. So maybe she was sure that Keiko was real but was too afraid to admit it.

"Frankie is my name." I told her. "And just like you, I am a Necromancer."

Ruby looked at me as if I was crazy. "Necro- who?"

"Necromancer. We can see ghosts. Keiko isn't in your head. She is real. Only people like us can see and talk to her. She is your Shadow, just like Joseph is mine. She is just trying to help you, and in return, all she wants is to be your friend." I gave her a minute to try and process what I was saying. "How old are you?"

"Seventeen." She glanced at me. "I have been inside that place since I was twelve."

"That would make sense as you would have to be twelve when Keiko came to you." I motioned to where Keiko was standing.

"Obviously, you know that because you read my file." Ruby bit her lip, while looking Keiko up and down a few times. Ruby was already warming up to her Shadow.

"Yes, however, I was the same age when Joseph came to my side. My daughter Jacquelynn is eight now and I know when she is twelve, she will also have a Shadow." I told her. "We can summon ghosts and talk to the dead as well. I have never met anyone outside my own family who was a Necromancer."

"My friend Roxann-" She turned around to face me. "Every time she comes to see me..." she trailed off.

"Every time Roxann comes, so does Zeke." Keiko told both me and Joseph. "And Roxann tries to talk to Ruby, but she is too out of it from the drugs they give her."

"They are always trying to put me to sleep." Ruby gripped her arms in both hands, looking at the ground. "I don't want to go to sleep anymore."

I gave a slow nod, Roxann is like Ruby and I. That made sense, Roxann did seem to hesitate when we met. She probably knew but wasn't entirely sure if I had any idea about her. "Where are your parents Ruby?" I asked her. I already knew the answer, but I wanted to see if she remembered what happened herself.

"I haven't seen them since I was eleven. I have been inside the institution since they had turned me over to the state. They never came back to see me." She looked saddened. "Roxann has been the only one to come to me frequently. She somehow found me. I'm not really sure, but..." She trailed off again. Roxann must have known how to locate fellow Necromancers nearby, I was sure to make a mental note for the next time I saw her.

"Roxann has been the closest thing to family." Keiko finished. That hurt me again, Ruby has had no one, but Roxann who was still but a stranger to her.

"Come on." I took her arm. "We should leave this building before someone else finds us here."

"Like who?" Ruby questioned me. She probably thought I meant those back at the institution.

"My colleagues. We live here in Golden Loch." I took her hand. "Everything is going to be just fine; I promise."

"Wait." Ruby stopped me. "I'm not going back to that terrible place. They aren't nice to me."

I gave a slow nod. "I won't take you back. That is a promise, Ruby. You can stay with me." She was going to need a place to stay, and hopefully in time, she will tell me what she knows about Elizabeth.

I walked back through town with Ruby by my side. Joseph was trailing behind us, and Keiko ahead, keeping an eye on things.

"You might lose your job for this." Joseph called to me. He was maybe ten or so feet behind us, his voice echoed through the street. It was late in the day, so it didn't matter as there was barely anyone out.

"Maybe, but I have to help Ruby. I won't let her fall victim to the human system again." I kept my head forward so no one would think I was losing it myself; it made it look as if I was chatting with Ruby instead of Joseph behind me.

"Will you keep it down?" Keiko looked over her shoulder at us. "We don't want anyone to see us."

"You mean Frankie and me." Ruby responded. "No one is going to notice you or Joseph." Ruby was right about that. If we were caught, it would look like the two of us strolling away from an abandoned building. Not that it would matter anyway, I was a detective and Ashley's partner who was also doing his job.

I hushed Ruby by putting a finger to my lips. We were better off not answering either of them right now. At least not until we had got back home.

After about a half-hour of silence between the four of us, we reached my house. I led Ruby up the porch stairs, unlocked the front door, and then went inside. I had shut the door behind us, but Keiko and Joseph had just walked in through the wall. They didn't need a door anyway so that didn't matter, if I had left the door open and Jacquelynn was standing right there, there would be way too many questions to answer right now. I was hoping to wait until she was at least eleven before I explained what she was going to grow into.

"Daddy?" I heard the patter of Jacquelynn's feet coming down the hallway. She appeared in the living area, already dressed for bed. "Who is this?" She had taken Ruby's hand and looked up at her. Both Joseph and Keiko disappeared when Jacquelynn came out, not wanting to interrupt.

"This is Ruby. She will be staying with us for a while." I led Ruby to the couch and had her sit down. "You will treat her like our guest."

Jacquelynn nodded. "Yes." She climbed onto the couch and sat next to Ruby. "I'm Jacquelynn."

Ruby smiled at her and looked at me a moment. Ruby had a look that said she wasn't sure if she could talk to Jacquelynn about who we were.

I shook my head; I knew she would understand. Or at least I hoped so. There was no way to really tell that we were thinking the same thing. She did know that my daughter was too young, however.

"Hi, Jacquelynn." Ruby smiled, pulling her legs up with her onto the couch.

They were going to get along just fine; I could feel it. There was no real need to worry about Ruby as she was just like myself when I was young. It is a very confusing time and She needs guidance to get her to where she needs to be with confidence. "I have to make a phone call, stay here." They didn't mind that I was leaving them alone for the moment, so I left to go out front and call Ashley.

"Ashley Aequitas." I heard her answer, while also making a hushing sound. I heard her step outside of her house, away from the noise.

I waited a moment for her to stop moving around to talk. "Ash, its me."

"Updates?" She asked. "I haven't heard anything from you all day. Mat, Roxann, and I called it day hours ago. I hope you are heading home soon."

"I am home, but there is something else you should know in the realm of updates." I paused, hoping she would have said something in return. After a few moments of silence, I just told her. "I have Ruby here at my house."

"I'm already on my way." She sounded as if she was ready to rush over here. That was not my intent, and I was hoping to handle Ruby on my own without anyone else.

"No." It came out much worse than I had intended it to, it sounded like I was barking an order at her. "I am telling you because I trust you not to tell Mathew or Luther."

"*Excuse me?*" I heard her start her car up on her end. "No offense Frankie, but that isn't how things work around here. I explained this to you earlier, here, we work as a unit, no secret B.S. that city folk carry. We cannot afford to keep secrets from one another."

I didn't answer immediately, I was debating on what to do next. Do I tell her the truth about myself and Ruby? She would think I am the one who needs to be put away, this wasn't the right time. "Ash, I think that Ruby doesn't belong there."

"Really? Why is that?" Her tone gave off the idea that she did not agree with what I was saying. She didn't understand.

"She isn't crazy." I was hoping that Ashley would listen to what I was saying, even if she didn't agree.

"Frankie, are you feeling okay?" She asked me. "Because if you need a day off from this case…"

"How is Ruby even connected?" I changed her train of thought, back to Ruby. I was not becoming the center of the topic.

"If you came back to the office, Mat and I would have told you. You didn't though. Has she told you she is seeing Beth in her sleep?" That much I knew, but I only found that out from Joseph. I couldn't tell her I knew that. Ruby had not even spoke on the matter. "Frankie?"

"I have to go." I hung up the phone. I had to play this out to see where it went and ask Ruby what she knew about Elizabeth even though I was trying to wait to let her talk to me on her own. I walked back into the living area where Jacquelynn was talking with Ruby. "Pumpkin." I interrupted their conversation. "Do you mind going to your bedroom?"

Jacquelynn slid down and off the sofa. "Work time." She took my hand for a second and smiled at me before running through the hallway.

I waited a few seconds before speaking to Ruby. I took my place on my chair by the fireplace. "You saw Elizabeth."

"Who-" She pursed her lips; I knew she would not be willing to talk about it.

"Ashley told me." I leaned forward. "You have about ten minutes to tell me what you know before Ash gets here and tells you that you have to go back." I wasn't trying to threaten her, but I knew that Ashley would not back off.

She hesitated. Her hands clasped together and her body tensing up. "You told her I was here and now she is going to take me back. That lady was trying to get me to tell her what I saw. Why would you go to an institution like that, just to get information on a killer? I don't get that." She shook her head. "Why did you tell her?"

"Ruby, I can't help you with this if you don't talk about what you have seen." I felt for her, I really did. She was feeling lost and didn't know who she could trust.

"Elizabeth asked me to help her. She said that a man named Frankie can help me and that I needed to find you. When Joseph came and said he was going to help me find you, I thought that there might be a chance that I was going to win this time. Now you are telling that lady that I am here, and she won't let me stay." She looked me in the eyes. "Elizabeth died you know."

"I do know." I let out a slow sigh. "Which is why we need to find her body so that Saidie, her sister, can finally grieve and move on."

Ruby's eyes shifted to the fireplace. "Promise me I won't have to go back." I could see tears starting to form in her eyes. She was afraid of what Ashley might do.

"Tell me what you know, then I promise you will not have to go back there." I wasn't taking her back, no matter what she said but I was still hoping she would tell me.

"She is stuck somewhere between life and death." Ruby replied, her feet fell to the ground. She wasn't so tense anymore. "I wish I understood what that meant."

"Did she tell you this?" I didn't know what that meant either, however, I am sure we would find out soon enough.

She shrugged. "I just felt it. I wasn't too sure about what I saw until this morning when Ashley and Mathew showed up. They started asking questions about her. Somehow they knew I was seeing Elizabeth and they wanted to know about it."

"That was when you knew something was going on here, wasn't it? Elizabeth told you my name, and Joseph came by, but something else was the real reason on why you left."

"Keiko was. She knew who you were and when Joseph came, it was just perfect timing, I guess. From the outside perspective you would probably say I am losing it all over again, but you aren't the outside perspective. Ashley and Mathew are." Why would a bunch of cops ask a teenage girl who has been locked away for years about a murder that she knows nothing about? Especially since she never met the girl." Ruby looked at the window behind her. "That's her."

"Yes, it is." I got up and went over to the door to let Ashley inside.

Ashley walked past me and over to Ruby. "You can't keep her here." She had her hands on her hips now and was looking at Ruby as if she was going to disappear if she looked away.

"Give her a chance, Ash." I shut the door and walked over to them. "She isn't going to run."

"She is crazy, Frankie." Ashley looked to me. "And she is a ward of the state. Her parents signed her over."

"What if I took her in, then?" I knew that it was going to come to this, I was not letting her slip through the cracks.

"Then I would say you are also losing it, Detective." Ashley shook her head. She knelt towards Ruby. "I'm also curious about how she escaped."

Ruby looked at Ashley, not speaking. She had to be feeling terrified again. I didn't blame her for that, after working with Ashley for the last few days, I have learned she was tough and didn't back off until the job was complete.

"She doesn't even talk." Ashley shook her head. "Mathew and I were with her for two hours, and she didn't speak to us once." She stood up and looked at me. "Please don't be foolish about this."

I sighed. "She is just scared. Give her a chance and don't make her look like a freak."

Ashley grunted at my comment. "This isn't right Frankie; we can't keep her here. You of all people should know that."

"Then what? We send her back? She-" Ashley had stopped me from talking back, I may have been doing this job longer then her, but she was in charge here. She had been on this crew for a much longer time. She knew how the law of this town worked way better than I did.

"Frankie." Ashley looked me in the eyes. "You cannot keep her. I'll give you until the end of the day tomorrow to get her back otherwise you are off the team." She went to the front door, slamming it behind her. I heard her car start-up, her tires squealing away from the house, and then her car was gone.

"Oh man, you made her mad." Joseph appeared alongside Keiko. He looked amused and very concerned at the same time.

"Thank you." Ruby stood up and hugged me. "No one has stood up for me like that before."

I put my hand on her back, letting her hug me. "What about Roxann?" I asked her.

She backed away and shrugged at my question. "Roxann may be my only friend, but she had no way of getting me out of that place. She said that she wanted to one day, but I never had any idea of when that was going to be."

"You had help." I said to her. "Joseph and Keiko were there to help you get out, but you had to have someone else. There was no way you did that without help from a physical body."

"I can't tell you." She shook her head. "I'm sorry Frankie. I just... I can't, okay?"

"Ruby, I am not forcing you to talk about it, but you and I will have to talk about this someday." One day she and I will need to talk about how she got out. It could be tomorrow or years from now. I would just have to be patient about it.

Chapter 5

I figured it was best to let Ruby rest for a while. It had been such a long day, and I didn't want to keep bothering her about how she escaped. She would also talk about Elizabeth when she was ready. It was almost eight when I decided to go out to chat with Payton and Lucius. I figured that it would be better to talk to Payton first since she was younger and would probably be in bed much earlier. I reached for my jacket and car keys when I felt a hand tug on my shirt.

"You are going back out, Daddy?" Jacquelynn looked up at me with tired eyes. "When are you coming back?"

"I will be home around ten, Pumpkin. Just make sure you are in bed before then, okay?" I picked her up and held her in my one arm. "Ruby is also sleeping on the couch." I motioned to Ruby who had been sleeping there for the last twenty minutes. "Let her be and get yourself back in bed." I kissed her forehead and let her down.

"Promise to come and see me when you get home." Jacquelynn puffed out her lips, crossing her arms. She may have been a child, but she sure had a huge personality.

"Of course, I will. Just like I always have." I slid my jacket over my arms. "I have to make a few house visits, and then I will come right home."

Jacquelynn nodded. "Okay, then. Be careful, Daddy." She hugged my leg before running down the hallway and going back into her bedroom.

I shook my head, smiling. I knew she was going to be fine. Ruby was here now, and I had a feeling that I could trust her with my daughter for a few hours. I went out to my car and got in. I looked back at the house, Keiko was nearby as well so even if something did happen while I was gone, I was sure Keiko would tell me.

I pulled up to the office, walked up to the door unlocking it, and stepped inside. It had a very eerie feel to it in the dark like this. I had quickly turned the lights on and sat at Ashley's computer.

Logging on, I looked up both Payton's address and Lucius' as well. I was sure that I would get my ass handed to me on Monday when I came back in, but there had to be information I could gather if I spoke with them, one on one. I took my sticky note, shoved it into my pocket, and shut the computer off. I stood out of my chair and turned to look at the office behind me before reaching for the door.

"Boo!" Joseph jumped out in front of me.

I was ready to slap him before stopping myself. He would not have felt it but it was the principle of the slap. However, I was spooking myself, so I completely deserved that one. I should not be so spooked by an empty office, but there was something lingering here that did not sit right with me at this time of night. "Not funny, Joseph." I pushed the front door open, locking it behind me, and climbing into my SUV.

"Oh, come on, it was funny. You are not used to being here late at night." He was now sitting in the seat next to me. "Besides, you caught yourself in that one." He chuckled. "I saw that look on your face. You were ready to slap me."

I rolled my eyes at his comment. He was right I was going to slap him. I looked down at the sticky note in my hand and then drove to Payton's home. It only took about three minutes to get there.

Once we had reached Payton's home, I got out of the SUV. Joseph was trailing behind me as we walked up her driveway. There was a large tree with a swing out front and two cars. I assumed the swing was for Alexa and that she and Jacquelynn's teacher was also here. I walked across the stone path that led to the door and knocked.

The door opened to a little girl, who I recognized as Alexa. She had these bright grey eyes and silvery blonde hair. She reminded me a little of Payton. "Hello, dear." I leaned forward and smiled to show I was friendly.

"You are here for my mommy?" She asked me, her head tilting to the side.

"Actually, I am here to talk to Payton. Is she home? I was hoping that we could talk for a few minutes. It won't be long." I thought she would listen to me and get Payton. I wouldn't want Jacquelynn talking to someone who she didn't know for too long. I figured Alexa was taught the same because it didn't matter who was at your door, kids should *always* get an adult.

"Yes. I can't talk to you because I don't know you." She told me. "Let me get her." She disappeared from their dining room.

"Smart kid." Joseph spoke to me. I looked at my watch, standing up.

"Detective." Payton came strolling over. She used her hand to get me to move away from the door so she could step outside. "What is it? I told you everything that I know. I barely knew Beth. I don't have any of the same classes as Saidie, so we aren't exactly friends."

"I don't expect you to know anything about Saidie. I was only hoping we could chat for a few moments." This was not going to be easy; Payton didn't even want to talk to me in the diner, what would make her change her mind now?

"Then what do you want, Detective? You should be out there looking for the person who did this, not wasting your time with me." Payton rolled her eyes and shook her head. "You don't think it was me, do you?"

"Of course not. I want you tell me about Malcolm and Delilah. I am almost ready to cross them off my list of suspects, but I want to hear from you first." I informed her.

"Delilah is a sweet woman and the best boss I have ever had. She wouldn't do such a thing to someone like Elizabeth." She worked her jaw. "And I can tell you it wasn't Malcolm either because he would never hurt a soul." She reached for the door. "Now please, will you go away? I am tired of being questioned by you and Ashley."

"Ashley was here then?" I didn't think Ashley would have come by, but if she did, then maybe we are crisscrossing each other without realizing it.

"Not recently, but before you came here, she was crossing names off the list. She asked me about them too. I don't even know why because I wasn't even an employee there at the time." She was ready to go back inside.

"Just let me ask you this then; Why do you think she asked you?" She must have known why. Ashley was supposed to inform her of why she was coming to see her.

Payton opened the front door to her house. "Probably because Saidie is in the same grade as me. There are not that many people in this town, so anyone in middle or high school has to go into Detroit for school. Most of the kids don't like us, so she probably thought that maybe I would have answers, but I don't. Sorry, Detective." She opened her door and went back inside, closing it behind her. A sure sign she was done talking to me.

"Ashley had to work every angle that she could think of." Joseph followed me back to my car and I examined my sticky note again for Lucius' address.

"Do you really think Malcolm and Delilah did it?" He asked me, concerned. "You don't. I have known you for a long time, Frankie. You know that they didn't."

"I still have to do this the right way. If I don't and go after who I think did it, then we could lose the case." I turned down a one-way street where all the houses looked just about the same with one large home at the end of the street. It looked more like a church but occupied as if someone was living there. I pulled into one of the driveways on the street, getting out I noticed how Lucius' home was the same color as the rest, blue. There were bushes giving privacy to the front porch and a pebble path that led to the side door. I pushed open the gate to the side door and knocked.

I heard some shuffling around before the door opened. "Oh, hello, Frankie." He smiled. "Just a moment." He shut the door and I heard him unlocking the chain that kept the door from opening all the way. "Please, come in." He led me through the hallway, past the two bedrooms, and into the kitchen where I saw the front door. "Sorry for the mess, I had company and have not had a chance to clean up."

"Don't worry about it. I am the one barging in on you." I answered. "Do you think you can spare a few minutes of your time to talk with me?"

"Sure." He motioned for me to sit on the sofa in the living room to our left. He then sat on his love seat and leaned back. "What's up?"

"I need you to tell me what you know about Malcolm and Delilah." Maybe Lucius would be more willing to talk to me.

"My bosses?" He smiled, shook his head, and leaned forward looking me in the eyes. "They are not bad people if that is what you are implying."

"No of course not, I just need to make sure they have their alibies straight. You and Payton are the two that can provide me with the information I am looking for. I know Payton was not working there at the time, she did however give me some information that I needed. Now I am hoping you can talk to me about what you know."

"What do you want me to say? I have nothing bad to say about them. They gave me my calling, and I make good money to pay for my home and to keep the church up the street running." He made a motion towards the wall, but I knew he was pointing towards the church.

"Then can you tell me where they were the night that Elizabeth was murdered?" I was calm about it. There was no need to force anything.

"At the diner. We were busier than normal that night. Elizabeth left after the rush with her boyfriend." He told me. "I didn't think that she was being odd or anything of the sort. I figured she was frustrated about the rush. We all were tired by the end of the night, especially after cleaning up, so we decided we would come in early the next morning to finish up anything we might have missed. Problem is, Elizabeth never showed. Malcolm and Delilah were worried, so they called her cellphone. When she didn't answer, they called Saidie who told them she never came home that night. That caused an alarm because Elizabeth is always punctual. She had never been late for anything. That was when we called Ash and Mat who came out to the diner right away and took statements. They searched all over town, but they never found her. They did however find her blood on that bridge."

"Yes, and her backpack in the river, but she was missing. There were no signs of struggle." I shook my head. "Malcolm and Delilah were not the ones who did this."

"No of course they were not, Frankie. I can attest that they were at the diner the entire night." Lucius stood up. "If there is anything else you need, please just stop by."

I stood up too. "Thank you, Lucius. You have been very helpful." We shook hands.

He then walked me back to the side door. "I wish you luck on finding who did this, Detective. I can't even imagine what Saidie is going through, the poor kid."

I agreed, Saidie wasn't doing well. She needed us to find Elizabeth. "Yes, we are doing everything that we can." Lucius said goodbye to me before I walked back to my SUV.

Once I got back home, I looked at Ruby, giving a sympathetic nod. She was having a rough time just as well, and I knew that I could help her. This was my personal goal. No matter what Ashley tries to tell me, Ruby is not going back to that institution. She will stay with me for as long as she needed to and that was a promise I was making to myself. I hung my jacket up, walked past her to go down the hallway to my own bedroom and then shut the door behind me.

"Then who did it? I know you have an idea." Joseph was sitting on my dresser.

"I have a list of suspects. It is still between Luther and Ashley. I know that sounds harsh, but I have a strong feeling it is one of my own." I pulled the covers back on my bed.

"That is why you are doing this on your own." He didn't say much more after that.

I was lying down in bed when the door creaked open. "Daddy, you said you would come and see me."

"Oh, I am so sorry Pumpkin, come here." I patted the bed next to me.

She crawled into bed next to me and cuddled up under my arm. "Remember when I would lay between you and Mommy, and we would all sleep in the bed together?" She closed her eyes. "I miss her."

I kissed the top of her head. "I do too." Jacquelynn drifted off into a sleep, and I shut the light off. "Goodnight, my little Pumpkin." I looked to Joseph who then got up to leave the bedroom. He was always great about that, leaving when I finally settled in for the night. He may be a pain, but he still respected my privacy. I closed my eyes and eventually fell asleep myself.

Chapter 6

It was Sunday, my personal day off. I signed up to work six days a week, with one day off. I decided when I woke up to make Jacquelynn breakfast and then take her to the farm down the road to see if we could get her, her very own horse.

"I want a pretty one." She said with her mouth full of food. "White and brown." She shoved her pancakes into her mouth.

"All horses are pretty." I was eating with her while waiting for Ruby to wake. "I'm sure you'll find one that speaks to you." I took a few sips of my coffee. My daughter is the one person keeping me grounded through this hard change. She is always full of excitement and some days I was not sure where the off button was, but I was slowly learning that she is the same as I was when I was her age. She also had my energy and enthusiasm about everything. I looked over when I saw Ruby walk into the kitchen and plop herself into a chair. "Hungry?" I pushed a plate towards her. "Eat." She looked at me as if I was going to poison her, shove her into the SUV, and take her back, but then decided she was too hungry right now to care.

"Thank you, I haven't had anything to eat like this in a long time." She cut her pancakes and drizzled her syrup on top.

"Daddy?" Jacquelynn spoke out. "Can Ruby come with us?" She bounced up in her seat. "Please!?"

I smiled a bit. "If she would like to." I put my cup down on the table.

"Where?" Ruby looked at me, curiously.

"Daddy is getting me a horse." Jacquelynn smiled wide. "My mommy always wanted one." She pushed her fork into another large amount of pancake pieces.

"A horse? That sounds really cool, Jacquelynn." Ruby put her fork on her napkin. "Where is your wife, if you don't mind me asking?"

I gripped my mug in both hands. It was a sensitive topic for me, as it had barely been a month and the wounds were still fresh. I still had not taken my wedding band off my finger. Call it whatever you want, but my wife and I were happy.

"She left then." Ruby sat back in her chair.

"No." I shook my head. "She passed." I wasn't afraid to tell people she passed away, but I wasn't ready to throw my entire story out there.

"Can I ask how?" Ruby looked down at her plate, ready to push it away.

"Cancer." I replied getting up and putting my things in the sink. "Finish up, put your things in the sink and meet me outside, girls. Please eat something, Ruby. Don't let this get you down." I walked out the front door and headed towards the lake.

"You need to grieve, Frankie." Joseph appeared. "You cannot keep running away from her death every time it is brought up in a conversation. If Ruby is going to be living here with you, she has a right to know."

I stood in front of the lake, looking out towards town. I put my hands in my pockets. "I am grieving. In my own way." I stared into the distance, making out the office on the other side and a few houses. I could see the diner in the distance on the other side of the homes.

"You talk to the dead." Joseph looked out with me. "You have a gift."

"Yet I can't even talk to my own wife. The woman who I was married to for fourteen years." I shook my head. "Life just isn't fair is it?"

"Daddy!" I heard Jacquelynn call me, the front door shutting behind her.

I turned around to see her running across the jetty towards me. "Let's go!" She took my hand and led me down back towards the SUV. I got into the driver's side, Ruby getting in next to me, and Jacquelynn in the back.

"Make sure you buckle up, Ruby." I heard my daughter. "You have to think about safety first."

Ruby put her seatbelt on just as Jacquelynn had told her to. "Is she always this full of energy?"

I smiled. "I wouldn't have it any other way."

I pulled down an old dirt road, past a sign that stated 'Wilson's', and then pulled into the farm's parking lot that held maybe six or seven cars. The lot was mostly grass with lines drawn with paint. We got out of the SUV and we're immediately greeted by a kid.

"Welcome!" The girl about fourteen, smiled when seeing us. "You're not from around here, are you?" Was it that obvious? Maybe it was the Florida tan or the fact that everyone knew each other around here.

I shook my head. "No, we are from the south. My name is Frankie, this is my daughter Jacquelynn, and this is our friend Ruby."

She grinned from ear to ear, pleased to have someone new around here. "I'm Sarah. What can I help you with?"

"I spoke to Bailey over the phone about adopting a horse." I informed her. Surely, she would know what to do.

"Oh your Mr. Dawson. Yeah, Bailey is my dad. Let me take you to him." She then led us to the house where a young man who had to be about Ruby's age, and a woman were sitting and having some lemonade that looked to be freshly squeezed.

"Mom! Gage!" She yelled, waving to her hand in the air as we approached.

"Sarah, who are these people?" her mom asked, intrigued that they had visitors.

"Mom, this is Mr. Dawson. Dad talked to them on the phone." Sarah answered her mother.

"Gage, go get your father." She looked at the teenage boy who grumbled and went inside.

"So, I hear you are from Miami." Their mom put her hand out. "My name is Jean. Bailey and I run this farm here together along with our son and daughter."

I gave a nod and shook her hand. "Yes, it was quite a long drive, but we made it."

"You will like it here, most of the folk are pleasant, you only have to watch out for a few of them." She turned her head as her husband came out.

"Ah, Frankie Dawson. It is so nice to put a face to a voice. Thank you for coming by." He walked up to me. "Let me show you the horses." He took us back outside, led us down a dirt path, and towards the back of the house. The barn was surrounded by a large fenced in area.

"Daddy?" Jacquelynn looked at me. She took my hand; I could see that she was excited to be here.

"Yes, Pumpkin?" I held her hand tightly.

"Mommy will be so happy. She is probably watching us from wherever she is and smiling." Jacquelynn let go of my hand, skipping ahead towards the barn, catching up to Bailey.

"You'll have to tell her soon." Ruby told me. "You don't want her to think she is going crazy." Of course, Ruby was right about this. There was, however, no need to tell her right now.

"She has a few years still. She is only eight." I wasn't going to drag her into it quite yet. She had so much time left without thinking about being followed around by a Shadow for the rest of her life.

"Keep telling yourself that and then next thing you know she is waking up as a twelve-year-old girl, confused." Ruby shook her head. No way was I letting that happen to my daughter, there will be a right time to talk to her about what we are and what she will become, but today was not that day.

Ruby and I watched as Bailey pulled three horses out to show us. Jacquelynn had moved back out of the way, her eyes full of glee. "Two mares and a gelding. I think the gelding would be better suited for a child."

"Child?" Jacquelynn looked up at Bailey, wide eyed.

"It will be easier for you to learn to ride if you had a young gelding. Our male is young enough to be learning still just as you will be. Plus, you will get to grow up with him, doesn't that sound exciting?" Bailey knelt to her. "When Sarah and Gage were your age, I made sure they had the perfect horse. I want the same for you as well, Jacquelynn."

She smiled and hugged Bailey. "My mommy always wanted a horse." She backed up and examined the gelding. "Can I name him?"

"Of course, you can name him whatever you would like." Bailey smiled. "He is yours so make sure you pick out the perfect name. It will be his forever." Bailey had touched the tip of her nose with his finger.

"How about Snow? He is white just like when the snow comes down from the sky." She circled the gelding and then jumped up and down. "Snow! Snow!"

Bailey smiled. "Snow it is, then. That name is perfect. Make sure you take great care of him." He looked my way. "I will need you to sign some paperwork so we can sign Snow over to you and Jacquelynn."

"Ruby, do you mind staying here with my daughter while Mr. Wilson and I do some paperwork?" I motioned to Jacquelynn.

Ruby was more than happy to help out. "I sure can." She walked towards my daughter, looking at her horse, giving it a pet, and lifting her up to pet the him.

I walked into the house with Bailey. "Thank you for doing this. Jacquelynn has been looking forward to having a horse of her own since her mother brought the idea up a few years ago. I am happy I can finally bring it to reality for her."

"She is a cutie with great manners." Bailey patted my shoulder. "You should be proud of her."

"She takes after her mother." I followed Bailey into his house and over to the island counter.

"It must be hard." He pulled out a folder from the drawer. "I could never imagine losing Jean." He put the paper down on the island and handed me a pen.

I picked the pen up and started reading the papers. "It is. I have been taking things day by day and staying strong, for Jacquelynn."

"Most of these folks know that you lost your wife. You can't come into a town and think no one will know about you. Of course, not everything is true, which is why it is best to keep my mouth shut until I hear it from the source." Bailey shrugged.

"Wise of you to do so. I wouldn't want anyone asking me odd questions anyway. Though I am sure no one else around here would want someone dropping in on them and asking them personal questions either. My wife was my rock. She held down the fort at home while I would work. Now I have to hope Jacquelynn is okay when I am not around." I shook my head.

"We could watch her." Jean came out. "There's four of us here, plus that would give her more time with… what has she named her horse?"

"Snow." I stood up straight. "She named him Snow. I also cannot impose on you like that." I was not forcing anyone to watch my kid when I was not around. It was my own responsibility to get her to school in the morning and watch her off the bus in the afternoon.

"Nonsense. Gage and Sarah are older now. They don't need someone to watch over them. When she gets old enough, she can certainly work here if she would like." Jean seemed happy enough to help out.

Bailey looked at his wife. "I agree, let the two of us help you out." He then turned to me. "You are working six days a week."

"She has school. You'd have to get her off the bus." I didn't want them to feel like this was an obligation and had to take Jacquelynn in under their roof when I couldn't be home.

"Easy." Jean put her arm around her husband. "I can have the school send the bus this way. They are very accommodating."

It didn't seem like too terrible of an idea, so I let them babysit her. "Thank you, I appreciate that. Speaking of which, do you mind watching her for a bit then?"

"Of course, not at all." Jean patted her husband's hand. "Why don't you show her how to lead her gelding around the fenced in area?"

Bailey agreed to work with Jaquelynn. The two of us walked back outside to Jacquelynn and Ruby. The two of them were brushing Snow and I could hear my daughter talking about her mother as if she was still here.

"Pumpkin!" I called, waving my hand to her.

"Daddy!" She came running as fast as her little legs could carry her over to me.

"Would you like to stay here for a bit?" I asked my daughter.

She nodded fast. "Yes! Is Ruby staying too?"

"Actually, Ruby and I have some work to do." I glanced over at Ruby, who was still standing next to Snow.

Jacquelynn looked sad, but I knew she understood. "Okay, can I play with Snow for a little while?"

I looked at Bailey who nodded and took her hand. "Your dad and Ruby have some things that they need to discuss." He led her to the horse. "But don't worry, you and I are going to play with Snow for a little while."

Jacquelynn giggled and let Bailey walk with her. She was going to be fine. I did not need to worry because Bailey and Jean were going to take good care of her when I had to work.

"We need to see Ash." I said once I was able to finally walk away from my daughter. Ruby didn't argue or say a word about it.

I pulled up to Ashley's home. It was sandwiched between two other houses, but she had yard larger than either of them. I noticed how yellow it was and how black the roof had been. I heard a dog barking as we walked towards her house. I reached up and knocked on the window. There was no answer, and the entire house looked dark, so I peered in and saw her sitting outback. I led Ruby to the back gate, hoping that Ashley would let us in. "Ashley." I peered over the tall wooden fence.

She looked over. "You brought Ruby along." She walked over, pulling a purple hoodie that had the letters GLPD over her head, and opened the gate. "Why are you here, Frankie?" She let us in and then led us to the patio.

The dog who we heard barking came running over. He was a small brown bulldog who had a giant tree branch in his mouth.

"Bruce." She said sternly, and the bulldog ran back into the yard with his tree branch. She then glared at Ruby, unsure of why she was here at all. "Please tell me you've made your mind up then, Detective."

"Yes. I have. It is our duty to protect." I sat down at the same time on the other side of the patio table from Ashley. "Which means I am going to protect Ruby."

"What are you getting at?" She called Bruce over to her. He had sat down in front of her, dropping the tree branch on the patio.

"I am saying that Ruby is staying with me, whether you like it or not. She needs me right now." Ruby was standing right next to me and I could see Ashley looking at her as if she was controlling me in some way.

"Right." She sighed and leaned forward, now looking me in the eyes. "What about your job?"

"You need a detective; I am a detective." I replied. "You could keep me on, or I can solve Elizabeth's murder on my own." I wasn't backing down.

"You cannot take the case for yourself." Ashley reached down to pet Bruce's head, not breaking eye contact with me. "The case was given to the department. That includes all of us."

"Yes, that may be so, but I also know that you need me." Sure, she could kick me off the case, but that would leave her with one less officer to take any leads that they would come across. "You need an extra head on this, that *is* why you hired me." She wasn't actually going to take me off the team.

"We hired you because you were one of the best in Miami's homicide department." She answered. "I have no idea why you took the job here, as we aren't paying you as well." She had tossed the branch into the yard, and Bruce ran as fast as his tiny stubby legs could carry him, barking a very slobbery bark along the way.

"It isn't about the money, Ash. I came here because, as I have said, you needed me. I also needed a change of pace. I miss my old home of course, but that isn't the point." I rested my hands on her table.

"Then what is the point you are making, Frankie?" I could see she was getting irritated.

"The point I am making is that we need Ruby and Ruby needs us. She has also told me that you came by to see her because she was seeing Elizabeth. Don't be so cruel, Ash."

"Do not make me force my hand in this matter." Ashley looked at Bruce. He was running around in circles with the branch that she had just thrown for him.

"You took your dog in because he needed someone." I was only speculating of course.

"I got him as a puppy on the side of the road." She looked at me. I needed to get to her soft side, and this was how I was going to get her to understand.

"Then why would you try and push Ruby away?" A person was no different than an animal, everyone needs help sometimes, and Ruby is the one who needs help this time.

She grunted, shaking her head and then letting out a smile. Bruce had come running back over to her with his tree branch. She looked down at Bruce. "Frankie Dawson, you are a pain in the ass." Her eyes met mine.

"Then Ruby stays." Bingo. I had gotten to her soft side.

"She can stay." Ashley gave a nod. "Just make sure she is okay and doesn't get herself into any kind of trouble."

"I will, and don't you worry, Ruby *won't* be getting into any trouble, not with someone like Jacquelynn around." I was only teasing, and I'm sure Ruby got that.

"I'll let Luther know our decision. What do you think we should do next? I am running out of ideas. This may become another inconclusive case." She sounded defeated.

"Another?" I looked at her oddly. With a town this small, there was no way there were that many cases that were left open.

"We have a whole folder of them. It's so frustrating knowing that Mat and I can only do so much. We don't have the same resources as the department in Detroit." She sighed. "If you weren't there the other day, Saidie may have not made it."

"I know." I looked at Ruby. "We got lucky." I was going to need to see this folder. There may be some information in it that I could use for this case.

"You are a good man Frankie, don't get me wrong, I am only trying to protect everyone here, as are you. I can, however, see we are going to make one hell of a team even if we don't always see eye to eye on every decision." She looked at Ruby as well. "And maybe one day you could help us with a badge."

"That would be interesting." Ruby tried to give Ashley a friendly smile, probably not liking the idea too much.

"You two are talking, then?" Ashley leaned forward, her arms resting on the table.

"She's a good kid, Ash." Ruby didn't have to prove herself to me, but she may have to prove herself to Ashley and everyone else around here.

"I can speak, I just don't like the idea of someone calling insane. Just don't do that, okay?" She glanced away. I knew she was looking at Keiko because I saw her too, Joseph was not here though.

"Okay, okay. We won't speak on that matter." Ashley agreed to Ruby's terms.

"Thank you." Ruby tucked her hair behind her ears. "I do appreciate you understanding.

Ashley reached across the table when her phone rang. "It's Luther." She pressed the talk button on her phone screen. "Yeah, he is right here."

"Frankie." Luther said over the phone. "Axel is here in the office. He said you wanted to talk. Also, next time make sure you are listening to your phone ring. I should not have to call Ash to talk to you. I don't care what you three are doing on your time off, just make sure you are answering if I call you."

"Yes sir. I'll be right there." I didn't admit that I had forgotten about this. I chose to leave Ruby with Ashley so they could get to know each other a bit better. I thought it would be a good idea for the two of them to warm up to one another, especially since Ruby was staying for a while. I was also hoping Ruby wouldn't talk to Ashley about Keiko. I had no doubts that she was going to stay quiet on the matter of seeing Elizabeth in her dreams as she didn't want to talk to her about it anyway. There was no need to freak Ashley out, make her think we were both insane, and in on some kind of conspiracy theory. We would only tell her what was important and kept any information on how we could talk to ghosts or even the dead between the two of us until we could fit it into the actual case. It was hard working with a partner who was human, but Ashley was growing on me, and I could tell we were going to be good friends. Maybe one day we would be able to chat about what I was without scaring her.

Chapter 7

Okay, so yes, I forgot that I was supposed to meet with Axel about getting a permit to have a horse on our property. I was too busy making sure that my daughter got the horse she wanted to remember the second half of being allowed to have the horse on the property. After about three minutes, I had reached the office. I got out and walked towards the doors when I saw Mathew sitting in his car. "Mat?" I was not expecting to see him out here on a Sunday.

"Frankie!" I guess I surprised him because he looked like he was focused someplace else. He stepped out of his Bentley that had to have been from 1984.

"What's bothering you?" I was concerned by the look on his face. "You look saddened."

"Oh, I was just thinking about Beth." He shrugged. "Miss the poor girl." He had leaned his arm on his car door that was still open.

I nodded, sympathetically. "I wish I could have gotten to known her."

"She was a great girl and basically a mom to Saidie." His face moved towards the door of our office.

"Whatever happened to their parents, anyway?" It wasn't in her file, just that they died. Someone had to have known something about what happened to them.

"You must be Frankie." An unfamiliar voice, but deep came from behind me. I turned around to see who was there. This unfamiliar face was standing there with Luther.

"Axel." He put his hand out. The man had dark hair and bright blue eyes. He wore a very expensive-looking suit and seemed like a germophobe.

"Oh yes, so sorry about earlier." I didn't mean to forget about our meeting, but I had, and I did feel horrible about it. I wasn't one to just skip out on something important such as this.

"No need to apologize, Detective, Luther was telling me how excited he is to have you on the team." Axel's smile seemed like he was trying to be friendly, but it also felt as if there was something, he was trying to hide from me. "And I'm sure Mat here along with Ashley are both happy to have you." His hand gestured out to Mathew.

"Yes. I am glad to be of help." It seemed that both myself and Axel were benefitting from my being here.

"Now about that horse. Have we picked one out yet? I am sure the Wilson's would be more than willing to help you out with that." Axel suggested.

"I only need a fenced in area for her new gelding. She has already picked him out. I think we have the space." I reached for my keys from my jacket pocket. "Let me get the paperwork out of the car for you."

"No need, I trust you. Your home does have enough space on the side of your house for this gelding." Axel replied. "But you also need a license."

"I figured as much. That is why I wanted to speak with you. If you can do that for my daughter, I would appreciate it." Jacquelynn's happiness meant everything to me. I wanted her to have something she could remember her mother by.

"Let me look into some things. Give me a day or two, and I will get back to you on the matter." He went to his car, not even remotely interested in what I have to say about Jacquelynn. His car was a blue '89 challenger and looked to be in excellent shape. I watched as he drove off, not taking my eyes off the car until it disappeared around the corner in the distance. "Interesting guy."

"He doesn't like it when people ask for favors." Luther told me. "He is the kind of guy that hopes we will do things on our own without having him come out here."

"He is the only one who can get Jacquelynn and I a permit to set up and get started with her horse." I headed towards my SUV, pulling the keys out of my pocket.

"And the only one scary enough to kick you out of town." Mathew got back in his car. "Enjoy the rest of your day off, Frankie. See you tomorrow."

"I'll see you tomorrow then, Mat. You too Luther." I got in my SUV and went to pick Jacquelynn up from the farm. On the way there, Joseph joined me.

"You look worried, Frankie. Jacquelynn is doing just fine, believe me. I have been watching her. Bailey and Jean can be trusted." He had informed me. "And just so you know, Ashley and Ruby are getting along fine."

I didn't answer him as we were pulling down the dirt path towards the Wilson's home. I was about to turn the car off and get out, but Jacquelynn came running out to me instead. She opened the door and got in the back on her own. "Hi, Daddy!"

"Hello, Pumpkin." I looked at her in the rearview mirror, then rolled down my window to speak with Jean. "How was she?"

Jean peeked through to see Jacquelynn. "She is a great kid."

"Everyone keeps telling me so." I knew she was as I rarely ever had any problems with her.

"She really is. She loves you. I remember when my kids were that age and had that much enthusiasm." She leaned to her side.

"Thank you for keeping an eye on her." I handed her a fifty.

"Please, no money." She put her hands up and shook her head.

"I can't let you watch her for free." I insisted, trying to hand it to her again.

"We want to do it for you and her, not for the money." She pushed my hand back into the car. "See you tomorrow, Jacquelynn." She waved to my daughter.

"Bye." She waved back to Jean.

We got back to the house, and I found Ruby inside sitting on the couch. I quickly sent Jacquelynn to get a bath so we could have a chat. Jacquelynn took off immediately with no argument.

"Wasn't expecting you to be back." I put my jacket in the closet and sat in my chair by the fireplace.

"Ashley offered to take me back. I could have walked, but she insisted, and I would have felt bad if I refused." She reached for the cup on the side table. "And she said if I come across anything to help the case that I can call her." She stood up, heading towards the kitchen.

"And what about the dreams?" I called to her.

"I didn't say anything about them. You know, it happens almost every night." She peeked her head into the room. "Coffee?"

"Every night? I only saw her once. The night before we met." So Ruby saw Elizabeth every night when she went to bed. I wondered if there was something more to this. "Yes, coffee sounds nice."

"Which means we both saw her then." Ruby popped back into the kitchen. I could hear her moving around, getting the coffee ready. She then came into the living area, handing me a cup before sitting on the sofa again. "What does it mean?"

"It means that Elizabeth is trapped somewhere, and we have to find her." I took my cup from her.

"How?" Ruby raised an eyebrow.

"I will chat with Joseph and see what I can find out." I looked around the room. "Joseph?"

Joseph appeared along with Keiko. They were both on the couch with Ruby.

"We need to talk to Elizabeth." I explained the situation to both Keiko and Joseph. I was sure they knew what to do in this situation.

"The only way to do that is with a third Necromancer. Which means we have to get Roxann." Joseph looked to Keiko. "We will need both her and her Shadow."

"Where does she live?" I looked at Ruby. "Has she ever told you?"

Ruby shrugged. "I have no clue, sorry."

"Then I will look into the records in the office in the morning." If I could find Lucius' and Payton's addresses, I was sure to get Roxann's. "Let's chat tomorrow."

"There's one other thing. We have to do it where she died." Joseph looked worried about this.

The next morning, I reached over to my cellphone and nodded that it was indeed Monday, the start of the week. Today, I had to report to the office, get Roxann's address, and give it to Ruby. I took Jacquelynn back to Bailey and Jean before going into the office. I got there early enough so I could have the office to myself before anyone else arrived. I got right on the computer and searched Roxann's address, immediately getting results. I took a photo with my cellphone and sent it to Ruby. She had promised to get a phone yesterday, and I helped her get plugged in. She had both mine and Ashley's numbers, and I knew it would only be a matter of time before she had other numbers in her phone as well.

We had to get Roxann on board with the idea of finding Elizabeth and calling to her spirit beyond the grave. I know Joseph has said she wasn't really dead, but if she wasn't then why were both Ruby and I seeing her in our sleep? Maybe we could find out what happened to her and solve this case faster. She could explain in detail what happened, and all I would have to do is collect evidence that led to her conclusion. It had already been a few days after her death before I had got here and a few more after that since I have been here.

"Good morning, Frankie." Mat came in with Ashley right behind him.

"Getting a head start?" Ashley pulled her chair out and sat down next to me.

"Something like that." I closed out of my search, there was no need for Ashley or Mathew to know what I was doing.

"Ash tells me you are housing Ruby." Mathew finally sat down in his chair.

"She needs someone to actually care about her wellbeing for once. I chose to take her in." I turned to face Mat.

"And we need her." Ashley added. "Just like you said, she can help us with this case."

I was happy that Ashley was finally admitting that Ruby will be staying. "What did you find yesterday, Mat? I know it was our time off but thank you for stepping up and working for Beth and Saidie."

"Hey, it's no problem at all. So, I talked to Saidie again, and she seems to be doing better. Then I got a weird phone call, and you know how we have to follow the lead even if it's fake." He looked at Ashley then at me. "Oliver."

"Who is Oliver?" I asked.

"Oliver is a friend of Malcolm and Delilah. I have a feeling they are screwing with us." She didn't sound like she wanted to be dealing with them again.

"Thing is, after meeting with Oliver, he looked panicked." Mathew shook his head. "Almost like he saw a dead body or a ghost."

I looked at the clock, then back at Mathew. It was crazy that I found not one, but two Necromancers living in this town. But three? Did Mathew know about Necromancers? He was only human, so I highly doubted it, but he talked like he believed it was real.

"Frankie?" Ashley waved her hand in my face. "Are you in there?"

"Oh sorry." I shook my head; I hadn't realized that I had stopped listening to their conversation. "What is it?"

"We were going to ask if you wanted to drive over to see Oliver." She looked at her watch. "He should be home." She then wrote the address on a piece of paper and handed it to me.

"I will go and see him then." I studied the piece of paper for a moment.

When I arrived at the address, there was a young girl about fourteen or so hiding behind a tree. I smiled and let her stay hidden while I knocked on the door.

"He isn't here." A boy about eleven appeared from around the corner of the house. He had light brown eyes, scruffy hair, and was fair skinned as if he was in the sun too long, he would burn. He had a rake in his hand.

I looked down to the boy. "Where can I find Oliver?"

"My brother is with Nathan." The girl peeked out from behind the tree.

"Who is Nathan?" I asked the kids.

"My dad. I'm Emmett." He seemed to be pretty proud of his father. This was Emmett, the boy who was in my daughter's class.

The girl walked up behind Emmett and slapped the back of his head. My eyes widened, concerned about the two of them.

"Hey." He rubbed the back of his head and pointed to the girl next to him with his other hand. "This is Addison."

"Kids, I need to find Oliver. This is important." I let the rough playing go for now.

"You a police officer?" Emmett asked.

I gave a nod. "Yes, and I am doing my job to protect you."

"Dad is in a meeting." Emmett shrugged. "We always get stuck here when the rest of our family gets to go to the meeting."

"Where is this meeting taking place?" They had to be somewhere nearby, his parents wouldn't have left him here alone otherwise. I was hoping at least.

"Malcolm's diner." Addison looked at me. She seemed to have much more confidence then Emmett did.

"Thanks kids." I decided to drive over there even if Malcolm didn't want me to. I had to do what I needed to solve Elizabeth's murder. I pulled into the parking lot and saw that the diner was closed. I walked around to the back and knocked on the door. It opened to a man at about my own height and looked like an older version of Emmett.

"Can I help you?" He asked me, his voice was a bit scruff.

"I'm Detective Frankie Dawson, I'm here on behalf of Oliver's statement, to Lieutenant Mathew Reames." I put my hand out, trying to be friendly.

He just looked at it and then laughed. "No need to be so formal, Detective. We all know one another around here." He let me in. Know one another? Maybe everyone here knew who I was, but I was still figuring out who was who.

Malcolm jumped up, pointing towards me. "I told you to never come in here again." Oh boy, he was angry.

"I need to see Oliver." I spoke calmly, I wasn't going down to his level.

"You can do this later." Malcolm seemed to growl at me, and it certainly didn't sound like a growl coming from any human. No, I was being crazy.

"Actually, when there is a complaint or something found, we have to act on it immediately." I raised my hands in surrender.

"I will not stand for this." Malcolm grunted. "Luther doesn't know when to stop."

"Malcolm." A tall dark-skinned man stood up. "Sit."

"I-" Malcolm tried to argue. He looked as if he was afraid of what this other man was going to do to him.

"Sit down." His voice was calm but demeaning.

Malcolm didn't argue and shrunk into his seat. I saw Delilah put her hand on his shoulder, trying to comfort him. She definitely cared for his well-being.

"How can we help you, Detective?" The man moved towards me. "Have a seat." He motioned me to the empty chair. I watched as the older looking Emmett stood near the door.

"That is Nathan." He told me, motioning towards the man who looked like Emmett. "Don't be frightened, we are good people here."

"I need to talk to Oliver about what he has found." I looked down the table, trying to see if I could figure out which one of them was Oliver.

"That would be me, sir." I saw the blonde man sit up much straighter. "I told Mat that I thought I saw Beth, but I can't be certain." His light grey eyes looked towards me. He brushed back his hair behind his ear, it was just long enough, down to his chin, to be kept behind his ear just long enough for it to fall back down into his face.

"Where?" I put my hands on the table, leaning over.

"By the bridge." He looked down, seemingly unsure if he should be talking.

"Where she was murdered then." I nodded, writing it down. "Last night, what time?"

Oliver moved in his chair. "Two nights ago, actually."

"So, Saturday night." Of course, it was, Oliver spoke to Mathew yesterday. "What time?"

"Three AM." He squirmed in his chair a bit.

"You shouldn't be out that late, but I will let it go for the sake of the case." I stood up straight and looked at who was apparently the leader here. "Thanks…"

"Nikolai." He put his hand out, smiling.

"Thank you, Nikolai." I shook his hand. "And thank you, Oliver. If you have anything else to tell me, please call."

"There is something." Oliver started to stand.

"Yes?" There was *always* something else. I could say he was on my list of suspects now, but I would take him off immediately because he is way too timid to even think about that, and he was more than willing to help me out without hesitation.

"I thought I saw her with Luther." He shook his head. "But I might be wrong." Does that mean that Luther was guilty? I still had Ashley to look into, they could be working together, and their bantering was just a cover.

I nodded slowly. "Thank you." I then went out the back door and got into the SUV. Elizabeth is dead, maybe Oliver saw someone else and mistook her for them. Oliver was willing to help. However, there was no real possibility that he saw Elizabeth, or was she alive?

"We are getting close to solving this case." Joseph appeared next to me. "Oliver has given you the information you need to make a conviction."

I started the car. "We are, but I don't understand what is going on. Some say she is dead and not coming back and then you have someone like Oliver who says that she is still alive and out there somewhere. I am not really sure what to believe at this point."

"Do you trust Oliver?" Joseph always knows the answers to his own questions, but he still asks them anyway because he wants me to answer them for myself. He wanted me to believe what I was thinking.

"I don't even know him, but I think so. He isn't guilty of Elizabeth's murder." I had already had my suspects. Everyone here did, however, seem to have their own personal motives. There was always some kind of new information to take in on the case, no matter how odd it may be. "Something about this town isn't right, and I intend to find out what it is before someone else loses their life. Ashley said we have a whole file on unsolved cases. This means we need to do some digging."

"Sir." I walked up to Luther at his desk. He was barely paying attention to me.

"Yes, Frankie?" He leaned back in his chair, his eyes on me now.

"Is it possible to look back on any recent cold cases?" I wanted to investigate the file that Ashley had talked to me about yesterday afternoon.

"What for, Detective?" He didn't sound like he wanted to give me the file, as if it was some secret that I wasn't supposed to know about.

"Well, I figured if I could get a look at them, I would be able to get some clues to Elizabeth's murder." I waited for him to reply to my request. He was not going to give himself up that easily, but he still had a job to uphold, and there was no reason as to why he wouldn't let me have it without outing himself as the killer.

He opened his desk drawer and handed the folder over. "Do as you must, find her killer." I had my doubts about him, but something deep inside my gut was telling me that he was at fault.

"Thank you, sir." I took the folder to my desk and started sorting through the files. They dated back almost fifteen years or so. "Where are the older ones?"

Ashley walked to the desk and sat down. "Older files get moved to another department in the city."

"They are in Detroit then." I moved over slightly, so she had some space of her own.

"Something like that." She shook her head. "Anyway, they take the files and put them in their own folder, hoping that the homicide detectives there will do something. They never do." She sounded a bit defeated.

I looked at the most recent murder from four years ago. "Who was this?" There was no information on what happened. It was eerie and disturbing.

"Some drifter who has never identified. Sad really." Ashley pointed to the photo as if she was trying to remember who they were.

"I was hoping this would have helped with Elizabeth's murder." I shut the folder. "But it seems like there isn't anything here to point me in the right direction."

"No, nothing happens here. Not to the people in this town anyway. We don't really get many outsiders, and when we do, they usually leave quickly."

"Can I ask why?" I looked at the folder, saddened by the idea of never knowing who that young teen boy was. His parents or whoever was part of his family would never know he was gone.

"They probably see something that scares them off. Not sure what, but it's common enough. People avoid Golden Loch for that reason. Maybe one day we can figure out who killed that boy and all the others in that folder as well."

"For now, we have other matters to deal with." Mat joined us in our discussion. "How'd it go with Oliver?"

"He saw her very early in the morning." I handed Ashley my notes.

"That isn't possible." Ashley looked at the information that I had written down.

"I know, that is what I said." I shrugged. "But he seems to believe it."

"What is he trying to gain from this?" Ashley had asked. That was a question that I wanted to answer myself.

"I wish I knew. Maybe he is protecting himself or someone he knows." I doubted it, but we still had to look at every angle before coming to a conclusion.

"Maybe." She looked at Luther who was staring at his computer screen.

Chapter 8

I sat on my back porch; it was almost ten. I had put Jacquelynn to bed already, and Ruby had joined me.

"Let me ask you something, Frankie." She started as she fell into a chair.

"What is that?" I could feel the cool breeze coming in from the front side of the house. The north was notorious for their winter snow storms.

"Once we call out to her, and if we find her, what then?" She looked at me, and I could see the sadness in her eyes. She wasn't sure what was going to happen, and I wasn't sure either, but I knew what had to be done.

"Well, then we arrest the one who murdered her." I looked out into the woods beyond the trees. There was something big living out there. Moose maybe? I wasn't far enough north, but you could never be so sure.

She sat there quietly. I assumed she was thinking, or she may have even heard the sounds coming from out in the trees.

"You know, I'm sure everything will turn out to be just fine." I tried to assure her, taking her attention back to the conversation.

"And what if it isn't?" She started leaning forward, her arms on her knees. She was still focused on the woods. Maybe a ghost then?

"Then we adapt, I know you can do that. You seem to have adapted quickly from being inside the institute they were keeping you at. I do not see how this would be much different. All we need to do is summon Elizabeth and then find the way to report on the murder."

"I did speak with Roxann and Zeke." She shrugged, still seeming to be unsure of all of this. "Keiko came along too."

"What did you find out?" There was probably something that we could use to our advantage.

"You will need to get a piece of evidence from your office." Ruby finally looked at me. "It is the easiest way to summon someone from beyond."

"I have done it before, many times really, without a piece of their belongings. There is no way I would have to do it now." Why did I suddenly need to bring something that belonged to the dead?

Ruby didn't know how to answer because this was all still new for her. She still needed to process everything that was going on in her own head, and now she had to figure out what was going on in this world as well.

"Okay." I broke the silence again. "I will do it. I just think that we could try and do this without having to go into the office this late at night."

She sat back in her chair and pushed her hair behind her ear. "Hey, I am only going by what Roxann said to me. I honestly wouldn't know anyway. I would pop over there and do this myself without the need of any kind of materials, but I wouldn't even know where to begin."

"And our Elizabeth is trapped someplace." I shook my head. "I guess that is the reason we have to do this." I stood up. "Do you mind doing me a favor?"

She started to stand as well. "What do you need?"

"Keep an eye on Jacquelynn for an hour or so while I go to the office and get what we need." I walked inside with her behind me.

"I'll be here but make it quick. This place gives me the creeps this late at night." She rubbed her arms.

I laughed a little. "Don't let Sebastian, our ghost of this house, scare you. He is harmless, and he certainly can't do anything to you."

90

Joseph appeared behind me. "But if he wanted, he could come after Keiko and me. I haven't banished him yet, so he is still here. I also think if you are doing this, you will want some backup."

"You mean yourself." I looked at Joseph. I knew he would be coming along, he always had, and he probably always will.

"Of course, I mean me, Frankie." He looked at Ruby. "Frankie and I will banish Sebastian soon."

"I will?" I grabbed the keys to my SUV. "Surely you are joking. I have never done that before."

"Of course, I know you can do it." Joseph walked through the front door.

Ruby smiled and made her way down the hallway. "Be careful going there this late, Frankie."

"Don't worry, I will be super careful." I went out my front door, locking it behind me, then walked over to my car where Joseph was standing.

"Let's go break into our own office." Joseph went into the passenger side.

I got into the driver's side and started the car. "Break-in? We were just there the other night, and here we are going back. It isn't the same as when we would go in late at night back in Miami. There was always someone there at the office.

When we arrived, the entire room was dark. I unlocked the front door and shut the alarm off. If anyone asked in the morning as to why I was here, I was going to tell them that I wanted to double check on some things. They probably wouldn't though, as they didn't even question me last time. I guessed that I had their full trust on this.

I went into the back room and picked up the backpack. I hadn't seen it in front of me before, but looking at it through the clear plastic bag, I could see there was no blood on it once so ever. It was as if her bag was taken from her before she had been thrown over.

"What is wrong?" He was looking over my shoulder at the bag.

"There isn't a single drop of blood on it. That makes no sense." I shook my head and started for the door. Even if her bag was taken from her, there should have been fingerprints, but the file said it was never touched. This case was getting stranger and stranger with each new finding.

"Which is probably why Ashley and Mathew are very frustrated with this case." Joseph followed me out. "They are having a hard time with this just as you are."

I looked at my desk and the computer before going towards the front door. "There has to be a reason for all of this." I knew there had to be, even if that reason was that one of my suspects are just a coldblooded killer. I reached for the door handle and pushed it open. "There is something not right about all of this."

"And I know you will figure it out." Joseph told me. "You always do."

Ruby, Roxann, and I couldn't summon her tonight as it was getting too late, I had to be back here in a few hours and get Jacquelynn up and ready for school. I drove in silence, trying to think of what I was going to say to Elizabeth when we saw her. What was I going to ask her? How she died? She probably only had so many answers herself. Even if I could get a name or a face, that would help.

I woke to my cellphone ringing. It had vibrated from my bedside table onto my bed.

"Frankie!" I heard Mat yell into the phone once I had picked it up.

"What is it?" I tried to rub my eyes to focus, sitting up in bed, unsure as to why he was calling me.

"It's Ash." He whispered. "She isn't answering her phone, and she isn't at her house. I checked the office, and I am on my way to your place."

I swung my legs over the side of the bed, suddenly focusing. Mat had hung up before I could answer him. Changing into my clothes, I ran into the kitchen.

"You're leaving quickly." Ruby looked up from the coffee pot.

"Ashley may be in trouble." I didn't say much more on the subject. I kissed Jacquelynn on the forehead. "Can you get her to Bailey and Jean?" I looked at Ruby as I put my jacket on.

"On it. Be careful." Ruby repeated what she said the night before, she obviously cared.

I ran out the door as Mathew pulled up. "We are checking the bridge first." He swung the passenger door open.

When we arrived, we found her standing in the spot where Elizabeth was pushed over. She seemed lost in her thoughts, probably saddened or feeling guilty herself. Was she guilty? I was starting to think that she was as confused and frustrated as Mathew and me.

"Ash!" Mathew came running up to her. "You scared us both. Why didn't you pick up?"

She turned to face us. "Sorry, guys. I thought about what you said, Frankie. Those other cold cases." She looked so full of guilt. She must have hated that she could never solve them. I wanted to tell her that was how it went sometimes, but I figured it wasn't going to make her feel any better. "Most of our cases happen here." She pointed behind her to the bridge. "Which is odd, but this is where people come. That was how we knew to check here first for

Elizabeth. You were in evidence last night. Why?" Ashley asked me. "Your turn to answer some questions." Did she think I was the one who hurt her?

"You what?" Mathew shook his head. "Man, you should not have done that. If Luther finds out-"

"He won't if Frankie tells us why." Ashley put her hands on her hips.

"I took Elizabeth's bag. I felt that if I was going to solve this, I should see the backpack she left behind." I shrugged, knowing that it was half-true. They didn't need to know about the other half.

"Right." Ashley backed away towards the stairs. "And then what?" She kept watch of me as she moved away from us.

"There is not a trace of blood on the bag, yet there it was on the railing?" I asked her. "So, does that mean someone took it off her before she jumped and then tossed it in with her? If so, then why is there no fingerprints or any kind of sign that someone else was here."

"I don't get it either, Frankie, but that is how things go around here." She peered down the steps. The wind started blowing.

"Snow is coming one of these days." Mathew tried to make things less tense.

"You aren't used to that, are you, Detective? Living in a place like Miami, you probably have never seen snow." Ashley turned back to us and walked towards Mathew's car.

"Only once, when I was young. It doesn't exactly happen." I have never seen a real snowstorm in my life.

"Let's get back to the office and look at this again." She climbed into the car.

I looked at Mathew, who then shrugged and patted me on the back. "She is as frustrated as the two of us. Don't let it get to you."

The three of us sat in our chairs, quietly. No one seemed to want to speak on the matter anymore. I had a bad feeling that Ashley wasn't sure if she could trust me. She was hunched over some paperwork, ignoring both Mathew and me. I could hear her clicking her pen, probably thinking to herself. I sat back in my own chair, waiting for someone to say anything. When no one did, I spoke. "Hey." They both didn't even look my way. "Ash, Mat." I called again.

They both glanced up slowly. "Look, Frankie. I know you think that this might be another easy case, but it isn't." Ashley looked at Mathew. "Don't be surprised if Luther closes the case on us."

"He can't." I looked at Mathew for a moment. "Really, how could he?"

"He is in charge here." Ashley told me. "And he makes all the final calls. If he thinks this isn't getting anywhere, he will let us know, and he will close it."

Mathew gave a slow nod. "Happens to about half of our cases."

"That is insane. What about Saidie? We promised that we would find her sister." I looked at the front door as Luther walked in.

"Then keep that promise, Detective." Luther said to me as if he heard our entire conversation. "You still have time to figure this out." He moved to his own desk on the other side of the room.

"I will keep that promise. I won't let Saidie down." I looked at Ashley. "Are you with me or not?"

She sat back in her chair, putting her pen down. "I will keep doing my job. There is no way in hell I wouldn't."

Mathew agreed. "We are a team, and we will do this together."

I let out a sigh of relief. They were still with me not against me. I knew for a fact that we were going to close this case one way or another, no matter how long it took or how far I was going to go to bend the human rules.

Back home, I had some time before Jacquelynn would be returning. I looked up at my wife's photo in the center of my fireplace mantel. "I will reach you one day, I promise." I reached for the photo as Ruby came in from the back porch, shutting the door behind her.

"Sorry, I did not mean to interrupt." She scooted past me to go down the hall.

"No, no." I told her. "It's quite okay."

She looked back at me. "I know you miss her. I wanted to give you a moment."

"Everyday." I gave a weak smile, holding back any tears I had. I need to be strong for my daughter.

"So, Cancer, hu? She is pretty." Ruby approached me from behind.

"Yeah, she looks like Jacquelynn, doesn't she? My daughter gets her looks from her mother." I thought about the day Jacquelynn was born and how exciting it was to become a father.

"What was her name if you don't mind me asking?" Ruby looked my way.

"Layla." I sat down on the sofa. This was the first time in weeks that I said her name out loud, and I needed to process it.

"It is good to talk about these things." Ruby sat next to me. "At least that was what they told me inside those walls. I'm not so sure how true it really is."

"They are right about that." I looked up at the photo. "I haven't spoken her name to anyone since she passed."

Ruby put her hand on my shoulder. "You are making progress then." She looked over at the photo. "I'm sure Layla would be proud of you."

"She always stayed home with Jacquelynn while I worked." I let out a small sigh. "She was good to her."

"She sounds like she was a good mom." Ruby shifted towards the other side of the couch.

I had a feeling she was getting upset, so I changed the subject to keep her from thinking about her own mother. "So then, is Roxann going to meet us there?"

She nodded, looking down at her hands. "She and Zeke will be there waiting for us when we arrive."

I stood up. "Then, we go after dinner." I put my hand out to help her stand so we could start on dinner.

Chapter 9

After asking Bailey and Jean to watch Jacquelynn for the night, Ruby and I went straight to the bridge. I would come for Jacquelynn tomorrow after school had dismissed her. We got out of the car, moved to the steps where I saw Roxann waiting.

"Hey, Roxann." Ruby called. She turned around. "This spot is not what I would call ideal." She looked slightly younger than a few days ago when we first saw her. "Did you bring it?"

I handed the bag over to her. "It was hers at the time of death, but there is no blood." Maybe she would know something.

Roxann examined it. "Frankie, right?" She asked flipping the bag around.

I nodded slowly. "Yes, that is me."

"We didn't formally meet." She put her hand out. "Names Roxann, but you already know that. You also probably already know about Zeke."

"You and Ruby are friends, why have you never tried to get her out?" Surely, she had a reason for not wanting to break Ruby out of the institution.

"Once a ward of the state, that's it." The Shadow who I assumed was Zeke had appeared.

"Hey, be nice to the man. He is new around here, Z." Roxann glared at him. "There is no reason to be so rude. How would he know how that works? He isn't from around here."

"The man is a detective, Roxann. He should know what the law is." Zeke sounded like he didn't want us here.

Ruby looked at me then at Zeke. "I won't go back there."

"Course not." Keiko appeared, and so did Joseph.

"You must be Joseph." Roxann looked at him. "Keiko says you are pretty much a deputy."

"More like a sidekick." I joked and smiled.

"I do all the dirty work, and that is what I get. A sidekick." He shook his head at me. "I am old enough to be your great great grandfather." He looked at Zeke and Keiko. "Both of you as well."

Keiko shrugged. "You can have whatever title you want. I am only here to help out."

"Can we get started, then?" Ruby shifted to one foot, anxious to start.

"Someone's in a hurry. Okay fine. Get in a circle." Zeke sat down on the bridge first. Roxann sat right next to him.

Ruby, Joseph, Keiko, and I then took our places. Roxann sat the backpack in the center of us. We closed our eyes and repeated after her. What seemed like hours to try and call upon dear Elizabeth, really was only mere seconds, and for some reason, it wasn't working. We all breathed, taking a moment, and tried a second time. Still, it didn't seem to work.

"Third time, then?" Ruby was determined to talk to Elizabeth. She was probably tired of seeing her in her sleep.

"What is the rush?" Zeke leaned into the circle towards her.

"She comes to me in my sleep, yet when I try to come to her, she ignores it." Ruby stood up.

"Then, she might not be dead." Zeke sounded so sure of himself.

"Then explain my dreams?" Ruby crossed her arms. "Frankie had them too."

Roxann looked at me, surprised that I saw Elizabeth too. "Is that true?"

I pursed my lips and nodded. "It is, but only once. She seemed to fade away after that." I would have liked to see her again, but I haven't. This was the perfect back up plan.

"So, not twice?" Roxann looked at Zeke then to Joseph and back at me like seeing her once was a message that I should have picked up on. This was the first time I had seen someone in my sleep this way. It was very real compared to any other dream that I had before.

"Why? Does that mean something?" I scratched my head, sure that meant something. She wouldn't have asked otherwise.

"You have never dealt with this before, have you, Frankie?" She looked concerned. Should I have? Was it because I was older than she was, that it meant I should know more than her?

"No, never. Every human I had dealt with in Miami was easily explained. This, well, this is crazy, and I don't know where it's going." I looked at Joseph. Did he know what was going on and decided not to tell me?

"Frankie and I usually could solve a case in about a week or so. He was well regarded by his colleagues." Joseph told Roxann. "Even if the Captain hated some of the methods he used."

"Your Captain knew?" Roxann asked me. She sounded surprised as if I shouldn't have told him to begin with.

I shook my head. "Not at first, but over time I couldn't keep explaining away what I was doing and why. He caught on eventually. It was better that way."

"Was he human then?" Roxann looked concerned. Was it a bad idea to be talking to humans about what we could do?

"He was, which is why I found it interesting that he let me work alone most of the time. As long as I told him what I was doing, he was fine with it. He would take care of things on his end as long as I did my job." I tried to redirect the conversation back to Elizabeth. "Maybe we should try this again."

Roxann smiled. "I like you, Frankie. You seem to work on the side of caution, but you trusted your Captain enough to tell him about yourself." She closed her eyes. "Okay, let's do this one more time, and then we will conduct a physical search for her."

The rest of us also closed our eyes and then repeated Roxann's words again, and as the first two trials, it failed.

"So, she isn't dead." Roxann stood. "Do we rule this as she survived?" She looked to me for guidance, full of hope that we would find Elizabeth.

I stood up, taking Ruby's hands, helping her stand as well. "We should go and search for her."

"I agree, but it is not safe to go alone." Roxann investigated the woods behind her. "You never know who is lurking out there."

"You and Ruby go together then. You have Zeke and Keiko." I told them, I would rather they were teamed together and be alone myself.

"What about you?" Ruby asked me, concerned for my wellbeing.

"I will be fine. Go on." Even if it wasn't safe, just as Roxann was saying, that did not matter. I felt better they were together.

They both walked into the woods, and I made my path down a different direction. I could hear creatures moving around me. Owls, rabbits, squirrels, birds. They were probably making their way back to their nests and burrows, just like I should have been, but I wasn't. I was out looking for answers on where our Elizabeth had gone.

I started to think about Daeron and Illyanna and how they lived somewhere back here. I thought about the way they spoke and the way they had gotten me to talk before I thought about my own words. I shivered at the idea of running into them again. Last time I had Ashley to pull me back, and they just disappeared into thin air before either of us could blink. I thought about how they may have been ghosts, but Ashley knew them, so that was scratched off my list of possibilities. I didn't want to be out here alone, but we needed to split up. We had to search before the sun came up, and I had to be back at the office. I had heard a sound and turned to try and see what it was. I reached into my pocket for my phone to get my flashlight on, but something had hit me in the back of the head before I could.

When I woke, I found myself next to a fire outside a home, made of what seemed to be wood and glass. I didn't see anyone, so I tried to stand but realized that I couldn't move. I wasn't even tied down, but my mind couldn't control my own body. I called out to Ruby and Roxann, but as I yelled, I couldn't hear myself. It was almost like my voice had been turned off. I suddenly felt a hand on my shoulder.

"Don't be alarmed, Detective." The soft hum of a girl's voice. She leaned over and smiled. "We only want to help." She was now in front of me. I heard a giggle from behind me. I tried to look, but the girl who was speaking to me had my eyes locked on her. Her hair was long, and an orangey color. Her green eyes made it clear she wanted my attention.

"Tell me, what brings you to our side of town?" Her voice was so soft you could barely hear it. However, I was able to with no issue at all as if I had the volume turned up on a TV.

I swallowed. She was talking to me, but I still couldn't speak.

"Oh yes, you can talk when I am speaking to you." She smirked. The giggle from behind me again.

"Where is Elizabeth?" I demanded, tired of her games.

"Oh, come on now, don't be mean. Let me help." She leaned towards my face. "I am only a friend."

"Good luck with that." The girl giggled again, and this time she showed herself right in front of me. It was Illyanna. "Remember me?" Her finger slid under my chin. "We met last week." She looked at her friend.

"So, you are acquainted then. Good." The other girl put her hands in her pockets.

"You girls know something. Start talking." I grunted; I hated this game, and there was no need to drag this out.

102

"Maybe it would be better to show you." The orangey haired girl leaned towards me, putting her cold fingers on my face as if that was going to make think of something that I hadn't before. These girls didn't think it would work, did they?

"Wait." A man's voice shook through me. He sounded angry. "Illyanna, Lily, go inside."

The girls looked up. I couldn't see the man, but I could tell he wasn't happy from their faces. They then both ran across the wet grass, and the fire went out as soon as the door shut behind them. The man had then sat right next to me. "Sorry about that, Detective Dawson." He snapped his finger.

I looked at him. His eyes were as bright as the girls, but his hair was sleek and black. I also noticed how perfect his skin was. "What is this?"

"My children don't like outsiders too much." He stood up, helping me stand as well. My legs felt weak and my arms had the tingle feeling as if they were asleep. "It will wear off. It is nothing more than a sedative."

"And you are?" I asked, waiting for a name.

"Winston." He put his hand out.

I hesitated before shaking it. "I should get going before my friends worry too much." I really didn't want to hang around here any longer then I had to.

Winston agreed with me. "No, that is a good idea. You don't know what could be lurking out here. Go on, Detective, you are free to go. The bridge is to the east."

His attitude seemed genuine enough, so I took his word for it and went on my way back towards the bridge. When I reached the crick, I was hoping to see Roxann and Ruby. The backpack was still up there on the bridge, and the sun was starting to come up. I called Ruby to find out she and Roxann had gone back home. It seemed a bit strange, but it did make me feel better. I made my way up the stairs, grabbing the backpack off the ground. It was too late to go home and get any sleep, so I chose to make my way back to the office instead.

When I had gotten there, Ashley and Mathew were waiting for me outside. They looked at me with a concerned look on their faces.

"What is it?" I approached them. Surely, they were upset about something.

"Go put the bag back, Frankie." Ashley told me. Her arms were crossed, and she looked tense.

I sighed, doing as I was told. I put the backpack back in the container I took it out of and made my way back out front.

"We can't solve this." Ashley said to me. "And Luther wants someone to pay for it."

"I thought we had something going here. We can't just go punishing anyone." I looked towards Mathew. "Or are we just going to pick someone?"

"That seems to be the case here." Ashley shrugged. "We are going to have to make a conviction because we are out of time. If we don't, Saidie will not get the satisfaction that she needs." That sounded wrong. We couldn't put someone away for no reason.

I bit my lower lip. "So, what is the plan then?"

Ashley and Mathew looked at one another before looking back at me. "Frankie Dawson, you are under arrest for the murder of Elizabeth Keaton." Ashley read my rights and placed handcuffs over my wrists.

"What?! Have you two gone mad?!" No way this was happening. Did they hire me just to arrest me? Something was very wrong here.

"You have been working on the case on your own without consulting anyone, that sounds like a guilty man to me. The backpack, for example." Mathew told me.

I shook my head. "No. You both know I am not responsible for any of this."

"Tell it to the Judge." She pushed me forward towards her Ferrari. "Come on Mat, we have a drive to make into Detroit."

Chapter 10

I sat in the cell and tried to trace my thoughts back to the day I got here. Was this just a ruse to get an outsider convicted of murder? How would they even prove I did this? I know I had not done it, but for some reason or another, both Ashley and Mathew had turned against me at the last second and put me under the knife. Now I was sitting in a cell in Detroit, waiting for my trial. I was in prison, along with so many others who were probably humans. I was a detective for a little over ten years, and I had always upheld the law, even if I had done so alone. I never strayed from breaking any kind of rule. Yes, I may have bent them, but I refused to break them, that would have cost me my badge. My wife Layla always supported my choices and let me do as I needed. She never asked questions as she knew I wouldn't be allowed to answer any of them anyway. Cases were not something you could discuss with those who were not part of it. However, it seemed that in Golden Loch, everyone was in on the case, and as a detective, you were only solving it.

When my daughter was born, I was away from home more then I should have been, but we needed to keep our income if Layla was going to be a stay at home mom. She did an amazing job as a mother to Jacquelynn. I would never take her place in my daughter's life, but I knew there was no way I wasn't going to be the best father for her. Now, what was I going to do? I needed to be home for my daughter, and I needed to show her that her daddy is a good person, not a cold-blooded killer.

I only knew Elizabeth from photos and what everyone was telling me, as I had never met the girl before. I heard a whistle from down the hallway, and I leaned close to the bars in front of me, gripping them. They were cold, and the ground was wet. I tried not to lean in the unknown substance below me.

"Hey, you." I heard. "New boy."

I looked around, but it was pitch black in here. There were no windows, so I had no idea what time of day it was.

"New boy, over here." I heard again.

I finally realized he was in the cell next to mine. "Yeah, I hear you."

"Good, that means that it's working." I saw his hand reach to me, and I fell back. I had fallen on the concrete floor and into the nasty substance. It smelled like mildew water. I did not want to be in here anymore.

"Don't hurt yourself." He said after a few moments. "You need to keep calm if you want to make it out of here, okay?"

I wasn't sure what he meant by that. "If you say so, just don't try and grab me again." I was uncertain about his motives, so I decided to stay on the side of caution. I couldn't see his face, so I wasn't even sure he was real.

The man in the cell across from us hushed us. "Quiet. The guards are coming."

I tried to stand, but the lights came on and blared in my face, sending me onto my backside again.

"Come." The bigger of the two guards said to me. "You can make your phone call now."

I stood up and let them lead me to the phone on the other side of the door. On the way out, I got a glimpse of the man in the cell next to mine. He smiled at me sympathetically and nodded wanting me to keep my calm. Once on the other side, we were in a second room, which felt like an enclosed space with no windows. I picked up the phone that was attached to the wall and called my own house.

"Hello?" It was Ruby.

"Ruby, it's me. Take care of Jacquelynn until I sort this thing out, okay?" I was hoping she would at least help my daughter in this time of crisis.

"I can't help you anymore, Frankie. I am leaving town and not coming back. You are on your own." She hung up.

"Ruby?! Wait. Please." I muttered, gripping the phone in my hands. "My daughter." I did not want this to be real anymore. I squeezed my eyes shut, hoping that everything would just go away.

"She will be turned over to the state." The smaller guard spoke. "If you are convicted, she will be put up for adoption." No, this was my worst fear coming to life. I was losing my daughter, and there was nothing I could do to save her.

I looked at them both, feeling the need to cry. "This is insane. I didn't kill Elizabeth."

"It's you against your own police force. You must have." The bigger guard pushed me back towards the doors. I walked in, and they pushed me back into the cell. I hit the far back wall.

"What a sad existence." The smaller one said to the larger one as they both exited the hall. The door slammed behind them. I felt pity for myself and I was ashamed.

"What is your name?" The man next to me spoke. I swear he wasn't there a moment ago.

"Frankie." I said quietly, I didn't even want to be talking to him, but he was the only one keeping me sane.

"You are a detective." His voice came back a moment later.

"How would you even know that?" Maybe word got around here already, or he overheard one of the guards.

"You and I are both from Golden Loch." I heard him move closer to the wall between us.

"Who are you?" I had called out. Surely he knew about Elizabeth if we were both from the same town.

"My name is Zane." He then stopped talking as I started to lean on the back wall that I had hit. Things got quiet again, and I started to think about how this shouldn't be happening. I knew that I was going to be put on trial, yet for some odd reason, I wasn't even given a chance at an interrogation. They must have thought the odds were in their favor and there was nothing that I could say or do that would sway them in either direction. I had to come up with something and fast before I was taken out there in front of all those people from both Detroit and our town.

Ruby had abandoned my daughter and me, even after I took her in. She probably feels like I betrayed her trust and there isn't anything I can do to convince her to stay because I was inside this prison. I needed to get out and solve this case before it was too late, but to do that I would need Zane's help. "Zane." I said loudly enough.

"Yes, Frankie? Are you finally ready to do something about this?" He made it seem as if we were in here for longer than I thought.

"Finally?" I asked him.

"Yeah, how long do you think you've been there? You were quiet for quite a while there. I was starting to think you had lost hope." He replied, seeming sincere. "Don't lose yourself in here."

"Minutes?" I was sure it wasn't long, it sure didn't feel like it.

"Try about an hour." He said back. "You went quiet, and I tried talking to you, but you weren't responsive."

Was this a cruel joke? I didn't find his humor very funny. "Then we have work to do if that is how it is going to be. I will prove my innocence and break free from this."

"I know you will." His voice echoed in the room.

We got to discussing the plan about how we were going to get out of this mess. Every time I asked him to tell me about what he did to get in here, he would push the subject back to my issue as if he wasn't ready to admit to his own.

Zane and I had stayed quiet for another good hour after our discussion. Those two guards came back and opened the door to my cell. "Time to go." The smaller one told me. "We have some things to do."

"Things?" I got up and moved towards them. "What things?"

"Your trial." The smaller one gave me a wide smile. "You are going right now."

"Now?" I shook my head. That was not how trials worked. I gave in anyway, letting them take me down the long hallways and into a room. I was then put next to a tallish male who reminded me of Winston. I looked down at the floor in front of us.

"Your lawyer has been given to you." The judge spoke loudly, and his voice boomed through the room. At the other table, I saw both Mathew and Ashley along with Luther. I also saw Axel with them. Was Axel also a lawyer? In came who I now realize was Zane. He somehow got to be in the stands of people. I shook my head; something was very wrong here, and I didn't like it.

"We will make this trial quick and easy." The judge spoke. "But first, we will hear what our police force in our small neighboring town of Golden Loch has to say." He looked at their table. "Ashley Aequitas, please come up to the stand and give your statement."

I watched her stand up and walk over to the stand. "We hired Frankie Dawson for the sole purpose of finding Elizabeth Keaton's murderer. What we were not expecting was to find out the murderer was the same man we hired. He had been going around behind our backs, using evidence to his advantage, while Mathew and I sat at the desk trying to solve the same murder that he had committed. He knows what happened to Elizabeth, and he knows he is the one who did it." She sounded confident in her words and was very calm. From the moment I met her, she was always aggravated about the case and had never been calm. She wasn't her normal self.

"I did not kill Elizabeth!" I jumped out of my seat. I was not going to sit here and let them get away with this.

"Mr. Dawson." The man who looked just like Winston said my name. "You need to sit down." He put his hands on my shoulders.

"This is not a fair trial." I tried to explain myself. "You cannot use random ideas and expect them to stick." I felt him push me back into the chair.

"But Ashley is right." Mathew stood. "I am Lieutenant Mathew Reames, and I know that Ashley is right. She is always right in these situations. She has never once failed to convict someone of a murder or any kind of crime." Mathew was not a follower. He didn't just agree with whatever Ashley said. He wasn't right, either.

"That is a blatant lie." I looked his way. "You two showed me all the unsolved cases the other day. There is no way I could make that up."

"You took that folder from our Luther, our Captain." Ashley said loud enough for the whole room to hear. I could hear gasps behind me.

"No." I shook my head. "Luther let me have that folder, he knew I was only trying to find Elizabeth, and I did not just take it." My head held low. I was only trying to defend myself.

"Do not talk back in this court room, Mr. Dawson." The judge had hit his hammer. "If you cannot control yourself, you will be held here for another day. Do not push it." He made it sound like that was worse than wherever I was going to end up.

"I-" I felt my lawyer's hand on my shoulder. "I didn't kill her."

"Just let them finish before we make our case." My lawyer whispered to me. "You can trust me."

Could I? I wasn't convinced he was here for my support. He was probably hired to keep me quiet until they convicted me. It was one huge, cruel act.

"Go on, Ms. Aequitas. Tell us about why you hired Frankie Dawson." The judge seemed satisfied that I was staying quiet now.

"Well, sir, we hired him because we needed help in our squad, and he seemed like a pretty decent man. He knew his way around the law, and he had been in his spot for quite some time." She explained. "But it seems that the law finally caught up with him, and now he is being put to the test for the actions that he has made."

This is not how a trial goes; I know that much. Someone here knew that I was innocent, and I wasn't sure who to trust. Was is my lawyer? Maybe. Zane? I wouldn't know, but I was ready to find out.

"And what about you, Mr. Reames? Tell us about your part in this." The judge waved for Mathew to speak to the jury.

"Ashley and I are a team, and we have been for a long time. We both trust one another; she had picked up on Frankie since the day he got here. We just needed time to let him think he was solving it." Mathew had sounded very confident in what he was saying about me. Great, I was screwed.

The judge was silent for a moment. "And you, Captain?" He asked Luther to speak last. Luther looked ecstatic about putting me away.

"I trust my Lieutenant and my Detective. If they think Frankie Dawson did this, then so be it." He looked at the judge. "Put the murdering bastard away."

I looked from the judge to Luther, then to the judge again, who looked at my lawyer. Luther was telling the judge to get rid of me, and there would be no final verdict chosen by the jury. I looked around the room, realizing that there was no jury here. My chance was taken from me before this had ever started.

"Go on." The judge told my lawyer.

"Frankie Dawson knows the man who did this." My lawyer said aloud after standing. "And you and I both know it was him."

I stood up so fast that my chair fell over on the floor. "Wait. No." I gripped the table in front of me. My hands turned into fists. "You have this all wrong. Really."

"Then it is decided. Frankie Dawson, you are sentenced to prison for life." The judge ignored my plea and sent me away with the guards.

"NO! I didn't kill her! It wasn't me! I swear on my wife's grave!" I tried to pull away from the guards; I looked back at Zane on the way out. He had a look of regret on his face; this was not his fault, and he shouldn't feel that way.

"What a sad existence." I was ushered through the doors as I heard Ashley speak. I spotted Zane on the way out; I had no idea how he got here again. I was not sure what was coming next, but I did know for a fact that it wasn't going to be pleasant. Being a detective in prison, it isn't safe. I can also say for a fact, that prison wasn't where you would want to be as a detective. If you were to run into someone you had put away, good luck surviving.

The judge didn't even give me a chance to defend myself; he went by heresy. This was wrong, and I hated every second of it. This entire situation was making me feel sick. I wanted to go back to the way things were supposed to be; the right way of living.

I was suddenly shoved back into my cell. "Good luck with things." The larger guard spoke to me. The guards disappeared again, and the room went dark.

I was alone with nothing but my thoughts to keep my company. I tried to call out to Zane, but he didn't answer, and considering that I saw him in the halls, he probably got sent home. I was going to prison without someone to consider even as an acquaintance, and I knew I was never going to see Jacquelynn again. That pained me more than anything. My daughter was going to see her hero father as some kind of monster who destroyed her entire world. First, her mother was gone, and now I was too. She probably would never understand why I was gone so suddenly, that I should have tried harder to make it out. I closed my eyes in hopes that things would be over before I knew it.

When I woke, I found myself in the back of a truck with other men. I was chained to the floor and could not remember any of this happening. They had to have done it while I was out, there was no other possible explanation for this. I looked around at the men, and I thought I spotted Zane. "Zane?"

His face looked up at mine. "You are awake, good."

"I thought you were gone." I muttered. "I thought you were going home."

"Ha yeah, that would be the day." He looked at the ceiling of the truck. "You and I are stuck together like glue, Frankie."

I felt a bit of relief when he said so; maybe he was supposed to be here. My head hung low towards the ground. I didn't convict him in my mind because I always went with the innocent until proven guilty. Some, however, slip through the cracks. I had always hoped I didn't become one of those statistics, yet here I was. I had fallen so fast and hard, I wasn't sure what was real anymore, but maybe I was foolish. Maybe I did hurt her, and I was in denial about any of it happening.

"Hey." Zane had leaned towards me. "Don't lose yourself on me here."

"Hm?" I glanced up at him. "Are they right about me?" I felt a pang of depression hit me.

"No." Zane shook his head. "You know who did this."

"Yeah. Me." I looked around at the others in the truck with us. "We are all going to be stuck there for a while, aren't we?"

"They put you away for life, Frankie. Doesn't that stink of something bad?" He asked me. "You are innocent."

I didn't answer; I wasn't sure of what to say. I just wanted to go to sleep for eternity; that way, I wasn't living in this hell. I felt the truck stop unexpectedly, and the back doors open, letting us out one by one. We marched to the doors of the prison and moved right inside. They strip checked us to make sure we weren't carrying anything illegal. After, they sent us to shower and change into these brown jumpsuits.

"They are going to assign us bunks." Zane stood very close to me.

"You there." The guard took my arm and pushed me to a bed. "That is your cell." He then grabbed Zane. "Share it." They shoved Zane inside and locked us in.

"At least we are still together." Zane leaned on the wall. "That is a good thing for the two of us."

"Yeah, sure." I sat on one of the beds. "I never thought I would find myself on the other side of these bars."

"Frankie." He leaned towards me. "Please tell me you know who did it." He wanted to get me to talk about the case.

I glanced at him and then down at the floor, putting my hands on my head to cover myself from anyone seeing my face. I wanted to be left alone; to never hear or speak to anyone ever again, not even Zane.

For the next week, I ignored everything he was saying. I would lay in my bed, facing the wall. I didn't have a care in the world about his enthusiasm and what he thought of the system. I was only another statistic to the outside world at this point. People will forever know my name and associate me with the loss of Elizabeth. I was the one who made her disappear, to never see her again.

I suddenly felt Zane touch my shoulder. "Hey, pay attention to what I'm saying. This is important, Frankie."

I rolled over to face him. "What?"

"I know you are grumpy, and you hate being here, but we will get you out. Trust me on this one. I know we barely know one another, but it is important to keep your spirits up." He was way too cheerful for being stuck in this place.

"You asked me if I knew who did it." I sat up slowly. "But I can't be certain."

"Then figure it out in your head. You know the truth; you have known for a while." Zane was trying to encourage me.

"How do you know that?" I was sure I knew who Elizabeth's killer was, but why would it matter? I was in here and they were out there on the loose. They were not going to be the one who got put away. Ashley and Mathew have probably shut the case down already.

"I know because you know." Zane smiled a bit. "It's just a matter of trust and patience."

"Then answer me this." I looked him dead in the eyes. "Are you real?"

"'Course I am real. I am just as real as anyone here." He stood up. "And you are real too, Frankie. Don't let this place get to you." He walked towards our door, and just like magic, it opened. "Now, let's get ourselves something to eat before we both start to feel the depression of this place." He led me out of the cell and down to the dining hall.

Chapter 11

We sat down with our food at an empty table. Only about seven or eight of us were allowed to eat at any given time as the room was not large enough to accommodate too many of us at one time. Zane and I always had picked a table to have to ourselves where we could privately have our regular conversation. Zane always asked me the same question every time we sat down to eat, making me replay the events of the past week in my head.

"So, start from the beginning." Zane opened his juice box. He ate his food before he drank the juice as the food, we had was always so dry.

"You know the whole story, Zane." I tried to avoid having to tell him the story again. I felt like I was a toddler, who was receiving punishment, even though I was innocent.

"Tell me again, anyway. Start from the day you first spoke to Ashley." He was not going to let it go.

"Okay then, fine." I reached for my bread. "I got a call from Ashley and she had me do an interview over the phone with her and Mathew. I succeeded, and they asked me to come as soon as I could. So, the next week I packed up, said my goodbyes to my friends and colleagues, and made my move up north." I saw Zane stare at me as if this was all it took to make him happy. I looked down at my hard-crusty bread and started pulling it apart. "Then I started at the office. I learned about Elizabeth, and Ashley let me go about trying to solve her case. We visited her sister, Saidie, and I saved her from jumping out of her window."

"Suicide." Zane sighed. He already knew the answer to this, but he wanted me to keep going anyway.

"Yeah, suicide. She was grieving, and I can see where she is coming from, but there is never a reason to make that jump. She has so much to live for; Ashley and I did not want her to throw that away." I dropped the bread on my tray, looking back to Zane now.

"Just like how you are grieving about Layla." He reached for the bread. "Your wife."

"Just like Layla." I drank from my bottle of orange juice and pushed my tray to him so he could have my bread. "Then I made a trip to the diner with Ashley, spoke to Payton, and then finally got interrupted my Malcolm. Afterwards, I went to the town bridge to try to see what I could find. I went alone, running into Illyanna and Daeron. Ashley made it sound like they were made of some kind of evil, but I wasn't sure."

"Okay, so you now know them, what next?" He asked, finishing the bread he took from me.

"Next, I took my daughter to dinner at the diner. The next morning, however, Malcolm wasn't happy. He came to our office and told us we couldn't come back." I placed the empty orange juice down on the tray and sat back in my chair.

"And yet?" Zane knew what was coming, but he was asking me anyway.

"We met Ruby, who helped with the search for Elizabeth, and then Oliver came along and tried to tell us he saw her with Luther." I shook my head; I was starting to feel like this wasn't worth talking about anymore. "There was no way, so I took his statement anyway, but he still seemed convinced. I was way more concerned as to why he was out so late into the morning."

"But you let it go, and you used the backpack to try and find her." Zane made it sound like my problem was lying with the backpack.

"Yeah, I did, but that didn't help much. There was no way to find her with it. I also think that maybe if I didn't take it, I wouldn't be here right now, and I could still be looking for Elizabeth." I knew there was nothing I could do to change things; this was my own doing.

"You still have a chance to make things right; you just have to be willing to grasp it. Don't worry, Frankie, everything is going to work itself out. You will see." He got up and tossed his food into the trash. "Time to get some exercise."

I followed him to the trashcan and dumped my excess food inside before putting the tray on top.

Once outside, we decided to walk the track. "Why do you think Oliver was out so late?" Zane looked at me.

"Oliver was out late because he wanted to be. I can't see a reason why otherwise." I was feeling frustrated with Zane's constant questions. Why did he care so much? Oliver was his own person; he can do what he wants; it wasn't like he was breaking any kind of laws.

"You know, his entire family loves to go on long walks and to take runs along the riverbank." He made a motion with his hand. "That bridge is a perfect spot." Was he trying to make it seem like Oliver was a fault?

"In the water? No, Oliver is innocent too." I know Oliver did not commit murder; there was no way he could have done something like that.

"Then who did it, Frankie?" He really was not going to stop asking me, was he? Even if I did tell him, it wasn't going to get me out of here.

"There is no proof that my last suspect had even done it." I used process of elimination for this one, but that system does not hold up in court. They want to see facts, and without facts, we were at a loss.

"You know the answer." Zane started jogging ahead. "And I won't stop until you say his name." He called back to me.

"How do you know it's a male?" I ran to catch up with him. I wanted to stay in shape even if I was stuck in here.

"How do you know that?" Zane was not giving me answers, just more questions.

"Zane, quit drawing circles around me and give me some answers already." I was getting annoyed with the game he was playing.

"Then don't doubt yourself, Frankie. Look, you can't keep pretending that this is your fault. You and I both know it isn't true." Even if it wasn't, everyone back in Golden Loch wanted it to be.

I looked out at the field of grass and beyond to the road that seemed miles away. I thought about my daughter and where she might be right now. I wasn't allowed visitors, so there was no real way of knowing where she may be. I was only hoping that wherever it was, she was happy.

"You are that close to solving this." He motioned to the road; it was just out of reach. "You just need to put forth the effort to get there."

I let out a breath, maybe Zane was right. Maybe I was being a fool; I needed to get myself out of here before the real killer struck again. I just needed an excuse to get over that fence, but what? Where would I go? Who would I turn to? Back to Miami? Golden Loch?

"You are thinking again, Frankie. I like it." Zane put his hand on my shoulder, shaking me around as if trying to wake me from this nightmare. "Come on, put it together."

"Zane, I know who killed Elizabeth, I just don't know how to get there." I shook my head in defeat.

"You let me take care of that part; you just get over that fence and get the hell out of this place." He pushed me forward. "Go on, get out of here."

"What about you? I can't leave you here." I was not leaving without Zane. He never actually told me why he was in here, to begin with.

"Don't worry about me; I will meet you on the other side." He sounded so sure of himself. "Put our murderer away."

I ran to the fence and jumped over. I looked back to see Zane trying to hold off the guards. Somehow, they were not even able to get near him as if there was a barrier around him. Everything inside me told me to run, but I couldn't leave Zane. I went to go back, but suddenly something was stopping me; it felt like an outside source, so without thinking, I went for the road.

There was a car coming my way as if this was coincidence and perfect timing. An older man greeted me, telling me to get in. I didn't think twice about it, that same something that told me to run also told me this man was on my side. I got in and shut the door behind me. I was sitting in the back seat when the man in the front looked to me in the rearview mirror as he hit the gas, and we started going 70 mph in about ten seconds.

"Are you okay, Detective?" He asked, focusing on the road.

"Who are you?" Out of breath, I buckled the seatbelt.

"Gregory. Everything is going to be okay; we are going to get you back to Golden Loch." He sounded sincere, like it was a promise.

"We?" I looked back at the prison. "I left Zane." Zane did tell me to run, and as much as I wanted to go back and save him, this car was drawing me in. This man in the front seat felt like that outside source. Who was he? What was he?

"Don't worry about him; he will be fine. When I say we, I mean Zane and I." He pulled over and turned to face me. "You know who did it then. You would not have got out of there, otherwise." He sounded so sure of himself. I *was* the one who jumped that fence and got away. What was odd about this was that there were no police chasing us down, even now as we are sitting here, we looked like prey out in the open.

"I do know, and I am ready to face him. Let's get going." I was tired of sitting here, and if I had a chance of getting myself back to Golden Loch to make this right, then I was going to take it.

"Good plan, Detective." He turned back to the steering wheel.

I heard him speak something under his breath in another language. I fell asleep not too long after. When I woke up, I was on a couch in what looked to be a mansion, but I then realized I was in the church at the end of Lucius' street. I saw his home on the right side, three houses down.

"He is up!" I saw a little boy jump up from the chair by the fire on the other side of the room.

Looking around, I realized I was in a large room made up of bookshelves on every wall, completely covering every inch of space that was not the window in front of me and the fireplace. However, there were books lined up on top of the fireplace, and there was a desk that had more books on top of it. This must have been the church's library.

"Oh, good." I heard a very familiar voice come from behind me.

"Zane?" I was sure that was him. How did he get out of prison?

"It's good to have you back." He sat down on the coffee table right next to me.

"How-" I paused. "Never mind, I just need to go and..." I shook my head. "Ashley and Mathew don't know I escaped."

Zane looked at the boy. "Finnigan, go get our Priest."

The boy ran off into the other room, no argument. He was about my daughter's age, but this kid had bright blue eyes and almost white hair.

"You have a daughter, Jacquelynn. So you know what it's like not being able to tell the young ones about who they are." How would he know that? Maybe he just meant his job.

"I do." I looked at him, waiting for more. He seemed to know more than he was willing to let on.

"The entire week was in your head, Frankie." I looked over to see Gregory. He was dressed in a white robe and had nice shoes on his feet. His hands had white gloves as he reached out to greet me. "I know we have already met, but I should formally introduce myself to you. I am High Priest Gregory."

"The whole week?" I looked from Gregory to Zane. "Everything that we talked about was in my head?"

"I was there, just not physically. I know what we spoke about, as does my High Priest." Zane made it sound like it was so simple. "I had to get inside your head to make sure that you would get out of there."

"So, not one thing that happened was real?" Now, I was concerned. One of us was losing it, and I was sure it wasn't me. It had to have been one of them, but I wanted to hear them out, so I let them talk on the subject.

"Oh yeah, don't think that any of that happened. You were never convicted. We found you out cold by the bridge." Gregory sat in the large chair at the desk that sat right in front of the window.

"What about Ruby and Roxann?" I was worried about them now, what if they had something similar happen to them.

"Ruby is at your home with young Jacquelynn, and Roxann is at her own home. Everyone is fine." Gregory assured me. "They were concerned when they couldn't find you. We called Ash when we found you."

"Is she here?" I started to stand up.

"She is at home." He handed me the backpack. "Here. You are going to want this."

"So even my encounter with Lily and Illyanna isn't real?" I was hoping he would say yes.

"No, that part is real. Just be careful and don't mess with them. Just stay out of that area, and you won't have to worry about them." Zane was starting to sound like Ashley. "Now, go and solve this murder. I only know what I saw in your head; it is your job to convict him." Not a single piece of this made any kind of sense, and I was sure going to figure this out after I put my suspect away. I want answers, and I was going to get them.

I took in a deep breath. I never enjoyed bringing it down on someone who I knew personally; it made the job that much harder. I went outside and made my way across the lot towards the front gate. I checked the time on my watch, realizing that only a few hours had passed since going to the bridge. I pulled out my cellphone to make a call to Ashley.

"Detective Ashley Aequitas." I heard her on the other line. Bruce was barking in the background.

I was just about to answer, but after today's events, I chose to hang up the phone and go home to think it over instead.

"Long day?" Ruby pointed to the clock with her thumb as I walked in the door. Jacquelynn was fast asleep and had her head laying on Ruby's lap.

"You were out cold." Joseph appeared. "I was trying to reach you all day."

"Yeah, I can't explain what any of it was, but it helped me put my final pieces together. I have a theory that I want to discuss with Ash." I sat in the chair across from Ruby and Jacquelynn. "Thank you for staying."

"Why wouldn't I? You are good to me, and I love little Jacquelynn." Ruby brushed her fingers through Jacquelynn's hair.

I smiled; she was right. I had been a good host, and what I heard her say to me was not on a phone but was in my head. I wasn't entirely sure how any of that worked, but it did somehow, and Zane knew what it was and pulled me out. I was forever thankful to him for that. I was also feeling extra thankful for both Ruby and my daughter. They were my rock, and I wasn't going to push Ruby away. "You need a family."

"What? I guess you and Jacquelynn are my family now." She wasn't leaving; I could see that.

"That includes me." Joseph said to her. "I am part of this family, even if Jacquelynn can't see me. I'll be that uncle that is there for her even when she doesn't know it."

"Oh!!" Keiko appeared. "Does that mean I am her sister?" She looked like an excited child getting their first sibling.

"If that is what you want." This family had grown by two. Ruby and Keiko were part of this family, no matter what.

"I only want stability, and you have already given it." Ruby was thanking me for letting her stay in her own way.

I wanted to give her more; I wanted to be her forever family. I knew what I needed to do and that was to get the paperwork to sign her as my own daughter. I would get it done and then only hope she would take our last name. Ruby and Dawson go together so well, and she could use someone to be a father to her, especially since her last one disowned her. She deserved better, and I was determined to give her that better. A second chance at life, that was what it was going to be, and I knew that was how it had to be. I laid my head back, I wasn't tired, but it felt nice to have a family who trusted and who believed in me. I was met with a familiar face as I had drifted off into sleep.

"Help me." She muttered; her voice echoed in the trees.

I looked down to see her in the water below. "Elizabeth?" I ran down the steps and into the water below towards her, but she was gone. "Elizabeth!" I yelled into the woods.

I was abruptly woken up to Ruby hushing me. "No school." She pointed to the window. Outside you could see the snow coming down from the sky. It was as beautiful as I was told it was going to be, the way it made the ground white, uninterrupted by footprints. "Snow day."

"Snow!" Jacquelynn ran to me and climbed into my lap. "Daddy, can we please go outside in it?"

"When it gets deep enough, okay, Pumpkin?" I patted her head. I reached over and handed the matches to Ruby. "Why don't we get a fire going?"

Ruby took the matches from my hand and crouched over the fireplace. She had lit a match and started a wood fire. "Did you ever get one of these back in Florida?"

I smiled. "We did, but we only used it at night when we sat outside on our back porch."

Jacquelynn curled into my lap. "Have you and mommy ever seen snow before?"

"Not like this." This had been the first time since my early childhood that I had seen snow, and even then, I hadn't seen this much. "It is my first, too."

Ruby stood up and looked out the window. "I used to watch it fall from the windows in our community room. I was never allowed out in it as it was deemed dangerous."

"Why?" Jacquelynn looked her way; she stretched and got even more comfortable in my lap. We had not discussed Ruby's situation with my daughter yet; I wanted to wait until she was a little older. I was afraid she wasn't going to understand and also felt it was better to let her keep her innocence for now.

"My family didn't think it was a good idea." Ruby knew better than to tell my eight-year-old daughter about her recent life. Ruby was doing much better now and bounced back pretty fast.

I glanced up at Joseph and Keiko as they appeared. They were both watching us, just like they always do.

126

"Do you have to go to work?" Jacquelynn asked me. She looked sad like she didn't want me to leave.

"I will call Luther and see what he says; maybe I can work the case from here." I leaned over to grab the phone out of my pocket. When Luther picked up, he sounded like he had just run a 5k marathon.

"Hey, Frankie." He sounded even more tired as he spoke. I heard a female voice in the background but couldn't make out what she was saying.

"Sir, my daughter is off from school due to the snow. Do you mind if I work from home today?" I waited as he was quiet.

"Yes, go right ahead. Just keep checking in with Mat and Ash, alright?"

"Yes, of course. I will keep in touch with both of them." I then hung up the phone. "Snow party."

Jacquelynn sat up. "Yay! That means all three of us can hang out together today!" She wrapped her arms around my neck.

"I still have to work, Pumpkin." I looked over at Ruby. "Why don't you two go get something to eat?"

"We had breakfast already." Jacquelynn told me. "And we made you some." She got up. "Come on." She took my hand and led me to the kitchen. She showed me the plate of eggs. "I helped Ruby."

I sat down as she climbed into the chair next to me. "Do you think Snow is okay?" She had a worried look on her face.

"I am sure that he is just fine." I picked up my fork. "In fact, if you want to check on him, you can call Mr. Wilson."

She jumped out of her chair and ran to my cell phone that I had left sitting in the living room. I could hear her asking about Snow.

"I was trapped." I told Ruby as she grabbed a second cup of coffee and joined me at the table.

"Where?" She reached for the sugar on the table, mixing it in.

"I'm not entirely sure, but it felt real enough. Ash and Mat convicted me and put me in prison, but somehow, I got away. When I woke up, it turned out to be completely in my head. It felt like an entire week went by, but when I checked my watch, only a few hours had passed." I looked out at the snow. "And you left town for good."

"Sounds like you were afraid of something." She sat back in her chair, with her hands wrapped around her mug. "We need to turn the heat up in here." She put her mug down to walk down the hallway.

I looked over as Jacquelynn came back. "Snow is good." I could see the smile in her eyes. "Mr. Wilson said he is going to keep Snow warm in his pen."

After breakfast, I had Jacquelynn grab her gloves and hat and to change into something warm. I looked at Ruby, who was getting herself bundled up. "Thank you for going out with her." I started to settle into my chair.

"She wants you to come." Ruby opened the back door. "Please join us as soon as you can." I could feel the rush of cold air coming into the room.

I gave a slight nod as I saw my daughter come running out of her bedroom and right out the back door. "I will be there as soon as I possibly can."

Ashley and I talked on the phone; she said that we would bring the matter up tomorrow as soon as we both could get into the building. No one was getting outside today, and she promised to check in with Saidie as soon as she possibly could get a hold of her. I got up after speaking with her, getting on my coat, gloves, hat, and scarf. I slid on my boots and went outback. I watched from the back porch as Ruby was teaching my daughter how to make a snowball big enough to build a snowman.

"Daddy, look!" Jacquelynn called waving to me. "Come help us build a snowman!"

I walked across the snow-covered ground. I listened to it crunching beneath my feet. Never seeing this much in my life, I let out a smile. "Layla would have loved this."

"You think so?" Jacquelynn handed me a little snowball.

"Your mother was born in Delaware. She moved down to Miami in her early teens." I took the snowball and examined how it was already melting in my warm hand.

"Mommy never mentioned it." I saw how she shuffled around, unsure if this was good or not.

"Hey, don't get upset, Pumpkin. She was looking forward to telling you all about it. She wanted to take a family trip there one year and introduce you to her family." I nodded. "Now, let's build that snowman."

Chapter 12

I sat in my car; I couldn't remember the last time I felt so tense about going into work. This was it; we were counting on this moment. I had to do it, and Ashley agreed on the phone yesterday. She wanted me to tell her about who I thought it was in person, in case someone overheard us. So that is what I am going to do; I was going to go in there and tell her my theory on this entire puzzle. Of course, this was just a theory, and even if I knew who killed Elizabeth, I can't just convict someone without actual proof. My next move was to go back to the crime scene and look at it from another angle. Getting out of the car, I watched my step as the ground was still a bit icy from yesterday's storm. I slowly made my way to the front door and stepped inside. I wiped my boots off on the front rug and hung up my coat. I looked over to where Ashley and Mathew were sitting. "Morning."

"Hey, there he is." Ashley looked up from her computer to me. "So, tell us your theory. Who do you think is responsible?" She sat back in her chair, patient about my movements to my chair. I pulled it about ninety degrees, so we sat in a triangle. They were both focused on me; Ashley had a mug in her hands.

I put my hands in my pockets; it was freezing in here. "No heat?"

"Nah, it doesn't work when it's below 20 out there." Mathew leaned all the way back in his chair. "We just have to bear it out."

I looked back at Ashley. "Last night, I went down to the bridge and tried to see if I could put the scene back together. Unfortunately, I didn't get much. I also went out into the woods to see if I could find anything else that may have been useful."

"You ran into Illyanna and her family, didn't you?" Ashley looked at me, concerned.

"I did, they didn't bother me any this time." I lied; they were bothersome. Zane had the answers I wanted, but he wouldn't give them to me.

"So, then what?" Mathew got closer to his desk, wanting to hear as much as he could.

"So, then I had a realization about who it was. Who in this town can cover up a crime like that?" I asked them both.

Ashley and Mathew sat there silently, waiting for me to finish. That was their cue to answer my question, as they were supposed to know the answer, but they didn't take the bait.

"You two are supposed to answer the question, not stare." I shook my head. "Anyway, there are four of us here who are capable of doing such a thing."

"You mean, Ash, Luther, you and me." Mathew pointed out.

"Yes, and we know that it wasn't me because I had got here not too long ago, and I don't even know the girl." I looked at Ashley.

Ashley sat up in her chair. "And it wasn't me because I was sleeping; I have security cameras to prove it." She explained to me.

"Exactly." I looked at Mathew.

"Wasn't me because Ashley knows where I was." Mathew admitted.

"And where was that?" I smiled to get him to keep going.

"Here in the office. Some nights we have to stay late." Mathew looked over at the front door.

"He isn't coming." Ashley assured Mathew. It took her a moment before she came to the realization as to who I thought it was. "So, you think it was Luther."

"It has to be." After much thought, there was no one who could have done this.

"What gave you that conclusion, Frankie?" Ashley was intrigued. I could see that she wanted me to explain it, even if she knew the answers already.

"It is my gut feeling. We have not come across anyone else who has been in a situation where they seemed guilty. Anytime we asked Luther for help, he seemed to hesitate. He didn't want us to figure it out, and he certainly wasn't ready for an outsider to come here and figure it out in about a week." I waited to see if they had any input, and when they didn't, I continued. "Of course, we still need to gather some evidence before we can approach him, but as far as we are concerned, Luther is our man."

"We should probably tell Saidie we have a suspect." Mathew decided. "Who is going?"

"Frankie and I will take it; Mat stay here and wait for Luther to come. Keep an eye on him, okay?" Ashley stood up and grabbed her coat. "Let him keep doing what he's doing; don't raise any kind of suspicion.

He nodded and picked up his pen. "Research; got it."

I followed Ashley to her Ferrari. "Perhaps we take my SUV with the slick roads?"

"You just want to drive, don't you, Detective?" She shook her head and put her keys back into her pockets, giving me a wide smile. "Alright, go on then."

I got into the driver's side, and we drove down the icy road. "Ash, you knew all along, didn't you?"

"What makes you say that?" She fiddled with her zipper, trying to pull it down as the car was starting to get warm.

"You didn't have a look of surprise on your face when I told you and Mat. It seems that you had your suspicions this entire time." I looked at her a moment before looking back to the road. "You were hoping I would have eventually made the same jump that you did."

"I guess you are right, I did know." She shook her head. "But that is what makes me a good detective. I hate the cold cases just as much as you or Mat, but we can't do anything about them."

"We will do something. We can't just ignore all of those victims." I knew she was still worried about our cold cases.

"Then we better get this done and find Elizabeth's body before Luther shuts us down." She finally sat still.

"You hate not being in control, don't you?" I pulled into Saidie's driveway. It was only about a five-minute drive from the office and a ten-minute walk, but no one walked this time of year. I guessed they didn't like how cold it was; I sure didn't.

"What do we say to her?" Ashley sighed. "Come on, big-city detective, I've never had to do something like this before. We never told victims about who did it before we had the convict."

"It was the routine procedure back in Miami. We always had to tell them what we knew and what we found. Even if it wasn't always correct, the higher-ups thought it was the best way to give them the closure they needed. Sometimes I wasn't entirely sure that was true, but we did it anyway."

Ashley's shoes crunched in the snow on Saidie's front porch. I just stepped in her footprints to avoid too much snow on my shoes.

"You aren't fond of it, are you?" she asked after knocking.

"Fond of what?" I asked curiously. I knew what she meant but asked her anyway.

"The snow. You do come from the sunshine state." She teased lightly.

The door opened. "Detectives!" Saidie motioned us to come in. She had her pajamas on still, even if it was late in the morning. "Did you find my sister's killer?" She seemed to be a bit happier this morning.

"We have an idea of who it may be, but we can't bring justice to Beth until we know for sure." Ashley told her.

"Sit, please." Saidie took a seat at the kitchen table and then motioned to the chairs across from her. "Who do you think it is then?"

Ashley looked at me, waiting. She seemed clueless about what she was supposed to be telling Saidie. I chose to take charge to make this easier for her.

"Luther." I leaned forward to put my arms on the table. I clutched my hands together, waiting for her to tell us we were either crazy or to start crying and admit that it had to be him. That was how it went, we told them about who we thought it was, and they usually knew right away or didn't want to believe what we were trying to tell them.

"No offense Detective Dawson, but how could your Captain be the one? He has been in that position for a long time, and he has always been so friendly to everyone." She looked to the window. She knew that we were right.

"Saidie, please." Ashley reached out to her. "Frankie and I both have come to the same conclusion. We are going to make sure we get the proof we need before we do anything." Even if she didn't know how to start, she was still a detective and knew what to say to Saidie to help her.

I gave a slight nod. "Ash is right. We won't peruse any type of charges unless we have the evidence."

"And how will you get it? You both said her body is missing. How do you convict someone without the body or evidence? How do you know who was there with her?" She didn't look at us. I knew she was feeling disheartened about never seeing her sister again.

"Just trust us. We will." Ashley looked at me. "We won't stop."

Saidie finally looked at us. "This is going to be another unsolved case." She got up out of her chair. "I don't know how much longer I can live in this place for." She started to the living room. "You can let yourselves out."

Ashley and I looked at one another before getting up. We headed out the front door, Ashley had shut it behind her. "That went well…"

"She is disappointed." I walked in the footsteps back to the SUV.

Ashley got in behind me and adjusted her coat before putting the belt on. "Mat and I have been struggling for years to get any kind of help."

I started to drive back to the office. "What are you doing about it?"

"We have been begging Luther to get us a third for a while, and he finally caved." Ashley looked out the window. Flurries were coming down.

"It must snow here a whole lot." I turned the corner.

"Yeah, it certainly can, especially now that it is February." She gave a nod in my direction. "What's it like down there right now?"

"Sixty and sunny most likely." I shrugged. "Jacquelynn and I would be dragging my wife to the shore to enjoy the cool breeze if I wasn't working."

"That sounds nice right now." Ashley looked at me. "And who knows, maybe we will get lucky, and Luther will admit."

"They never do, Ash." I pulled into my parking spot. "I do." I got out of the SUV.

"You do what?" She looked confusingly at me as she followed me to the door.

"I am not fond of the snow. It isn't easy to navigate." I investigated the sky. "It looks nice coming down, but look in the road, it looks like mush. My daughter, however, loves it."

She lightly hit my arm. "Alright, beach boy, get used to it. This is Michigan; you are going to see snow." She pushed the door open, and we went to our desks.

"He never came in." Mathew handed us each a bagel. "I had Zane drop off some bagels for us, though."

I gave Ashley a weird look, and I knew that this was a bad sign. Luther must have known that we were getting close to him.

Mathew looked at us both with a puzzled look on his face. He waited for one of us to explain.

Ashley was the first to speak. "Now, we will need to look at the evidence and try to connect it to Luther; of course, there is only so much we can do from our desks until he gets here." Ashley reminded Mat. "We can, however, use the backpack."

I realized the bag was still in my house, right where I had left it. I had forgotten to grab it on my way out this morning. "Oh, crud."

"What?" Ashley looked at me as if I misplaced her badge.

"It is still at my house." I sighed. "I left it right on my kitchen table." I started getting up.

Ashley shook her head and waved her hand at me. "Nah, leave it. We can get it later." She started to eat. "Zane and Romeo sure know how to make the perfect bagel. Try it, Frankie."

I bit into mine; she had made it to seem as if the bagel was better than any bagel I have ever had. "Oh, wow, they are good."

"See." She smiled. "Grow up in a place like Miami, and you don't know what you are missing." She reached for her napkin.

I shook my head; she was right. Get to know some people and they get to know you. Maybe living in such a small place wasn't so bad after all. This move may be the best thing I have done for Jacquelynn and myself since Layla's passing.

"So, what do you think happened to Beth; from the top?" Ashley asked me first. "Since you weren't here when the incident took place, you should go first."

"Considering her age, they may have been a couple, secretly. I think they would go out at night together and maybe have a few drinks or so. They were probably together for a few months before Elizabeth wanted to call it off. Luther didn't like that, and he was probably stalking her until he eventually got mad enough and pushed her over." I looked at them; they looked as if they had no idea what I was talking about. Someone you know or are close to is usually your killer.

Ashley sat back in her chair slowly and put her bagel down on the desk. "Luther is at least ten years older than Beth. She was twenty-four." She looked over at Mathew. "Mathew, after recent events, what are your thoughts?"

Mathew bit his lip; he seemed to be a bit nervous about the entire situation. "I cannot see how Luther would or could have done this, but for this, let's say he had. How did he make it look like an accident? What made you conclude that he and Beth were a couple?"

I shook my head. "I see the way he looks at us when we talk about her. He looks at us with sorrow and annoyance. It is almost as if he knows. He probably feels terrible about the entire situation."

"You got that from his facial features." Ashley shook her head. "You are starting to sound crazy, Frankie." She was ready to write me off, even if she did believe me.

"Then we ask him." I answered. "What about you? What do you think?"

"I think that Beth got herself into trouble and tried to get out of it. She ended up throwing herself over in an attempt to get out of it." Ashley shrugged. "And to be completely serious, I doubt it had anything to do with an argument." That was not what she told me earlier, but maybe she wanted to sound like she was following evidence exactly when she was in the office.

"Then we get him to talk, Ashley. We won't know until we confront him and put him on the spot." I knew this wasn't going to be easy; it never was. What we have to do now is to get him to tell us what he knows and how far the two of them went with their relationship until she went over the edge at the bridge that night. There had to be an answer to all of this, and I had a strong feeling it was Luther. After speaking with Zane in that strange state of sleep, he knew I knew, and I had to prove it, one way or another.

I went home to get the backpack off the counter and had run into Ruby, who was on her way out.

"I was not expecting you to be back." Ruby reached for the door.

"I also didn't plan on coming back, but we need the evidence, and here it is sitting on my counter. Just be back for dinner, alright, Ruby?" I followed her out the front door and down the porch stairs.

"I'm only going for a walk. I need to get to know the town if I'm going to be staying a while." She then walked down the gravel path that led to the road and disappeared around the corner.

I was hoping to make her stay a more permanent one soon. There was no need for her to feel like she was only a guest at the house for much longer. I wanted her to feel fully welcomed and as a part of the family, without any kind of weirdness between us. I knew I shouldn't be forcing her into any new situations, but with her bad home life with her birth family and how they had abandoned her with no explanations, I wanted to be there for her. Even if they did know what was happening to her or not, they should never have abandoned her as a kid. I was not going to pry her story out of her. That was something that she would be able to keep to herself until she was ready to tell me. I wanted her to keep her own life; it was her story, after all, not mine.

Once back at the office, I stepped up to the final step to be eye level with the Ashley and Mathew, who had a very disconcerted look on their faces. "What is going on?"

"Luther called." Ashley's hands went into her back pockets. "He is on his way and wants us all to go home."

"You are joking." I knew they weren't; I was only hoping they were. This couldn't be over; we had to get Elizabeth the justice she deserved.

"Sorry, Frankie. I'm sure he is closing the case as soon as he gets here. It is his call; he is in charge here." Ashley looked at Mathew when he spoke up.

"Just think of it as time off." I could see the pain in Mathew's eyes. He didn't want this to be over either, but not one of us had a choice.

"When a case was closed back in Miami, it was handed off to another department to try and figure out. They were specialized in closing cases when we couldn't." I handed the bag to Ashley. "And I know we don't have the man-power in a small town like this, but we have to do something."

"What are you saying? We go behind Luther's back and do it anyway? He is our Captain, Frankie. We can't do that." Ashley took the bag from me. Why was she changing her mind now?

"Then, we become P.I.'s." I looked to my SUV. "I'm not giving up on her." I started walking away. They could help me if they wanted to, but I wasn't sure that they would.

"Frankie." Luther pulled up in his car and got out. "The case is closed." He grabbed my arm.

I turned to look Luther in the eyes. "We can't give up on her. What else are we to do?"

"Move on. It's just one more for the folder." Luther went to the office doors. He took the bag from Ashley. "Go home, all of you." He went inside.

Chapter 13

And so, that was that. Luther closed the case on us, and there was nothing any of us could do. We all were sent home and told to come back next week. We were to work on any petty crimes that we can easily solve to keep our numbers up. All Luther cared about was that we had good numbers. There was zero justice for those who deserved it. Every case that this town has in their folder are all murders. Why was the rate high for such a small town? What was happening here?

"You seem to be deep in thought." Joseph appeared on the couch in front of me. He looked very saddened. He must have known. "What are you going to do, Frankie?"

"You mean since I can't get into the office now? Luther locked us out and wants us to take the next week off. I am going to work around the clock to solve Elizabeth's murder. I will not leave it alone." I had Joseph; this was not his first time either. We would work as a team once again. He and I were going to bring Luther down.

"So, you do think it was Luther." Joseph raised his eyebrows and leaned forward, so his elbows were on his knees.

"I have a strong feeling that it was. There is just one problem; there is no way to prove it." I looked at the fireplace from my chair.

"What do you think she would say right now?" Joseph asked; this was his way of getting me to talk about her and open up. He knew every girl I had dated from the age of fifteen to my proposal; he even helped me do that. He was there when we said our vows and was there when Jacquelynn was born. He was there with us until Layla's death. He stayed with me and comforted me, while the rest of Miami thought I was mourning by myself, I wasn't. I had a friend, even if no one else could see him.

"I think she would tell me to do what I thought was best. I would then proceed to explain that I wanted to keep looking, and she would support me completely." Layla was my rock through every case and kept me focused. Since losing her, I had to find another way to solve this case. I was just getting to the bottom when Luther kicked us off. He must have known what we were doing and stopped us beforehand. He must have figured out that we knew it was him, and we were going to get him convicted. He shut us down before we could.

"She definitely would have. She would tell you to get out there and solve that case. She would know you would get it done, one way or another. She never questioned how. Layla had complete faith in you." Joseph was always reassuring me when I doubted myself. This was one more for him; he never seemed to mind it, though.

"I think I know what to do." I got up and went to my bedroom. I picked up my old badge from Miami. I was going to make it look like I was P.I. even if it cost me my new job. I would solve this one alone, just like many of my old cases back in Miami. This was no different, only this time I was working in a new place, and there was little to no evidence present anywhere.

Joseph came into the bedroom and looked at the badge. "You carried that for a long time. What are you going to do with it?"

"I will become a P.I. or at least temporarily. Ready to be a team again?" I was feeling good about this; I was still following the law, but now I was doing it without any police procedures. I had a new set of rules to follow instead.

He looked at me, shocked. "You want me to go into places and get information for you, like before."

"You have always told me it made you feel good to solve a murder. You would love to get another killer, right?" Of course, he would. Joseph always looked forward to solving a murder.

"Who did it?" Keiko appeared, and I knew Ruby was home.

"He thinks it was Luther for sure." Joseph answered Keiko.

"You are doing this alone, then." Ruby leaned on the doorframe. "Please don't."

"I cannot just sit here for a week and hope that it just gets swept under the rug." I waved my hand into the air. "Elizabeth's body is out there somewhere, and I will find her."

"And when you do?" Ruby asked.

"I will communicate with her and ask her what happened. It is the best route to take." I moved past her and into the kitchen.

Ruby followed me. "And you are sure that will work?"

"What if you never find the body?" Keiko asked me.

I looked at Keiko. "There is no way she isn't in this town somewhere. She must be. You can't make a body disappear into thin air."

Joseph touched Keiko's shoulder. I was never sure if they could actually touch one another, but they sure acted like it. "Don't worry, the two of us used to do this all the time in Miami. It isn't anything new to either of us."

"And your boss let you." Ruby looked away a moment. "I should get Jacquelynn, and you should get dinner started. Do not go running out on us right this second."

"My clock is ticking-"

Ruby cut me off with a stern look on her face. "You will eat first and get some sleep. Do not argue with me on this." She walked out the front door, taking my keys with her.

"She is really coming out of her shell." Joseph paused, unsure if she was going to snap on him next. "But she is right, Frankie. You need to sleep and get something to eat. Don't skip either. You know what happens when you do."

"Yeah, I know." I muttered. It wasn't pretty either. I somehow always end up bringing unwanted ghosts, and Joseph has to fight them off. They saw I was weak, and that was a chance to take Joseph's place. Neither of us wanted that to happen. I didn't want to screw this up.

Ruby had come back home with Jacquelynn at her side. My daughter had come running towards me. "Daddy!" She hugged my leg.

"Hey, Pumpkin." I patted the top of her head. "Hungry?"

She nodded and jumped into her chair. "I am."

I sat down at the table with her and Ruby joined in. "How was your day?" I asked my daughter. She had to of had it better than I did.

"I got to play with Snow all day!" She raised her arms in the air. "It was amazing."

"Does Snow like the snow?" Ruby looked to me then to Jacquelynn.

"He is a little afraid, so we stayed inside the barn." Jacquelynn shrugged. "But that is okay; he is my new friend." She frowned when she saw my saddened face. "What is wrong, Daddy?"

"Oh, nothing, Pumpkin." I shook my head. "Everything is fine." I was not going to put her in the middle of my investigation. She knew I was a homicide detective, and she knew what that meant. She understood that I solved murders and put the killers away. To her, I was always a good person, and I couldn't do anything wrong. I wanted to keep her purity that way, but I knew that in less than four years, she was going to be pulled in with me. My daughter was going to understand the reasons for so many things that I have done in the past.

Jacquelynn finished her plate. She got up out of her chair, walked over to the sink, and put her plate down. "Can I go to my room?"

I kissed her head and let her go. "Of course, you can."

She then ran off to her bedroom down the hallway.

"Hey Ruby, can you keep an eye on her? Course I can, Frankie." Ruby said before I even asked.

"I do appreciate it." I looked down at the table. "She is only in third grade."

"I know, I know. Please promise to spend some time with her after you finish with the case." Ruby looked at me with sorrow. "Do not forget you have a family." She got up and started loading the dishwasher.

I got up too and handed her my plate. "I'll unload it when I get back."

She looked up at me and then shut the dishwasher door. She stood up straight, hugging me. "Please don't do something to hurt yourself again."

I was taken back by her hug. I then slowly put my arms around her. "Ruby, I will be fine. I promise to sleep when I come back."

She pulled back and smiled, tears falling down her face. "After what happened, you said you were trapped."

"I was, but it gave me what I needed too. It was strange." I looked at Joseph, who was standing outside the front door, waiting. "I will be back by morning." I assured her and then went out the front door.

"Do not give false promises, Frankie. You are a P.I. Dawson now." Joseph got into the SUV with me. "Jacquelynn and Ruby are looking to you to solve this and come back alive."

"I will come back; there will not be any dying." I shook my head. "I couldn't do that to my daughters."

"Plural?" He asked curiously.

"I said what I said. I am serious about giving her a place she can call home without any problems or difficulties. I want her to have a family, and that is going to be Jacquelynn and me." I buckled up. "Let's get going to the bridge; we will start from scratch." I started backing out of the driveway and made my way downtown.

I got out a pen and a notepad when we reached the bridge a few minutes later. I walked down into the crick and wrote down what I saw, from the blood on the railing that no one bothered to clean up to her hair being stuck on a rock downstream. Ashley and Mathew had said they got rid of it all, but I saw traces of what had to have been her hair. I followed it until it was gone.

"Hey, Frankie." Joseph called to me from the top of bridge. I went back to the stairs and walked up. He pointed to the other side. "Have they even looked over here?"

I looked to where he was pointing. There was a female's shoe. I looked at it and took a photo. "Maybe it was hers." I had knelt by the shoe; it was a sneaker.

"Possibly. What was her shoe size?" Joseph asked, examining it from behind me.

"Seven." I remembered seeing that on her profile.

"Well, it is a seven." He looked at me. "So, she was definitely here. She must have come from the other side." He stood up.

"That is outside of town. We can't go out there." I let out a long sigh. "No, we will do it anyway." I walked with him down the road. The road eventually turned into dirt, and we stopped when we saw a cabin.

"Someone's home. Maybe they saw something." Joseph suggested.

"Why didn't Ashley and Mathew come this way?" Something was off about this shoe.

"It isn't part of their jurisdiction, you said it yourself. They can't take that into their hands." He told me. "I'm more curious as to how they didn't see her shoe."

"I bet we have the other one in evidence." I pointed out, even if I didn't see it, it had to have been there. We walked down the slushy path towards the cabin. I raised my hand to knock, but then stopped. This house was way too close to Winston's colony, only a mile away, and we would be there.

"What is it?" Joseph saw the hesitation in my face.

"We go about ten minutes east, and we would be at that Winston's home along with the rest of those sparkly eyed people." I shuddered.

"Oh yeah, let me take a peek." Joseph went into the cabin, leaving me outside. I waited there for a few minutes while he poked around inside. "No one is home."

I pushed the door, and it opened on its own. "Hello?" I called. I wanted to prove that I wasn't just entering. I went through the living room and saw a cat sleeping on the sofa. There was a fire going, a sure sign someone was here. No one had abandoned this home; whoever is living here will be back. I had to be quick about looking around. I walked through to the bedroom and found books on different animal species and notes on wolves. I figured this person must have been a wolf specialist. They probably had wolves in this part of the country. I put it in my notes but had a feeling that Elizabeth was never actually in this home. She had come from somewhere even further. I decided to leave the cabin with Joseph behind me.

"I found nothing to point out that whoever was here, knew Elizabeth." Joseph shook his head.

"I have not found a thing either. She wasn't here." I looked at the back of the cabin when I heard a sound. It sounded like someone was chanting. I was not going to be a witness to a cult; it would be stupid to confront whoever they were alone. "We should get out of here." We ran back to the road and walked further away from town.

"That had to have been Winston's people. It was coming from their direction." I informed Joseph, who seemed to agree with what I was saying. "That would make sense, that was coming from where they live." The further we walked, the less we found. "We should probably head back. We aren't going to find anything this far out."

"Are you sure about that?" Joseph was only trying to push me further along.

"We can come back in the morning."

"Any luck?" Ruby was up waiting for me. She was leaning on the railing on our front porch, watching me come towards the door.

"We found a shoe and some of her hair. Ash and Mat must not have cleaned up the scene very well." I pushed the front door open and stepped inside.

"You keep going that way, and you'll end up finding the place I left." She shuddered.

"I know, and there was no way to tell if she was that far away."

"What do you plan on doing now?"

"I will have to come up with a new plan in the morning. I will probably ask Saidie a few of my own questions." I went towards my room. "Good night, Ruby." She was right; I should have slept first and then went out after. I was in too much of a rush, and the adrenaline was still running through me. What was out there in the woods? I had a hard time falling asleep; I kept twisting and turning until I finally felt myself drift off.

Chapter 14

The sound of banging on my door had awaken me. I rubbed my eyes, got dressed quickly, and ran to see who was here.

"You like to sleep late or something?" Ashley looked as if she was ready to get going. "Or was it because you were out there by yourself last night?"

I looked at the time; it was almost nine. "I am usually up by now, and yes, you are right. I went to the scene." I wasn't going to hide what I was doing from her. She was still my partner, even if we didn't agree on the plan of action right now.

"What is your next plan of action, P.I. Dawson?" She had a teasing tone to her voice.

"I am starting the entire case over from scratch. Today I plan on talking to Saidie. She might have some answers." I told Ashley.

"Coffee first." She handed me a cup. "Let's go, then." She gave me a smile. "I want to see how you do things. Besides, you are better off if you had someone watching your back. What kind of partner would I be if I wasn't there to make sure you were not getting yourself into trouble?"

I hesitated but agreed. She wanted to be a part of this, and I was going to let her. There was no stopping this now, and there was no way she was going to let me go alone, so she was on the job.

"I hope you know I can't pay you." I got into my SUV.

"Oh, that is fine. I don't need your money, Frankie. What I want is to help Beth in any way that I can." She took a sip out of her coffee cup.

We pulled up to Saidie's home, and I knocked on her door. Ashley had promised on the way over to let me do most of the talking. I had already written down some questions I wanted to ask of Saidie.

When there was no answer at the door, I moved around to the side of the house and peeked into the window. "Does she ever go anywhere?"

"Rarely." Ashley shook her head. "Not since her parents passed away."

"She is still living here." I tried to open the window. "I will have to pick the lock on her door." I moved around to the front to pick her lock. I knew what I was doing; this wasn't the first time I opened a door this way. Once it was unlocked, I pushed it open and found Joseph standing there waiting for me.

"She isn't home, Frankie." Joseph informed me.

"I'll check upstairs." Ashley went up the steps to the bedrooms. I moved down the hall to see what I could find. I heard her yell that things were clear up there.

"In the bathroom, Ash!" I yelled back. I was looking at the bathtub.

She pushed the door open slightly so she could stand behind me. "What do you see?"

I shook my head, "Saidie has probably gone to find her sister on her own."

"What makes you say that?" Ashley sounded confused as to how I came to that conclusion.

I handed her a note that I had found sitting on the side of the tub. "I thought that she was going to be in there, but this is her way of saying she was going to find Elizabeth even if it kills her."

"Oh, Saidie. I will find her and stop her." Ashley put the note into her pocket. "We can't have her getting hurt."

"Thanks, Ash. When you do, let me know. I am going back to the bridge to check for anything that we could have missed." I started out of the bathroom.

"Wait. What do you mean?" Ashley grabbed my arm. Her voice was full of alarm.

"The shoe. The hair in the stream." I shook my head. "How did you and Mat never see it?"

"We combed that bridge. Someone is setting you up." I could hear the distaste in her voice.

"Are we sure about this? Ash, she is a size seven, and the shoe was a seven." I was so sure that they had missed it, but what if Ashley was right about this?

Ashley looked down at my notepad then into my eyes. "You think that we would not have found those items? Really, Frankie?"

I didn't speak; I was busy deciding if it was worth the argument. It wasn't, so I chose not to answer her questions.

She let go of my arm then. "I will go find Saidie, okay? She could not have gone far." Ashley left me at the house.

"Ashley seems so distraught." Joseph waited until Ashley had left to say anything.

"She is just as annoyed as I am about all of this." I put my hands into my coat pockets. "A girl is missing, and no one can seem to find her. No one has a single answer as to what happened. There is something very off about this case. Doesn't any of this bother you?"

"Someone knows something." Joseph shook his head. "Someone had to have seen it."

We both knew it was Luther who did this, but we had to prove so. To do that, we needed to head back to the scene again. This time when we got there, the shoe was gone. Ashley was right; someone must have planted it the first time. This game was of running circles was getting old.

"Hey, Frankie. Your phone is ringing." Joseph pointed towards my pocket.

I reached to grab it. "Hey, Ash."

"Found her." Ashley told me. "She was at the diner with Roxann."

"I can be there." I felt better knowing that Saidie was okay. "You were right, by the way. The shoe is gone and so is the hair, it is almost like somebody wanted me to find it."

"Luther, you think?" She asked me.

"He is playing with us. He probably thinks this is a game." I got into the SUV. "Where do you want to meet?"

"Come to my place." She told me.

I hung up the phone and sat there in the SUV for a moment, thinking. "Luther is trying to push us away from the case. He doesn't want us to close it." Luther really did know that we were following his trail.

Joseph appeared next to me. "You are getting somewhere."

I looked at my Shadow. "He is always late to work."

"What else, Frankie?" You got this solved, don't you?" He knew my face, and he knew what it looked like when I had put all of the pieces together.

"I need him to tell me how. He definitely did it. First, however, we are getting Saidie to talk with us on the matter. It also seems that Roxann is jumping in on this." Roxann had helped me try and find Elizabeth the other day, and now she was working closely with Saidie. It was probably to see if she could get answers without asking and having a badge.

"Saidie needed someone to talk to about all of this that wasn't police most likely. She is a human; she doesn't have a Shadow to help her through her problems." Joseph told me.

My phone rang again. "It's Ruby. Hey." I waited to see what she wanted from me.

"Where are you?" She sounded distant.

"At the bridge. I'm heading to Ashley's place; we are going to talk to Saidie." I spoke into the phone.

She didn't answer right off the bat. This was concerning. "Ruby?" I asked, hoping to hear her again.

"I'm still here. Please be careful." She then hung up in what seemed to be a hurry.

"I will." I said into the deadline. I started the car and drove away. When we got to Ashley's house, I pulled into her driveway and went up to the front door. I heard Bruce barking inside then the door opened, Ashley had let me inside. There at the kitchen table were both Saidie and Roxann.

"Good morning, ladies." I said to them both; it was only eleven.

Roxann smiled at me. "How is Ruby holding up?"

"She is doing great." I assured Roxann, as I sat across from her and Saidie. I didn't mention the phone call that I had just got from her. I wasn't going to bother Ruby about it right now; she would probably tell me to stop worrying about her so much and then hang up again. That did not stop me from worrying about her, anyway.

Ashley sat next to me. "Alright, Saidie. Tell Frankie what you told me, from the top."

Saidie shook her head. "She had a boyfriend."

I looked at Ashley; I knew it. "Go on." Ashley said to Saidie. "This is all new to me as well."

I looked right back at Saidie; she was going to tell us what she knew. She seemed to be ready to talk on the matter. "My sister had a boyfriend, but she never told me his name. She seemed to be fascinated by the way he lived and his whole family. She would see him all the time, mornings, nights, and weekends. She was waitressing at Malcolm's until she disappeared, and then one day,

Ashley told me she was most likely dead. I just want my sister back."
She looked at us. "Please tell me you found her."

"Not yet, no, I am sorry. What do you think happened then?"
I needed her to tell me everything that came to her mind on the
subject.

"I'm not sure; they were so happy. I never met him, but from
what she told me and the way she expressed herself, they seemed
happy enough. They were going out for a few months. I'm not
saying he killed her, but I wish I knew who he was." She shrugged.
"I also think they may have had some kind of argument one night
because she came home crying, but she seemed to be okay, and they
continued to see one another."

"It isn't enough for someone to kill another human." Roxann
said to us.

"You can't always explain why people do what they do."
Ashley informed her. "Sometimes, people think they are doing a
good thing, even if they are not."

"She is right." I added in. "Some killers believe they are
doing something right even if it isn't. How long after this argument
did she pass?"

"A few weeks. The day she left for work, she seemed on
edge. She wouldn't tell me why, so I let her be. That night instead of
Beth coming home, it was Ashley and Mathew who came to my door
the following day." Saidie rubbed her arm.

"Let me ask you something." I leaned forward to Saidie.
"Was your sister suicidal?"

"Not that I ever knew about. She was probably one of the
most down to Earth, sweetest girls, ever. She was never afraid to
help someone who needed it." Saidie told me. "She had inspirations
of moving us into Detroit and getting a job as an attorney."

"She would have been a damn good one too, Saidie." Ashley
comforted her.

I gave the room some silence before I asked another question. "Can I ask what happened to your parents?"

Saidie bit her lip. "They died in a car crash on that same bridge. Beth had to grow up fast, she was my big sister, and a mom to me."

Ashley looked at me. "That was about seven years ago. Beth was seventeen."

"That puts you at nine then. Not much older than my daughter is now." I knew how hard it was on my daughter to lose her mom, but to lose both parents, I couldn't even fathom.

"My sister and I helped each other as soon as I was old enough. She got her waitressing job, and the townsfolk helped us keep our home. They were not letting us fall into the cracks." Saidie looked to Roxann then back at me. "And now she is gone." Saidie's head fell onto Roxann's shoulder. "I miss her."

"And we will find her." Ashley informed her. "Frankie and I will not let this go."

I agreed. "No matter what, we will find Elizabeth and bring justice for her."

"I know, but I feel like we are running out of time. It has been so long already." Saidie looked at me with saddened eyes.

"Do not lose hope." Ashley told her. "You cannot lose hope. Not now and not ever. Beth is out there somewhere, and we will find her." Was Ashley only trying to be friendly, or was she feeling upset about Elizabeth too?

"Ashley, I am going to go do this." I had stood up and made my way out the door.

Ashley followed me out. "Frankie." She grabbed my arm. "Please do not go and confront Luther." She looked frightened, almost as if I went there, I was signing my death certificate.

"What do you want me to do? I cannot keep playing his game. This needs to stop." I was tired of this.

"You don't understand." She warned. "Please, just wait a minute."

"How long is that minute, Ash?" I asked her. "Saidie needs closure."

"You go there, then what? You might not walk away." I could see the pain in her eyes. She looked worried about me. She knew something, but she wasn't telling. I shook my head. "If you know something, Ash, please tell me now."

She pursed her lips. "I can't. You will have to trust me on this."

I shrugged. "Then, I'm going." I headed to my car and started down the road. What was Ashley hiding from me? Everyone in this town seemed to be keeping secrets. It didn't matter who I talked to; no one wanted to tell me the entire truth. I was starting to have a really hard time trusting everyone, even Ashley.

"Don't be upset with her, Frankie." Joseph was probably hoping I would listen to her plea.

"She is hiding something." I told him. "She has information and is hiding it from me. How can I trust her? How do I know she isn't in on this?"

"She is not in on it." Joseph looked away from me. "Don't go down that road; you won't like it."

"What do you mean? What are you saying?" I asked him.

"I am just saying that Ashley is only doing what she can to help solve this. She is not your enemy, so do not make her out to be so." Joseph disappeared after that. I had a feeling he was angry with me.

Maybe he was right; maybe I had been irrational. Ashley is probably trying to protect me. I turned down the road to Luther's house and saw something run right out in front of my car. I swerved towards the crick on the other side, trying to avoid the large animal. I ended up crashing the car into the trees, stopping me from falling into the water below. I heard someone coming, someone yelling to get help, and then everything went dark.

When I woke, I found myself in a bed, inside a bedroom made entirely of stained and carefully crafted wood. It smelled mostly of oak and pine. When I tried to stand up out of bed, I felt dizzy and sat back down, catching my breath.

"Careful there." I saw a familiar face leaning on the doorframe.

"Oliver?" I asked to be sure.

"Yeah, that's me; you swerved into the trees not too far from here." He shrugged and pulled a chair over. "Are you feeling okay?"

"I think so. What happened?" I was sure I knew what happened, but I figured that I should ask anyway.

"I called Ruby and Ashley to let them know you are okay. That was quite a crash you had there." He sat into his chair.

I looked him in the eyes. "I would like to stand, but that might not be possible."

"Lay down." A young blonde girl came walking into the room. It was Addison. "He shouldn't be sitting up, Ollie." She sounded as if she was trying to nurse me back to health.

He looked up at Addison, who now had a hand on the back of his chair. "Hey, he is going to be fine."

"Lay down, Detective." She ignored her brother.

I laid down on my back; I was still feeling dizzy, so laying down was probably a good idea. "What was that? What ran out in front of me?"

"Wolves." Oliver told me. "They live around here. You have to be careful; sometimes, they tend to run wherever they please." I saw the way he glared at his sister.

"Anyway…rest for now; okay?" She smiled. "Ollie and I are down the hall if you need us." She then grabbed him by the arm. "Come on, big brother."

"Addi-" he grumbled at her as the chair fell over, and she pulled him out of the bedroom.

I laid there, staring at the ceiling. A wolf? It was way too large, and it certainly was too small to be a deer. I was not entirely sure what I almost hit; it was too fast, almost a blur to even see for more than a split second before it had run off into the trees. How did Oliver and Addison even come to my rescue? I had not seen them anywhere. I was the only car on the road. "This is getting too weird."

"You are alive." Joseph sat at the end of my bed. "Are you still mad at Ashley?" He looked towards the window at the other side of the room, something outside had his attention.

"Frustrated. Maybe. Angry? No." I turned my head so I could see him. "I only want someone to start telling me the whole truth around here. I can't keep running around blind."

"Then maybe it is time to tell Ashley about me." Joseph looked at me. The only other time he suggested this was when my last Captain started asking way too many questions.

"Right, she will think I am just as crazy as Ruby." I sighed, sitting up again. "There should be answers, somewhere."

"You mean like how you are talking to a ghost?" Oliver came into the room. I was ready to tell him he was wrong. He continued talking before I could even get a word out of my mouth. "Don't fret Detective, I knew it from the moment you came into town. I could smell it on you; I wasn't sure how ready you were for all of this- or how much you knew outside of your own abilities."

"Ready for what?" I was unsure about what he meant. There was a long pause. "Smell???"

157

"Sleep for now; we can talk more about it tonight. We should take a walk around the bridge. I can tell you what I know from the scents I pick up and the ones I picked up the day she died. I know what happened to Elizabeth."

When I woke up later, I heard chatter coming from downstairs. I made my way down the steps towards the sound. Addison and Oliver were in the living room, along with two women who looked almost identical to one another. Oak and pine are what looked to make up this entire house. The craftsmanship of the staircase, the door, the floor, just about everything had seemed to be hand carved. It was probably one of the most beautiful homes I have seen in this town.

"He is up." Addison was standing over by the fireplace. "Good." She looked at Oliver. "Hey, Ollie."

Oliver was standing and reading a book by the window when he looked over at me. "Oh, hey, how are you feeling?" He moved past the girls sitting on the large couch and over to me. "You remember Zoey and Sophia from when you came into Malcolm's."

"I am feeling much better, Oliver, and yes, I remember seeing their faces when I was there. It is nice to meet the two of you." I smiled at Sophia and Zoey.

Sophia stood up and put her hand out. "We do appreciate you doing your job, Detective."

"Thank you, Sophia. Ash and I are doing everything we can." I looked down at Zoey, who was starting to stand up with help from the arm of the sofa. "Is she okay?"

"Zoey is my twin sister, but she is blind." Sophia told me. "She was born that way."

I gave Sophia a nod. "I understand."

"May I?" Zoey asked, leaning towards me. Her hands touched my elbows, and her face went into my shoulder.

"It is her way of getting to know you." Sophia informed me. Oliver did mention the idea of scent, so I had a feeling that she was getting mine.

Oliver touched Zoey's shoulder. "Zo, Frankie and I are going to take a walk now."

Zoey backed off slowly. "Sorry Detective, I didn't mean to scare you." She spoke so softly, touching her sister's arm.

"Nonsense, it is fine. Don't worry about it." I shook my head. I didn't want her to think I was angry. I then felt Oliver take my arm and pull me out the front door. "It isn't always easy living here." He was leading me down the gravel path towards the road.

I wasn't sure what he meant by living here. "You said you knew that I talked to ghosts." I stopped him from walking.

He shuffled around until he turned to face me. "I don't know much about it, but what I do know you can talk to the dead. I thought you would try to talk to Elizabeth."

"We did, but we failed to call upon her." I hated to admit the defeat, but it was true.

"Then, she is still walking around on her own two feet." He sounded so sure of his words.

"Alive, then." That was the only alternative to being dead, wasn't it?

"She doesn't necessarily have to be alive, Detective." His face looked into the distance, back at the house. He shook his head and turned back down the path. We turned the corner and saw my car with someone else who had their head inside the hood. "Don't worry; I will fix it up for you. Ethan and I are good at what we do."

Ethan waved at us when Oliver had told me this. Ethan looked to be no more than twenty-five. He had dark skin and light brown eyes. The garage that Ethan was working out of looked to be like it was a real business, and they probably had a good reputation among the people in town here.

Oliver waved back to Ethan. "He is pretty much my best friend. I trust him explicitly."

"Thank you, Oliver." I felt happy that Oliver and Ethan were going to fix my car up for me.

"We can take my truck up to the bridge." He pointed to the green pick up. "Let's get going." He got in, and I got in the passenger side. I looked in the rearview mirror into the back seat.

"There is a ghost in the back seat, isn't there?" He asked me curiously. He reminded me of when Jacquelynn learned she was going to a school friend's birthday party for the first time.

"How did you guess that?" He must have picked this up. Why hadn't he asked Roxann these questions?

"Easy, I see the way you look into certain places." He nodded.

"You smell it. Whatever that means." My arm rested on the door.

"I can't smell ghosts, Detective." He chuckled. "I can only find what that is in this plane."

"Meaning, you can't smell my ghost." I responded. Sure, that made sense then.

"No, I can't. I couldn't tell you anything about whoever is there." He motioned his hand into the back seat.

"Why didn't you just talk to Roxann if you were so curious?" Surely, he would have asked her, right?

"Roxann doesn't really live in town here." Oliver explained. "She is from Detroit and helps when we need it. She only rents a house here. Time to find your clues and bring justice to Elizabeth." He patted my shoulder.

There was that we word again. I could not wrap my head around who 'we' was meant to be. No one wanted to answer my questions until now. Oliver was the only one willing to give me the answers I wanted. "Can I ask who 'we' is?"

"Anyone like us, Detective." Oliver shrugged. "You know, me, my friends, Ash, you."

"You are telling me that Ashley is like you?" I was taken back some. "That smell thing or whatever it is?"

"Let's just get to the bridge, and I will answer all of your questions." He became silent after that, leaving me to let my thoughts wander.

Chapter 15

He pulled his pickup truck over to the side of the road, right before we had got to the bridge and pointed to the stairs that led us down to the river below. "Let's talk."

"Then start explaining, Oliver." I was now ready for him to tell me his side of the story; I followed him down that staircase and prepared myself for whatever crazy explanation he was going to give me.

He stared at the river as we reached the bottom of the staircase, his hands going into his pockets. It felt almost forever that silence he kept before actually speaking to me. "You are a Necromancer. I am a Werewolf." He sounded so casual about that explanation. "My sister, Zoey, Sophia, Malcolm, and Delilah are also wolves." He didn't bother looking up at me. "When you came into the diner that night, there were those sitting at the table. They are all part of my Pack."

"I'm sorry, what?" I didn't exactly believe what he was saying as there was no way he could be a Werewolf, surely, they were only fiction. "Werewolves turn under the full moon, don't go pulling my leg."

"That isn't true, we can turn into wolves as we wish, but if we turn under the moon, we have an advantage." He led me to the spot where Elizabeth landed and looked me in the eyes as he continued. "Ashley is a Half-Demon. She was trying to protect you from the madness that is this town." He looked up at the bridge. "And Luther is- well he is a Vampire." Oliver didn't seem to like saying the word Vampire.

"What about Illyanna and Daeron?" I asked. I was sure there was more to this. "Winston? Lily?"

"Elves." He shrugged.

Elves, Half-Demons, Werewolves? So it was true, I wasn't alone in all of this. There were others, and it seemed that there must have been more. "Then what about Zane?"

"A male Witch." He told me. "Zane and I talked about your trance." He knew about what happened to me. Zane had told Oliver what I went through. Oliver turned towards the woods and started heading off in that direction.

I walked quickly to try and keep up with him. We went right and were heading straight for the Elves. "Trance? Is that what that was? I don't know how that happened." I still had no idea what that was. I was confused as to how it happened or why, and now Oliver knew. Zane had answers too.

He stopped walking. "Yes, it is Elven magic. They can put you in a dream state with your worst fears and then make you believe it is reality. You were lucky to have Zane nearby to get you out of there."

I almost ran into Oliver as he stopped. Zane did save me; he was right. I guess I was afraid of getting the blame, even if I had not done it. It isn't the first time I had that fear either. Some days in my job, I thought that I was going to be the target after solving a case.

Oliver interrupted my thoughts. "See that?" He pointed up to the tree where there was a symbol marked, a triangle carved into the tree. "That is the marking that you are crossing into their territory. Elves do not like it when others come to their land. They are seclusive and would rather keep to themselves." He took my arm and turned me away.

"Why a triangle?" I asked Oliver. He kept walking me back to the bridge. He didn't even bother answering my question. Was he afraid of the Elves? "Mathew?" I tried to change the subject matter away from the Elves and their magic.

"Human as any human can get. I think he is frustrated some days. I wish I could tell you everything." Oliver didn't mention much more than that. Maybe he didn't have all the answers.

"Okay, so everyone here is some kind of supernatural being." I felt ready to face Luther head-on. "Meaning that I can go right to Luther and tell him I know what he did."

"Bad idea." He told me. "Addi stopped you from making that choice the first time." He knelt in front of a hill.

"That was Addison?!" So, it *was* a wolf who ran out in front of my car. He was only fixing my car out of pity and not because he wanted to.

Oliver hushed me and pulled me down with him. "You need to keep your voice down; you don't want anyone out this way to hear you." He pointed to the cliff. "Go that way, and you are heading to the cabin." He continued to move back towards the bridge.

I looked right at him with a surprised look on my face. The cabin was listening too? No way, this is too much. The cabin couldn't be alive, could it?

"Calm down. The cabin isn't alive, Detective." He sighed, seemingly worried for my sanity. "But the cat that lives in there isn't a cat."

Joseph appeared to give me a warning. "Oh, no. We need to get out of here, Frankie."

I looked at Joseph. I felt the need to acknowledge him, but I also felt that I should probably ignore him for the moment. "I am a Necromancer, yes. We don't just raise the dead when we want. We have what we call a Shadow. My Shadow's name is Joseph, and he has been with me since I was twelve. We get a companion, and they are usually with us forever."

"Oh, how cool. Hey, Joseph." Oliver waved, knowing I was looking at Joseph.

Joseph smiled. "See, Oliver is trustworthy. Now, we must get out of here. Quickly."

"He says hello." I told Oliver. "Now tell me about how you saw Elizabeth a few days ago." I wasn't ready to give up on this, and I wasn't leaving until I had all of my answers.

"She was with Luther." So that much was true. They were together at the time of her death. "But they weren't unhappy. I know it sounds crazy but hear me out. Maybe she wanted to be turned into a Vampire."

I shook my head. "And if she didn't?" Who in their right mind would want to be an undead corpse?

"Very possibly, she wanted to be with her lover for the rest of her life. So, she may have asked Luther to turn her into what he is." Maybe he was right then, but we would never know, not without Elizabeth. Her body was still missing. Ashley and Mathew have claimed that she is dead. They won't say otherwise until she had been located. "I did some sniffing around here, and I got a whiff of Elizabeth and Luther. I'm not sure if that is what you needed or if there is something else going on with your case." He shrugged. "But I swear that Elizabeth is probably okay."

"What if that wasn't her?" I shook my head; I wasn't quite sure if he was a Werewolf or not, and I wasn't entirely sure that Luther was some manic Vampire either.

"Then, I may need to get my nose checked because a Werewolf's nose is just about always right." He seemed to keep his calm. "Detective, listen, I am only trying to make things right here. I want to get this solved as much as the next person, but I need you to try and trust me. If you don't believe what I am telling you, then maybe I ought to show you."

I looked back at the pickup truck as we reached the river again. "So, what happened then? If you somehow magically know, how am I supposed to be sure you weren't involved?" I followed Oliver up the staircase.

"Luther pushed her over the edge. To turn someone, you must bite them and then kill them. Once undead, they need to feed on the one who turned them to live. They have about an hour to do so. Whoever turned them are now their sire." He led me back to the railing. "And here we have her touching her neck and then touching the railing before Luther pushes her."

"If that is so, then why aren't his fingerprints anywhere?" I bit my lip and leaned over the side. This was getting weirder and weirder. I was starting to miss the old days when I would solve a case that actually made sense in the human world and could send it right back to my Captain.

"Vampires don't have a pulse, which in turn they don't have fingerprints, and since they are dead, they cannot leave their DNA anywhere either." He must have believed his theory. I chose to keep following it to see where he was leading me.

"Then why don't we confront him? I do not see the reason as to why we have to keep running circles." I was still determined to go to Luther. Surely, he would have the answers at this point. I knew everything, or at least I was sure I did.

"As I said before, you can't. Not yet." Oliver shook his head, taking my arm and pointing to the truck. "First, we need a confession, and to do that we need someone like Ashley."

"A Half-Demon." There was no way some demon was going to be able to get him to confess. She was, however, a detective so, she would have some credibility. "How does that help us any?"

"She can get a confession out of him. She is Lucifer's daughter." He reached for the door handle of his driver's side, pausing a moment to continue talking with me.

"The fallen angel." I walked around to my side of the truck. "Then, he is real."

"Maybe not in the form you might be thinking of, but yeah, the guy is real, and he had a kid over thirty years ago." Oliver shrugged. "What are you thinking of doing about all of this, Detective? You now have new information that you did not have before."

"I am thinking we go talk to Ashley, as you said. We then get her to talk to Luther with us. Finally, we then get Luther to confess and possibly turn himself in." I responded, it seemed like a good idea in my head, but out loud it sounded foolish. I was teaming up with a guy who was a Werewolf, or at least says he is a

Werewolf, and now we were getting Ashley, who he claims to be Half-Demon to join up with us as well.

"He may not get jail time, especially with Axel around." Oliver told me. "Axel has too much power; he has been around for a very, very long time."

I wasn't sure how long Oliver was referring to, and I wasn't asking. The man didn't seem to be older than thirty. Oliver did say that they were undead, so he was probably as old as the day he died. "That explains why he is always late to work and why Axel refused to meet me anywhere but under the overhang outside my office." I looked at Oliver. "Vampires hate the sun."

"Well yeah, it kills them." Oliver rolled his eyes as if that much was obvious, and I should have known that from the start. "Luther takes the long way to the office to avoid the sunlight."

"And he keeps the curtains closed at the office." I nodded. I knew that something was odd about him. "It keeps him out of the sun. This is starting to make sense."

"I am glad you are starting to understand your situation here, Detective." He smiled. He seemed to be excited to help me solve this case. "I guess this makes us a team then."

"Not so fast, Oliver. You gave me crucial information, but that does not make us a team, especially since I cannot pay you as part of this investigation. How do I know I can trust you? How am I to be sure you are not working with Luther?" I knew he wasn't, but I wanted him to say it. If he wanted to be a team with Ashley and me, he will have to be on his toes.

"Because you and I both know that you know the truth. Zane even said you knew." He was quick to answer. He was going to make for a good teammate.

Zane did get me to finally understand that I did know who hurt Elizabeth, even if I wasn't ready to believe it myself. I never had to convict my superior officer before. "And I am to trust him too?" I asked.

"Hey." Joseph interjected. "Oliver is only trying to help, Frankie. He isn't trying to turn you around and push you in another direction. You already knew it was Luther, now let him tell you how it happened."

"Tell me about Elizabeth and Luther's relationship." I was also ready to hear Joseph's warning.

"Relationship? Oh no, you got it all wrong. Luther isn't dating Elizabeth. She is dating Felix, another Vampire." Oliver reached for the handle of his truck again. "And to be one-hundred percent honest with you, I think Luther was jealous."

"Luther? Jealous?" A female appeared. She had bleach blonde hair and dark brown eyes. That surely didn't go well together. She was wearing a bright pink shirt, boot cut pants, and brown boots as if this were the 70's. "You hear that, Julian? Luther was jealous of Felix." She giggled.

I tried to get into the truck. I had a bad feeling about our visitors. They didn't remind me of Winston, Illyanna, Daeron, or Lily. These visitors had a vibe that they have brought trouble with them.

"You are in our turf." A dark-haired woman was behind me and had grabbed my shoulders. Oliver looked at me through the car window, as if telling me not to move or say a word. "Quit coming down this way." I caught a glimpse of her face as she walked around me in a circle. She was Japanese and looked to be right out of Feudal Japan. She then gripped my shoulders.

"Hey, hey, calm down, ladies." The guy with the woman in pink had curly hair and wore a button-down shirt and dress pants. I assumed this was Julian. I then figured that they died in the clothes that they were wearing. That is depressing, to say the least. I thought about how I dress every day and thought about how I was now going to dress in the future. "The Detective here is only doing his job."

"And that job involves getting rid of Luther." The Japanese woman gripped my shoulders even harder. "Isn't that right?" She pushed me to my knees.

"Sora." Julian's New York accent started spilling out. "Let the man be; we will take the dog instead."

Sora grunted, pushing me to the ground. "Rachel always gets to play." She rolled her eyes and walked away from me. "The bridge is ours. Now leave." She and Julian disappeared.

The woman in pink smiled. "Come on, pup." She disappeared with Oliver.

Getting to my feet felt like forever compared to how fast they moved. I tried to follow them into the woods, but they were gone, and there was no way to know where they went.

"I warned you." Joseph let out an elongated sigh. "I really tried to."

I looked at him with regret. "We will have to walk back then. I am going to need help getting Oliver back from them."

"Vampires, Frankie. They have a name for their race." He talked as if he knew this all along.

"Race? I wouldn't call it that. We are all still human at the core. They were most likely human before someone came along and killed them." I moved past him, back to the path towards the Elves territory. "I'm going to Winston and getting help. The Elves and the Vampire share the space out here, so they possibly might not like one another. I also want to know more about that cat."

"Maybe a shape-shifter of some kind." Joseph appeared next to me again. "This is getting very interesting."

I rolled my eyes. "Interesting? Try frustrating. I know what happened to Elizabeth, or at least have an idea, but I won't know for sure if I don't have my witness and can't get Luther to confess." The only way to go right now was to get Oliver back.

"Hey, don't let this anger you too much. I'm sure this isn't the first time that any of them have gotten themselves into a problem or conflict." Joseph trailed behind me. "The difference now is that they have you."

I looked up, seeing that triangle and looked back at Joseph. "Maybe it would be better if you waited here."

He put his hands into his pockets. "I will be here when you come back, Frankie."

I knew he would be. He was always there when I needed him. I couldn't risk them seeing him, and I had a feeling he wouldn't get past. From what Oliver had told me and from what he wouldn't tell me, I had a feeling that Vampires and possibly anyone who was dead, would not get past. I know it sounds silly, but I was trying to be careful; I didn't want to lose Joseph. I wasn't sure what these Elves were really capable of anymore. I felt safer doing this on my own, knowing that there was no way they could get to him.

Chapter 16

I arrived at what I believed to be the home of the Elves. I only saw it from one angle before I had run away. I saw the fire pit on one end of the yard, and the large home which was made from glass on the other side. I pushed past the last of the bushes and trees into the clearing of their yard. No one seemed to be outside, and the fire was not burning. I looked up at the three-story house but saw no one inside there either. There was a possibility that they weren't here during the day. I looked around, noticing how trees surrounded the entire yard. I realized how anyone could either miss or accidentally stumble into a place so well hidden; even in the sky, you would not be able to see the house as the trees were entangled over-head. It almost felt like an enclosed garden without all the flowers. I braved my way up the stone path in front of me to the house. I was just about to knock when a small girl about the same size as Jacquelynn appeared. Her eyes and skin glistened, just like any of the others. I knew she was one of them, an Elf. She smiled at me, her bright grey eyes joining in. Her hair was long, all the way down to her ankles and a natural light brown blonde. She was wearing a white dress. My daughter couldn't wear white as it would have stained almost immediately, but this dress was in perfect condition as if she had just put it on along with her black boots. She pushed her hair behind her ear and then stepped aside. I looked inside, hesitating a moment before walking in. There in the room was a large table, big enough to fit at least fifteen. There were bar stools and a table on the left side and then the kitchen right behind it. The entire room was pure white, and in the white marble floor below me, I could see my reflection.

"Detective!" I saw Winston approach me with a smile. Behind him was another man with deep green eyes and a tan that made me think he could have been Hawaiian. "What brings you here?"

I looked at him, untrustingly.

"I understand why you wouldn't want to answer, but you came here for a reason." He motioned me to sit at the elongated table. "Reese, get us some tea, please." There was a mini garden that ran from one side of the table to the other, flowers I had never seen before were blooming inside it.

The man behind him nodded and went into the kitchen; I could hear him getting cups and boiling some water. Winston had looked at the little girl in the white dress. "Kailynn, go find Cassaveil and Keithro."

She smiled, bowed, and ran off down the hallway. Her boots clicked across the marble flooring, echoing through the hallway. She must have gone down another hall as I couldn't hear her any longer.

"She is my daughter's age." I started by trying to make things more comfortable for myself.

"She may look it, but she is much older than that. We don't age very fast." He informed me. "What would you pin me at, Detective?"

I looked at him. It felt like he was trying to get me to trip up. I wanted to say forty, close to my own age, but this felt like a game.

"Don't think on it too much. I won't be offended in the slightest. Everyone says something different. It is all on how you perceive it." He looked up at Reese as he gave us our cups.

"Sir, if I may, the Detective is here for a very specific reason. He seems to be unsure of his own self and situation." Reese looked at me. "He is disheartened and feeling lost."

Winston nodded. "Yes, thank you, Reese. Please, go see what is taking Kailynn so long." He shooed Reese away. "Now, where were we?"

"Your age." I adjusted myself in my chair. "I guess I would say around forty."

He let out a hearty laugh. "Oh, that is quite young, indeed. I haven't got that number in a long while. This tea must be working its magic." He looked down at his cup. "Something is bothering you, Detective. Would you care to share with me?"

I picked up my cup. "Oliver told me about you and your trance." I sighed. "I know what you are."

He smiled at me. "Ah, it is about time you caught up with everyone else. I was not the one who placed that trance on you. It was my dear Illyanna. There was no ill intent there; she was only trying to get you to understand your fear, and the truth came out because of it. She was doing her best at trying to help you."

I shook my head. "I would have been stuck there if it wasn't for Zane." I looked away towards the front door. "I would have never gotten out."

"That, Detective, is untrue. You would have seen it with time and realized what was going on, no matter how long it would have taken you to do so. You wouldn't have been in the trance for more than a few hours."

I looked back down at my cup. "If you are only trying to help, then you will help me find Oliver."

"Of course, that is why I had Kailynn go and get Cassaveil and Keithro. They are tiny and can get into smaller places, which will be convenient for you." He tapped my hand with his. "I share this area with Axel, and we agreed to stay out of each other's business, but this involves one of the humans here." So, he and Axel were in some kind of agreement just as I had thought.

"I appreciate that. Let me ask you this then; you knew what I was from the start."

"Since you moved here, yes. Daeron and Illyanna told me about you as soon as you came to the river." He smiled. "You give off the same wavelength as Roxann." He turned his head as soon as the three kids came to him. The two others were boys. Cassaveil was a light brown blonde like Kailynn and had a beachy tan to him. Keithro, on the other hand, looked as if he was an English boy with his light skin and brown eyes. "Darlings, do you mind doing a search and rescue of Oliver?"

"The wolf?" Keithro asked. "We can."

"Then you will help out Detective Dawson and get Oliver back safely." He talked to them like children, but he had told me they were much older. They probably were but were still the same as Jacquelynn in the sense that they had the minds of seven to ten-year-old children.

I walked back outside with the kids, in hopes that they would know the way. I certainly was unsure of where we were going, so I figured it was better to let them lead the way instead. It wasn't like I had a sharp nose or had the ability to use magic; all I could do was see ghosts, mostly just Joseph. He was my partner, though, so I guess that was something. We were always good together, even if we didn't always see eye to eye. I felt one of the kids take me by the hand and pull me across the yard and back behind the house. I looked back and saw no one inside again.

"You won't see them, you know." Keithro informed me as he continued to pull me along. "We are good at hiding." He led us through the trees and away from their home.

Cassaveil came up next to me. "Plus, who wants to see someone in their house anyway? Yuck."

"It is mostly for privacy, Cass." Kailynn looked at him. "Don't be so mean to the detective. He doesn't know any better."

I looked at Kailynn. She was acting like she was the mom, and I was the child. "Don't give me that look, Detective. We may look like kids, but we aren't, okay?"

I smiled slightly and nodded. "That is what Winston has said to me."

"Well, he is right. We aren't kids." Kailynn made sure I knew they were not children.

I thought back to when I saw the little blonde girl outside her house when I was seeing Saidie for the first time. "You can't read minds, can you?"

"Read minds?!" Cassaveil laughed. "What are we? We are more like empaths. We can see how you are feeling."

"Right, like how Reese did." I looked up at the sky; it looked hazy.

"Not rain." Kailynn shook her head. "You haven't been this far out of town yet, have you?"

I shook my head. Were they really this far away from the bridge? "No, I haven't."

"Well, the story goes that Axel kidnapped a witch, and took her hostage, and makes her keep the clouds in the sky." She pointed to the castle-like building. It was a shade of purple with red accents on the outside and three towers with one dead center looking towards us. "And that is where they live. In that dark, cold place." She shivered, and so did Cassaveil and Keithro. "Elves feed off of each other's emotions." She then went on to explain our procedure. "Well, let me explain to you how this will go. You go to the door, distract them, and demand to get Oliver back. Meanwhile, Keithro and I will go in and rescue Oliver. Cassaveil will keep watch out here."

"Do you think Elizabeth may be in there?" I was sure she had to be. Maybe I would finally be able to know she is alright.

"No." Kailynn shook her head. "She isn't."

"You can sense it?" I was sure she knew.

"We aren't Fairies, Detective." Cassaveil grunted. "We are Elves."

I wasn't sure what that was supposed to mean, but they all took his comment seriously. "Okay, I'll go in and distract them. How do I know when to leave?"

"Trust me, you will know." Kailynn pushed me forward. Once I got to the castle door, I knocked. It was Rachel once again.

"Hello." Rachel smiled, answering the door. I could see the blood on her lips.

I bit my own without even thinking. I was feeling concerned.

"Oh, don't be so afraid." A man with caramel dyed hair approached. I figured he was of Korean descent. His eyes were dark, and he seemed to be intent on getting me to leave. "It isn't wolf's blood."

I looked at him, pushing my way into the castle. The floors were made of stone and the walls too. I was intent on making a scene right here. "Where is he?!" I demanded.

"Whoa there." He grabbed my arm. "You cannot barge into someone's home like this." He wasn't happy, and his grip was tight, just like Sora.

"Be nice to him, Silas." Rachel said. "We need him."

"Why, so Axel can do what he wants? No way. We have an intruder." Silas sounded like he hated having to listen to Axel.

"He is also a Necromancer." Julian appeared. His hair still seemed to flop everywhere.

"You mean like that Roxann." Silas said to Julian. "Who cares?" He pushed me to the ground.

"I am not leaving until I get Oliver back." I hissed at the Vampires.

Julian took my arm and tossed me into the wall before I could fight back. "You will leave here and never come back; you hear me?" He lifted my chin so I would be looking at him in the face. "This does not concern you. You will go back to Miami."

I tried to pull away. "No! I am not leaving Oliver behind!" I was trying to fight back. "I demand to see Axel!"

"No one demands Axel." Rachel sounded bored. "Ever." She shoved her foot into my back.

I fell forward as both Julian and Silas let me go. My face hit the stone floor.

I woke, unsure of where I was, I noted the stone floor. I knew that it wasn't back with the Elves. It smelled of bleach in here as if they were intent on getting rid of a body. I tried to get up, realizing I my arms were chained to the wall and my ankles to the floor. I tasted old blood in my mouth before I spit it out. I was in one of the wings of the castle. I started realizing the room was dark, and there was no way out. I only hoped that Oliver got out safely. Somewhere in the room, I heard the doors open, and I felt someone touch my chin. Suddenly he had lit a fire above me. "Oh, isn't this a surprise?" His familiar voice filled the room, echoing off the walls.

I glared at him when I realized who it was. "Axel."

"This is my town, Detective. You will play by my rules and by my rules alone." He stood up, adjusting his suit.

"You mean to continue to let you and your friends get away with murder? No way." I was not letting him get away with this. This was my biggest battle yet. I had never come face to face with another kind that wasn't human, or at least I never thought I had.

"Murder? Oh, please. You are still alive." He smiled. I could barely make out his face in the firelight. He had a smug attitude and seemed to be proud of what he was doing. "I own this town. I am the one who makes sure that everyone is happy. Do not come here and try to change that because you will fail, just like everyone else."

I looked away. "You are a dictator."

"Call it as you want, Detective. I am only giving you the answers you have been seeking." I saw him putting out the fire and then head to the door. "Think about it for a while." The door shut behind him. I couldn't hear anything beyond the door, as this house seemed to be soundproof from between rooms.

I tried to break free from the chains, but I didn't have superhuman strength. I thought about Jacquelynn to get my mind off this dark place. I smiled, thinking about how well she had been adjusting to this small-town life, but when I realized what I was bringing her into, I frowned. This town was not what it seemed to be from the outside. Everyone was some kind of supernatural, then there were the humans, like Saidie and Mathew. I wondered if Kailynn, Cassaveil, and Keithro would notice any worrying emotions. If I am giving them off, would they come and find me? There had to be a way to get out of this. I had to believe I would get out of here. I closed my eyes; I was feeling tired, but I didn't want to sleep until I knew I would be safe, so I opened them up trying to stay awake, but I had no idea how long I had been here. Eventually, I drifted off.

When I woke up, I heard sounds from outside. Someone was coming, or was it something? I heard clacking sounds, like paws. Wait, was Oliver here? I then saw someone, or something come in through the window. The door was ripped open, and the two figures I could barely see ripped my chains apart, and I felt a wet nose push me to the window. I tried to climb out, feeling someone's hands lift me out of the window. I saw another someone there in the moonlight.

"Are you alright, Detective?" I barely recognized who it was. "We have to get out of here." I saw Malcolm, another woman, and a light brown wolf. "Get him out of here, Esther." He turned to me. "And get Luther's ass convicted. We are all tired of these damn Vampires taking control of our lives."

I nodded. "I plan to. Thank you, Malcolm." I felt Delilah push her muzzle under my hand, so I had it on top of her head and pushed me forward with her nose. Esther scooped me into her arms. "Ready?"

"Wait, what?" I asked as she jumped from what seemed to be five stories up.

Right behind us came Delilah.

"Don't worry, we are strong enough to handle a jump like that." She put me down. "Now, start running. Delilah will be right behind us, along with Malcolm. She started off in front of me.

I followed after her, catching up. I heard Delilah's paws hitting the earth as we ran. Suddenly, there was a blackish-brown wolf right next to me. That had to be Malcolm. He was bigger than Delilah, but she seemed to keep up without an issue. I felt Delilah push me as if she probably wanted me to run faster.

Malcolm let out a huff. I had no idea what they were saying to one another, but they seemed to agree on something and ran off.

"What was that?" I asked Esther.

"They agreed that it was safe enough, so they went to turn back into their human forms. They will meet us at home." She pointed to the green truck as we approached the bridge. "Oliver is fine."

I let out a sigh and tried to catch my breath as we got to the truck. Esther pushed me inside, stepped on the gas, and we drove off quickly. "Oliver has some minor injuries, but he will be quite okay." She smiled at me. "You look like you broke your nose."

I touched it. "It is sore." I wiggled it around. "Rachel must have done it as she pushed me into the floor."

She reached over and hit it. "Should be okay now."

I sneezed into my jacket, and blood came out. "Oh, that's great."

Esther laughed. "You'll need some tissues. Try in the glove box." She pointed down towards it. We were driving at about seventy now.

I opened the glove box and took some tissues. "Thank you for helping me, Esther."

She shrugged. "Yeah, well, we have been fighting Axel and his minions for years. We want them out of here."

I rolled the window down to get a feel of the late winter breeze in my face. "I'm just glad Oliver is okay." I then sat back, relaxing in my seat.

"We aren't done yet, Detective. Oliver wants to help you finish this, and now that our Alpha is considering letting us all in on it, you won't have to go alone. No more having to be a P.I. alone." She shrugged.

"Oliver told you." He must've, everyone knows everything it seems.

"Well yeah, when he woke, he told Nathan and Dominic everything." She answered. "Nathan is Nikolai's right hand, and Dominic is next in line for Alpha status, but that won't be for a long while." She pulled into the gravel driveway of my home and stopped the truck. "Come by tomorrow and work your own magic, Detective."

I reached for the door. "I don't know how to repay you."

"Don't you worry about that. Getting Luther convicted is all the pay we want." She gave me a warm smile. "Now go on, your family is waiting for you."

I nodded and opened the door, getting out. I watched her drive away. "Thanks again, Esther." I whispered under my breath.

"Daddy!!" I heard my daughter's voice.

"You've been gone for three days, Frankie." Ruby came out after. "What happened?"

"The case happened, Ruby." I picked up Jacquelynn and held her in my arms. "I am starting to understand what is going on around here."

Chapter 17

I woke up the next morning with something pushing against my side. I looked down and saw my daughter curled up next to me. I enjoyed the silence and comfort of my own home for a few minutes. Had I really been knocked out by Axel's friends for a few days? I tried not to think about it. I was home now, and it felt nice to be in my own bed. I reached down, pushing Jacquelynn's goldish hair away from her face and watched as she stirred awake.

"Daddy?" she asked. Her green eyes peered into mine. She stretched and cuddled up next to me. "Remember when Mommy and you would hug with me in the middle?"

I stroked her hair and closed my eyes, remembering. "I do. We would stay in bed for hours, undisturbed." It felt like forever since she was here with us.

"Until your phone would ring, and then you had to go to work." She laid her head on my shoulder. "But it's okay because Mommy and I would make you coffee and have dinner ready when you came home." I felt her hands wrap around my arm. "Now, I have Ruby."

I had realized where this was going in her little eight-year-old head. "Oh, Pumpkin, it is not like that at all. If you want to know a secret, I actually planned on adopting her."

She jumped up to sit on her legs. "Wait, really? A sister?"

"Shh." I put my finger to my mouth. "She doesn't know. It is a secret. We can't tell her."

She smiled big and nodded. "But that is so exciting. I get a sister, and she gets us!"

I patted her head. "I am glad you think so." I started getting out of bed. "Now, why don't you go get dressed?" I got up and scurried her out of the room. I shut the door, got changed, and brushed my hair.

"So, tell me what it was like." Joseph asked, appearing on my bed. "It has been days."

I turned around. "I didn't know how long I was there until Ruby informed me. I was out of it for so long before I woke up to Axel coming into the room."

"That is okay, Frankie. You lived. You got out with nothing but a broken nose." He pointed to my nose. "And you got that fixed already."

"Look, I know you were there the whole time." I went to my bedroom door and opened it. "Thank you for not leaving."

"Now, why would I?" He got up and followed me to the kitchen. "I may not have been able to see Winston with you, but I was able to go inside that castle without any kind of issue."

"Because he is feeling insecure." Keiko was sitting at the table with Ruby.

Ruby looked at me. "Are you?"

"I am not feeling insecure." I wanted all three of them to be clear on that. "I feel like this case has become so much easier, but so much harder at the same time. There is no certainty that we can bring Luther down and bring Elizabeth peace and justice."

Ruby looked to Keiko then to me. "Quit worrying so much and go do it already. You have everything you need, don't you?"

"I do." I was ready to put this case to a close, which meant Saidie could grieve for her sister with closure. "Tell Jacquelynn that I will be home on time tonight." I grabbed my jacket and went out the front door. The snow looked to have melted enough that I could walk without slipping. "We are getting Oliver first. He is our eyewitness."

"We don't even know where Luther is or where to find him, Frankie. What do you expect to do?" Joseph asked me.

"With Oliver's nose, I am sure we can track him down." I started walking towards Oliver's home, not speaking on the matter any further. When I arrived, I walked up the cobblestone path and saw Addison was on the porch outside, leaning on the railing watching as I was coming up the path. She looked as if she was out in the Sahara Desert. "Is Oliver in?"

She nodded, drinking a glass of water. "Sorry, Detective. I was out running." She pointed to the door behind her with her thumb. "It is unlocked."

I went past her and pushed open the front door. "Oliver?"

"In here." I heard him from upstairs. I went through the kitchen and up the wooden staircase. He was sitting on his bed, tying his shoes. "Good Morning, Detective."

"Good Morning, Oliver. How are you feeling?" I asked, concerned for his health.

"I should be asking you that. Esther was telling me about what happened." He got up off the bed, and his hand landed on my shoulder. "Don't worry; we will go get Luther."

"Oh, so now you are ready?" Right, he was probably feeling agitated since being kidnapped. I didn't blame him, but was he the one being impatient now?

"I am over the games, just like you." He went down the staircase, and I followed. "But I don't think we should rush into it."

"Then what?" I asked, frustrated with him. "While he is taking advantage of another human, I sit back and wait? What if it was Addison?"

He bit his lip, I was sure I had hit a nerve with that remark. "If it was Addison, then my pack would be handling this, not the police." He grabbed his jacket. "Come on, let's go to his place." I followed him to his truck. "You'll get your car back soon, I promise."

"You mean that we would have to turn our heads and look the other way while your friends and those Vampires go into an all-out war?"

He looked in the rearview mirror and then pulled out of his driveway into the road. "Listen, I know it isn't how things are supposed to work, but if they hurt one of ours, we can't sit back and pretend it never happened. This town works differently from the outside world. This isn't Miami, Detective. There is only so much an officer can do here."

"Then what's the point of having the police here?" I still needed to pay my bills every month; there was no way I was getting to stay in my home for free.

"Honestly, I don't know. If you and Ash were P.I.'s together, I am more than sure things would be fine." He shrugged.

"No way, that leaves Mat without a job. I am not doing that to him." I knew that was wrong. "We are being employed by this town."

Oliver shook his head. "Do you know where that money is coming from?"

"Detroit, I am sure of it." It was Detroit, right?

"Axel pays you. He controls your moves." Oliver gripped the steering wheel. "If you don't like that, then you will have to start putting people away without using the rule books from your cadet days."

He was right, for the most part. Ashley and I needed to get things done, and we couldn't do them the traditional way anymore. Maybe we were to tell Mathew that things were going to be different.

"One more thing, the humans have no idea about us, and we would all like to keep it that way."

This meant Ashley, Mathew, and I, would have to keep getting paid by Axel until we could figure something else out.

Oliver pointed up the hillside to the house. "And there it is, Luther's home."

Something about it gave me the chills. I don't think it had anything to do with what he was and more with the fact that we knew he killed Elizabeth. I was getting used to the idea of others like me, and it felt nice knowing I wasn't completely alone. Now we had to go up to the house and talk to Luther. Oliver started up on that hill, it seemed like a bit of a climb, but once we had hit the top, we were stopped before we could knock on the door.

"Frankie."

We both looked back to see Ashley standing right behind us. "Don't do it." She shook her head. "Really, it isn't worth the time."

I turned to face her. "What do you mean worth it? You told Saidie we would help Elizabeth. Do not abandon her now."

"Luther isn't here. He rarely ever is." She had a sound of defeat in her voice.

"Then where is he?" I was tired of everyone trying to stop me from finding Luther and putting to an end to this.

"Do not get snappy with me, Frankie. We need to think rationally about this. Luther isn't going to let you walk up to his door and put him under pressure. Not that he knows that you know. I have been on the lookout for him too. I think if we work together, then maybe, we would have a better chance. After you took off a few days ago, I was worried. I heard you ran your car off the road into a tree, and Oliver has been nice enough to fix it up for you. I came to your house, but Ruby told me you were out working." She bit her lip and looked away. "I just- we shouldn't rush him like this."

I looked at Oliver, who I could tell was getting antsy. He wanted to chase Luther down, probably quite literally, too. He is a wolf, after all. I sighed. "Then what?"

"Let's meet up back at my place. Saidie and Roxann aren't there, and you won't have to worry about Jacquelynn over-hearing." She looked at Oliver. "How is Addison?"

"Addison is doing just fine." Oliver walked past us to his truck.

"I really hope you are right about this, Ash. See you in a few minutes." I walked away and joined Oliver in the truck.

"She is tough." Oliver grunted.

"She can be, but that is just Ash doing her job." I watched as Ashley walked back to her car. "Hey, I have a question. There is a family that lives across the street from Elizabeth and Saidie."

"Oh, Scarlet. Yeah, stay away from there. Her kids are weird." He shook his head. I saw Ashley checking her phone as we drove away.

"Do you think Ashley is going to be okay?" I put my seatbelt on. I let the subject about Scarlet go; he didn't sound interested in talking about her and her kids.

"She will be fine. She knows what she is doing here, Detective. We do not need to worry about anything. Ashley has been doing this for years." He told me as we pulled down Ashley's street. She lived only a three-minute drive from Luther. We pulled into the driveway, right as she came behind us.

"Inside." She told us. "Now." She shooed us through the front door, as we were just getting out of the truck.

Bruce growled at Oliver, and Ashley stood between them. "Hey." She scolded him for his growl.

I heard Oliver let out a low growl back at Bruce. Bruce whimpered and ran off down the hallway.

"Sorry about that." Ashley shook her head, putting up the gate.

"Ashley." I started sitting down at the table. "Oliver told me everything."

Oliver sat down, right next to me.

Ashley looked at Oliver, annoyance on her face. She fell across from us. "What do you mean he told you, everything?"

"I know what he is, I know what you are, I know what Luther is. No more secrets." I was hoping she would nod or say something to go along with it, but instead, she just laughed.

"Oh, Oliver, what did you get yourself into?" She rolled her eyes.

"Ashley, I know you aren't exactly happy about your situation, but that doesn't mean the rest of us aren't." Oliver shrugged.

"Right, well, when the two of you decide to stop playing around, let me know." She stared at us for a good few minutes.

"Ashley." I finally said, breaking the silence. "Oliver is telling the truth; he isn't lying, and neither am I. I wish it weren't true. I wish Luther's friends didn't take me hostage for a few days, but here we are, and it happened."

Her jaw worked out what I was telling her. "Then, you know." Her voice dropped. "I didn't ask for this."

"Hey, I didn't ask to be stalked by Joseph, but you know what he has become my best friend." I pointed to the empty chair. He wasn't here at the moment, but it was easier to show her that someone had existed then to say it out loud without showing. I didn't expect them to understand without being able to put something physical to a name.

She looked over at the empty chair. "You really are a Necromancer then." She smiled slightly.

"Ashley, it doesn't matter who your parents are. No one cares about that; you are a good person, and that is all that matters here." Oliver added in, trying to make her feel better.

She looked back my way. "The easiest way to get this done is if I force him to confess, but first, we have to get him alone."

I figured when she said, 'force him to confess' she meant using her own abilities. "Then we better find out where he is." I wasn't sure where that would be, but I figured both Ashley and Oliver might have an idea.

"Remember that cabin I was telling you about?" Oliver asked me.

I gave him a nod. "What about it?"

"He is probably hiding there." Oliver looked over at Ashley. "And we both know that the cat is keeping him hidden."

Ashley let out a sigh. "Of course, we do. What else would it be?"

Joseph appeared. "It's Jacquelynn."

That was all it took for me to jump out of my chair. "My daughter." I said before I ran out of Ashley's kitchen so fast, I had Oliver's keys in my hand and got into his truck. The whole drive was a blur. I couldn't even remember Ashley and Oliver trying to stop me. They must have. They didn't understand though, neither of them had a kid. This was my worst nightmare; I couldn't lose my daughter. I drove up the dirt road of Wilson's farm and got out quickly, not even shutting the truck door behind me. I ran to their front door so fast, hoping it was open. It was, so I ran inside to find Jacquelynn sitting on a stool in front of their kitchen counter, with a bandage around her leg. I dropped down to her, taking her face into my hands. "Are you okay? What happened? How hurt are you?"

She hugged me. "Daddy I'm okay."

Jean and Bailey came in from the back door.

I stood up. "What happened?" Sure, she was okay, but I was still afraid things were much worse.

"She fell off of Snow." Jean walked over to me. "It happened so fast, but she will be fine."

188

I let out a sigh of relief. My heart rate started returning to normal. Jacquelynn was going to be fine.

"You didn't let me finish." Joseph said to me as he appeared in the house. "I was going to tell you she only hurt her knee after falling off of her horse."

I glared his way, annoyed at him more than anything else. I was going to chat with him later. In came walking Ashley and Oliver.

"There you are." Ashley shook her head at me.

"Hi, Ashley." Jacquelynn waved to her. "Daddy, who is that?" She pointed at Oliver.

"Pumpkin, we don't point at people. It is rude." I patted her head. "His name is Oliver."

"Hello, Oliver." She waved to him too.

I looked back at Jean and Bailey. "I have to thank you for being there for her."

"Hey, don't worry about it. She only scraped her knee. It won't be her last, especially if she wants to keep riding." She tried to steer us out of the house. "You should go do your job and let us do ours. Jacquelynn will be okay. We will call you if it is bad." She was shooing us out the door now.

"How did you know?" Bailey asked me, curious.

"Parental instinct." I shrugged and went to Oliver's truck. I handed him his keys back.

He took them from me. "I understand how you feel with your daughter. I would probably come running if my sister was hurt, too. That is why I am not going to be the next Alpha." He got into his truck. "You and Ashley go to the office; I need to go check in with Addi anyhow. She is still new to her wolf instincts." He started the engine and drove away.

I looked at Ashley. "You'll have to tell me more about your abilities."

She shook her head, getting into her Ferrari. "Just get in, Frankie."

I got in with her, and Joseph appeared behind us. "I would have told you if it was bad, Frankie."

"You can't start off with 'It's Jacquelynn.'" I crossed my arms, not looking back at him.

Ashley looked at me confused, but then caught on that I was speaking to Joseph. "Your ghost is here, then."

"He is in deep trouble, too." I looked out the side window.

"What are you going to do?" He asked. "Punish me?"

I didn't respond. I wanted him to know I was ignoring him.

"Don't be such a child, Frankie." He sighed. "If I could get Ashley to smack you right now, I would."

I looked at Ashley. "He wants you to smack me for not speaking to him."

Ashley laughed. "Oh, you two fight like brothers, don't you?"

"Imagine someone constantly bothering you all the time, and you can't get rid of them." I told her. "Like an annoying little brother who is always attached to your side."

"And if you could?" She asked as she pulled up to the office.

"Then I would have a different pain in the ass." I shook my head and huffed. "What made the two of you want to come here first?" I followed her inside.

"Well, we need the evidence." She walked to the closet door, opening it and going inside. She came back with the backpack. "I put it back in evidence after you gave it to me."

"But there is no way to know he used it. Fingerprints, remember?" I raised my hands.

"Maybe, but we can use it against him when we get to him. Trust me; I've done this trick many times before."

"I do trust you. Let's hope we can find him first."

She pushed the backpack onto my desk. "Let's go, Frankie. Oliver is meeting us at the cabin." She told me as she left the office and shut the lights out.

Chapter 18

Ashley pulled over at the bridge. We couldn't drive much further out because the dirt path would start narrowing, and her car probably wouldn't like that too much. It would be easier to get out and walk from here. Ashley and I walked through the woods, not doing much talking. We stopped when we found Oliver waiting for us against a tree.

"Hey, this way." His tone was impatient. He led us down the same dirt path that Joseph and I took the first time we came out here. As we approached the cabin, I saw the area where Joseph and I heard the trees the night we came here. Of course, that was at night. We were here in the daylight now, and it looked like something was running through here.

"Frankie?" Ashley asked. "Are you coming?" She asked at the front door. I realized I was staring at the clearing it was big enough to fit the form of anyone. I shook off the odd feeling and approached the front door. Ashley shook the handle and we found it was still open, so we cautiously walked inside.

"There is still no one here." Joseph told me. "I don't know why we are back."

I ignored Joseph. "I came by here before." I informed both Oliver and Ashley.

They both stopped snooping and looked at me.

"What?" Oliver asked me. "What did you find the first time?" The cat came over to Oliver and rubbed his leg.

"Notes on wolves, but now that I think about it, it must have been on Werewolves." I answered.

"Those a-holes. Those Vampires are taking notes on us." Oliver looked at Ashley. "They are planning something." So this cabin was owned by the Vampires.

"Then we better get moving because we wouldn't want them to find us here." She went to push us to investigate when we heard

192

footsteps in the back room. A little girl appeared and yawned. She had dark brown hair, dark brown eyes, and was wearing red pajamas. "You aren't my friends."

Ashley put her hands on her knees and leaned over to be eye level with the child. "Who would that be, dear?"

She rolled her eyes. "My name isn't *Dear. It is Diana.*" She may have been small, but she had a huge attitude.

"Okay." Oliver muttered. "Then who are you waiting for?"

She picked up the cat and let it go down the hallway. She turned to us, ready to answer Oliver's question, but Luther had walked in, interrupting.

"She is waiting for me." Luther looked around the room, at Ashley, then at me. "I would leave now if I were you, Detectives." He finally rested his eyes on Oliver. "I can keep you around, though."

Oliver growled and spat at Luther's shoes. "Keep that, you piece of dead crap."

Luther lunged at Oliver, who slid out of the way. Luther hit the wall, ready to go after Oliver again. He was seething before Ashley grabbed his arms, pulling them behind his body.

She spoke to Luther from behind. "You may be nimble, but you sure aren't always the smartest." She spun him around to look him dead in the eyes. "And now you are going to confess to killing Beth. Vampires are done getting away with their illegal activities." She looked to Oliver, who nodded, grabbing Luther's arms and put them into cuffs. "Let's go." Oliver told Luther. "Time is up."

Luther struggled against Oliver's Werewolf strength as Oliver pushed him through the front door. "You will not get away with this! I was doing everyone a favor!"

"Luther!" Diana came running out after us. She was just a kid, though; she couldn't possibly know what happened to Elizabeth.

I was hoping she wasn't going to be Luther's next victim. We didn't stick around to find out; we had to get Luther back to the office.

Ashley knelt and looked at her. "Stay here." She turned back to her car. I got Luther in the truck with Oliver while she was talking with Diana.

I drove back to the station with Ashley, who asked me to get the bag off my desk. She put Luther in his chair at his desk and tied him up.

Ashley sat on Luther's desk. Oliver leaned against the wall behind him, ready to open the curtain if need be. I grabbed my chair, pulling it over. I sat down in it, ready to see what Ashley was going to do.

"You know this bag." She put it on the desk next to her. "So, Luther, you killed Beth."

He looked up at Ashley. "You can't prove it."

"So, you did do it." I shook my head. "You were just yelling out that you were doing everyone a favor. Sounds like a murderer to me."

"How would you like it if we took your immortality away from you?" Ashley asked, looking over at Oliver.

"Do it. I dare you. Axel will come for you." Luther grunted. "He will get your ass fired."

Ashley nodded to Oliver, who then opened the curtain a bit. Oliver looked to be getting a slight joy out of it.

Luther let out a painful scream that sounded torturous. "Okay! Okay!"

Oliver shut the curtain. "Then what happened, really? What did you do to Beth?"

"She asked me to do it." Luther looked at Ashley. "For Felix. She wanted to be with him for as long as she could."

"So, she and Felix were a thing." I was jotting it down in my notepad.

Luther chuckled. "You don't know anything, Frankie. You haven't been around enough. Don't pretend that you understand how we operate here."

"I know enough to say that you were jealous. Or was it because you didn't want her around anymore?" I asked him as I continued to jot down notes.

Luther was unamused. "Why don't you ask them yourself? I am sure those two lovebirds would love to tell you all about it."

"If we knew where she was, this would have been over a long time ago. Start from the top, Luther." Ashley pushed Luther's chair on its back legs towards the sunlight with her foot. "Now."

He waved his arm to get her to stop. "Felix was madly in love, and Elizabeth wanted to be with him forever. She didn't understand what forever really meant. Felix would never have done it himself; he didn't want to control her."

Ashley pulled her foot away. "What do you want to do, Big City?" She crossed her arms, staring Luther in the face.

"We will have to take him to a judge in Detroit. Our lawyers will have to help us settle this. The judge will put an end to our case." I answered.

"So instead of Felix, you control her now. Sounds like jealousy to me." Oliver leaned on the arms of the chair to be face to face with Luther. "One more thing, quit researching Werewolves. When Nikolai finds out what you were doing, oh boy, he won't be happy."

"Then he will have to kill Diana himself because it was her. She is a curious kid." He smirked.

Oliver slapped him. "I am done here. Get rid of him already." He turned away. "Or I will do it myself."

"I would love to see you try." Luther mocked. "You want to start another war between our families?"

Oliver turned to hit him again but was stopped by Ashley putting her hand on his arm. "Hey, we are doing what we can for now. He confessed, and that is what we need. Now we have to get him to tell Mathew, and we are good to go."

"And how do we do that?" Oliver leaned on the desk next to Ashley. He looked extremely frustrated and annoyed.

"I'll call and get him here." I stood up and walked to my desk, using the phone to call Mathew. "Mathew, we caught Elizabeth's killer. Get to the office." I hung up before he could reply to me. I looked back at Ashley, who was staring Luther down. Oliver was pacing the floor now. He must have been getting impatient. I leaned over on my chair. "Mat's on his way here now." I assumed anyway. He didn't seem to be the type to miss out on bringing down our killer.

Ashley looked back at me. "We can't have him tied up here, but we can't let him leave either."

"I can stand outside, and if he tries to leave, he will have a wolf on his tail." Oliver suggested.

Ashley nodded. "We have no choice, it would seem. Do it, Oliver." I agreed with Ashley's choice; we were hoping that Luther wouldn't try to run from us.

Oliver walked out the back door while Ashley untied Luther. "We are not letting you go anywhere, Luther."

He looked at me, blatantly ignoring Ashley. "Why do you care that I ended Beth's mortal life, Frankie?"

"Because you killed her, that is why." I answered as Mathew walked inside.

"Luther did?" Mathew asked. "But why?"

"Jealousy." Ashley told him. "Get ready because we will have some paperwork to do, gentleman."

Mathew and I both looked at one another. Luther had said it as Mathew walked in, and that made things so much easier on our part.

"Tell him." Ashley warned.

Luther looked to the back door as he saw the muzzle of Oliver. He looked at Mathew. "Yes, okay, I did it. I killed Elizabeth for my friend Felix."

Mathew shook his head. "The cameras got that right?" He looked at the ceiling. "They did." He was so innocent and had no idea about any of us or what we did. The humans were the most amazing piece in all of this. They were clueless, yet still willing to help even if it was confusing. We had gotten Luther to confess, and that was what made the job worth it in the end. We were ready to move him to Detroit, where we would turn him over and get him inside a real prison. We knew it wouldn't hold him for long, but we would get him out of town, at least for a while.

"When do we leave then?" Mathew asked Ashley.

"As soon as we finish writing our findings." She pointed to the computers at our desks. "Let's get this in motion."

I smiled and sat down at my computer with Mathew behind me. We exchanged looks before we typed up our findings through this case. Computer work was the boring part of the job, but it also meant that we solved the case, and that meant we were able to close it down for good. The only problem now was finding Elizabeth. We had the confession but not the body. That part could wait for now, though. We had paperwork to do first.

After finishing up, Mathew and I printed our paperwork and put it in the file before grabbing Elizabeth's belongings. We then got into Mat's car, and Ashley sat in the back with Luther. I knew she would have a better time keeping him in line then Mat or I could.

"Ash always sits with our prisoners. She is good at keeping them in line." Mathew informed me.

Oliver was driving his truck and following us into the city. He was our eyewitness for this case, so we needed him to tell the judge what he saw what happened between Luther and Elizabeth. I know we said it was a bad idea, but this was the only way to bring justice for Elizabeth. We had prepared for Luther and his Lawyer to plead crazy. He would get put away barely an hour away from our little town of Golden Loch. For the rest of the drive, we sat in silence. The only sounds were coming from the car as we rolled up towards the highway that we take us into Detroit. Mathew had not even put on the radio as we all had agreed it would have been distracting.

I looked up every so often, glancing in the back to where Luther sat, who had not moved a muscle since being placed in his seat. I would also check to see if Oliver was still following in his truck, and he always was. Oliver never lost sight of us, no matter how far apart we became. I assumed it was that Werewolf instinct of his.

We soon reached Detroit and the obscene amount of traffic that surrounded us. If this was the time for Luther to escape, he wasn't taking it. The sun was going down, and all he needed was a split-second opportunity to get away. I have seen how fast those Vampires can be. They are there and gone before you even blink. No wonder why they live right outside of town; they know they can get in and out with ease and not have to worry about being late for anything. Except Luther was always late to work, and it was all because of the daylight. I was starting to see why he was on time when the sun was not out.

I felt the car come to a stop when we reached the cities courthouse. Mat had gotten out, and I then followed. The large brick building must have been built in the early 40's, by the look of it. There were steps that were starting to crumble apart that led to the front door. Ashley informed us she would take Luther around back and meet us on the inside. She then walked away and disappeared around the side of the building.

Oliver came jogging up to us and smiled. "Had to park down the other end. You know, being a civilian and all." He shrugged. "Anyway, where is Ashley?" I knew he knew where they went, but he had to play it like he hadn't since Mathew was here with us.

"Ash took Luther inside." I pointed with my thumb. "She is meeting us inside." I looked at Mathew, who smiled slightly.

"I cannot wait for this to finally be over. I am tired, and it will feel nice to close the case for good." Mathew motioned for us to follow him to the front doors. We followed him inside the brick building and around the first corner.

"This place smells like Clorox bleach." Oliver muttered into my ear.

"Well, they have to keep it clean somehow." I whispered back. Oliver could smell the chemicals in the building; I assumed that was another characteristic of being a wolf. I certainly would not want to have to smell every detail of every single place all the time. We watched as Mathew talked to a woman behind the counter and then told her his name, and then explained that Ashley was coming with our man from the back. She buzzed us into a room on the left side of the desk. I followed both Mathew and Oliver inside the room. The room, along with the two chairs and the table were made completely of metal.

"Our Lawyer is going to meet us here." Mathew sat down in one of the chairs. "He is pretty cool. You'll like him, Frankie."

Ashley came in and shut the door behind her. "Mathew, can you do me a favor? We left Elizabeth's belongings in your car. Do you mind getting them?"

He muttered under his breath before walking out. He seemed a bit upset about her asking him to do that, but we needed those things so we could talk with the lawyer.

"He says he hates having to do the boring work all the time." Oliver looked at Ashley.

"Oh, believe me, I know what he said." She smiled and pulled a chair over. "Sit, Frankie."

I took the chair and sat down. "So, who is our lawyer?"

"His name is Rhett Suez. Amazing Lawyer. He has been working with Mat and me for years." She handed me his card. She then took a seat in the second chair.

"Well if it isn't my favorite Half-Demon." The man who I assumed to be Rhett had entered the room. He had a very defined jawbone, along with black hair and sky-blue eyes.

"Hello to you too, Rhett." Ashley shook her head at his comment.

"And who might this be?" Rhett sat down in the chair on the other side of the table.

"This is Detective Frankie Dawson." Ashley introduced. "And you remember Oliver." She pointed to Oliver with her thumb.

"Of course, I do. He is always a help to you and Mat." Rhett smiled a bit at Oliver. "Can I ask what you are?" His attention was turned back to me.

I looked to Ashley, waiting to see if it was alright to tell him what I was. He may have known what Ashley was, but this guy may have only been a human asking what my job position was.

"Hey, go on." Ashley smiled. "He is one of us."

I gave a slight nod, trusting her. "Necromancer."

"Whoa, that is definitely someone you don't come across often." He leaned forward. "I'm a Demigod."

"Rhett is the son of Zeus." Ashley added in. She smiled a bit at the idea.

"Trust me, it isn't as great as it sounds." Rhett shook his head at Ashley. "Now, who is the man that we are convicting in court?"

"You won't believe it." Ashley crossed her arms and sat back in her chair. "It's our Captain, Luther."

Rhett leaned forward, his hands clasping into one another. "And how did you come to that conclusion?" Of course, he was curious; he was a lawyer and a god. What better combination to get someone undead like Luther into a jail cell? He looked to be full of so much excitement. He must not come across cases like this often.

"Vampires don't have fingerprints, right?" Ashley asked. "There is no evidence pointing to a killer, but Oliver can smell the entire incident, it is almost like he was there. The jury won't know the difference. Plus, we have Luther confessing to killing Elizabeth."

Rhett looked at Oliver. "Then, we go to trial." He handed Ashley a plastic card. "Here. Get settled in our downtown hotel and we can discuss this tomorrow."

Mathew walked in and put Elizabeth's things on the desk. He made a face at Ashley, not wanting to have to make that walk across the parking lot again.

"We are getting a hotel for the night." Ashley told him, standing up. Mathew looked at me and shook his head as Ashley walked out of the room. I patted his shoulder as I also got up and left the room.

We reached the hotel almost ten minutes away from the courthouse. The lobby was full of people coming and going. It took another five minutes to get into the elevator off to the right side of the lobby and another three to reach the sixth floor. Once we had, we went into room 617 and settled in for the night. I made my way to the sliding door on the opposite side of the room and out into the deck. I took in the smell of the city as I leaned on the railing, almost remembering home. It was dark, but you could see the streets were still busy, below.

"You miss Miami." Joseph appeared next to me.

"This city doesn't have the beachy smell to it, but it is very similar." I looked over at Joseph. "Do you think it is possible that we have come across others like us in Miami?"

Joseph shrugged. "Possibly. I can't see why we wouldn't have. Miami is a pretty big city, but we would not have picked up on it, that's for sure. We didn't have the knowledge to figure out." He motioned his hands at the streets below us. "There are no palm trees here, Frankie."

I laughed at his frantic motion. "Unless we came across another Necromancer." I looked out into the sky. "But I don't think we have even done that. If we had, their ghost should have seen us."

Oliver came out and handed me a glass of water. "Figured you would need it." He stood on the other side of me. "Who are you talking to? Joseph?"

I looked back at Joseph. "Yeah, we were just having a chat."

"I can leave you two be if you want, but don't think I can't hear you from inside." Oliver smiled, patting my back.

"You are welcome to join us. We were just reminiscing about Miami." I responded, looking into the starry sky.

"This city reminds you of home, then." Oliver leaned his back on the railing.

"In a sense, yes. Minus the beach and the palm trees. Oh, and the sunshine." I smiled with a small laugh.

"Maybe one day, we can all visit Miami beach." Oliver nodded, giving me hope. "I'm sure little Jacquelynn would like that. She would get to see her old home again."

"One day." I answered back. One day, possibly.

Chapter 19

The next day, after we all had eaten breakfast, we were sitting in that same enclosed room, but this time Rhett brought two extra chairs with him so Oliver and Mathew could sit with us. We were about to discuss the case with Rhett and what we would bring to trial.

This was it; this was the day we were going to bring Luther down to give Elizabeth and Saidie the peace they so desperately needed. They deserved that much, and we were finally giving it to them. We had to discuss this case as if not even one of us had a nose and ears like a wolf or a Shadow who could get into places without consent and give details on a subject. I still was not entirely sure what Ashley's abilities consisted of, but from yesterday's events, I had a feeling she was able to get someone to tell her the truth.

"Frankie came not too long after Luther pushed her over." Ashley explained to Rhett. I kept watching her as she spoke on the matter. "His big city instincts kicked in, and he solved the murder in a little over a week."

Rhett looked at me. "You were watching Luther then." He was writing down everything we were telling him. He had the paperwork that we had already written up yesterday, but as with any case, it is always good to go over it one more time before you go into court. You want to have everyone on the same page, so when we gave our side of the story, we all were in agreeance with one another. There needed to be a small amount of variance between us.

"Everyone I came across who has been in contact with Elizabeth is someone I considered watching until I could narrow down who did it. It came down to Luther and Ash in the end." I looked at Ashley. She didn't seem to mind my method. "I was able to rule Saidie out immediately with how distraught she was. Malcolm and Delilah have proof that they were in their diner, along with Lucius. In the end, it came down to Luther. Oliver, who is our eyewitness, had seen him push her over."

Rhett looked over at Oliver. "Then you will be able to tell the jury what happened. You will know that what you say will sway them one way or another. Be careful today."

Oliver nodded. "I will. Believe me, I don't have any intent on screwing this up. I want to help Saidie."

"Does she know the four of you are here?" Rhett asked us.

"I called her last night." Ashley answered. "She got on the next bus here to Detroit. She is happy that this is going to be over soon."

Rhett nodded. "Once we get this settled, I suggest finding Elizabeth's body. I am sure Luther will know exactly where she is."

I shook my head. "And if he doesn't tell us?" I was sure Luther wasn't going to tell us, not without a sentence reduction.

"Then, we will have to press him until he does." He glanced over at Ashley. Ashley got him to confess the first time; maybe she would have a chance at getting him to tell us where Elizabeth was.

"We will do what must be done." Ashley put her hand on my shoulder. "There is no need to worry, Frankie."

I knew she was right. Ashley was good at what she did, and so was I. There really was no reason to worry. Mathew was also a great cop, but he was still human. We had to tell the judge how this went from the beginning without mentioning our abilities. I was able to do it for myself, but I have never had to do it with a Werewolf and a Half-Demon before. "What about Luther's lawyer?"

Rhett shook his head. "No need to worry about that. He has a lawyer given to him."

"Rhett is our lawyer. He will not represent Luther because he is getting convicted in the courtroom. He pretty much doesn't have a lawyer now." Mathew looked my way. "Meaning the city gives him one, and they are not always the best. Rhett *is* one of the best lawyers you can find."

I bit my lip, unsure. Luther could get a great lawyer; it was just the luck of the draw. There really was no way of knowing who he was getting. "Then we move forward with the case."

Ashley nodded. "Good idea, we are just about ready, one more thing, however." She looked at Rhett. "If Luther's lawyer pulls the fact that Luther is nuts, then what?"

"Then, we still have won, but you will have him real close to Golden Loch." Rhett shrugged. "Sorry, Ash." He looked back at Oliver. "We are going to have Ashley explain the case first, then we will have you come onto the stand as a witness. After, we will call Detective Dawson and have him explain how he came to his conclusion. Mathew and I will stay at the table and work it out from there."

We all had agreed to what Rhett had asked of us. It always sounded so much easier when we discussed it. Putting forth the actual plan always came circled back at us. We had no idea who Luther and his lawyer were going to be pulling out and what kind of conclusion they are going to draw for him. There was also the fact that there is no proof he was at the scene; fortunately, we had him on camera saying he did it; after we let him go. Luther did not have access to this anymore, and there was no way of getting it to his side of the case before this was over. We were sure we were going to win this.

We braked for lunch and decided to go to a local restaurant. It looked like a very popular spot to be. The young men and women working were wearing bright orange t-shirts and blue jeans. They were moving pretty quickly between the crowds of people standing around, waiting for their tables. Oliver looked uncomfortable standing while waiting to get to a table, but once we had, he seemed to have settled down.

"Sorry." I said to him. I felt terrible about making him come to such a crowded place full of humans.

"Not your fault, Frankie. I am a bit claustrophobic." He looked at the others at our table before whispering to me. "Nothing to do with the wolf." He then sat back in his chair.

"I actually found that a bit uncomfortable myself." Mathew shook his head. "I guess when you grow up in a place like Golden Loch, the city feels tight."

"You get used to it." I glanced at the waiter as he came to us. We each ordered our food before the waiter walked away.

"We aren't here very often." Ashley then informed me as the waiter came back and put a bowl of bread on the table. "No one in this city is going to look at us like friendly faces and know what we are thinking. To them, we are just some small-town cops who think they know things."

"Believe me, most of them are not even aware you are the police." I picked up a piece of the bread and put it on my plate. "Even in Miami, they didn't look at me unless I had my badge. Folks just don't pay attention to others unless they need something. Sad, really, but that is city life."

Ashley shook her head. "And yet we don't carry our badges unless we are leaving town. Everyone at home knows who we are."

The food came to our tables, and we ate in almost silence. We weren't allowed to speak on the case outside of the courthouse, and with Mathew here, Ashley and Oliver didn't want to speak on themselves either. It gave me a chance to think the case over in my head. The crime scene was the only thing on my mind the entire time and how distraught Saidie had been when we came to her door for the first time. What if I wasn't there on time? Joseph sure would not have been able to save her. I may have been able to talk to her in spirit, but that would not be my first choice. It was better to have her alive anyway. She needed to live her life. She was only a teenage girl, Ruby's age. I thought about Ruby too; she didn't have a family either, but her circumstances were not much different from Saidie's.

Ruby was left to fend for herself alongside Keiko, while also being told Keiko was not real.

We had arrived back at the courthouse and met up with our lawyer. He looked a bit displeased when we approached. "Guess who is here."

Ashley and I looked at one another then at Mathew. We were all sure we knew the answer, but Mathew asked the question anyway. "Who?"

"Your favorite Mayor." Rhett grunted. "He is negotiating with the judge as we speak."

"No." Ashley had then run off into the courtroom angry, the doors slamming behind her.

"I will go with her to make sure she is fine." Mathew had then run off after her.

Oliver grabbed my arm. "What now, Detective?" He looked as if he wanted to go after Ashley as well.

"Good question, Oliver." I looked at Rhett. "Is this trial going to work, or are we done for?"

Before Rhett could respond, Joseph appeared behind me. "You may want to get yourself in there, Frankie. Ashley isn't exactly in the right state of mind. Remember who she is."

I grabbed Oliver by the arm, and we pushed the courtroom doors open only to be greeted by Mathew, who looked a bit dazed and confused. Joseph walked into the courtroom to have a look around himself.

"Mathew?" I asked as he stumbled into my arms. "Mathew!" Something was not right here, and I assumed it had to do with Axel and Luther. I felt something fly past me, possibly fur. I didn't look up, too concerned about Mathew. He had holes in his neck like he had been bit by something. I couldn't stop them. Axel must have taken Luther. I then felt a hand on my shoulder.

"As long as he doesn't die on us in the next twenty-four hours, he will live." Ashley told me. She helped me stand up. "Oliver is already on their scent. I will stay here with Mathew if you follow after Oliver."

I saw Joseph nod to me as Ashley suggested I follow Oliver. "I will catch up with him." He had then disappeared.

"Joseph has gone ahead. I am going to go out the back and follow as best as I can. Call me when he wakes." I informed Ashley.

She sat down on the bench and put Mathew's head on her lap. "He will be fine, now go."

I took off to find out where Axel and Luther had gone. I ran out of the parking lot and down the busy road until I came to a stop at the end of a crossroad that led me into a park. I went that way, running past people going about their daily lives. Joseph appeared by my side and ran with me as I continued forward. "Oliver has Luther by his leg, and we were not able to locate Axel." Joseph told me. "Frankie."

I stopped running. "Where are they?"

Joseph led me to the spot. Oliver had Luther's leg just as he had said. They also looked as if they were in a fight. Luther was covered in blood and leaning against a tree with his forearm trying to stand. Oliver's fur was also covered in blood. However, he was the victorious one here. I heard a growl come from Oliver's throat as Luther fell to the ground.

"Alright, Luther." I knelt to him. "We can make this easy, or we can make this hard. Oliver isn't exactly happy with you, so let's not piss our Werewolf friend off anymore then he already is."

"Let me go, and I will tell you where to find Elizabeth." He looked me in the eyes. Was he actually being serious?

"You will not come back to town, ever." I warned.

"Then, deem me to be dead." He tried to continue negotiating with me.

Joseph shoved his hands into his own pockets. "This is like watching an old movie."

I looked to Oliver, who let go of his grip and ran off to turn back. "Luther, you have maybe three minutes before Oliver comes back."

"Then, you will never find Beth." Luther grunted. He reached for his leg. "A Werewolf bite to a Vampire is nothing compared to a Vampire bite to a Werewolf." He tried standing but fell back down against a tree. "And you and your ghost are some duo who thinks that they are good at solving crimes. You couldn't even find Beth."

I bit my lip, trying not to talk back to him but was immediately saved by Oliver walking back towards us. "Ashley is waiting for us; Mathew is awake, and Rhett wants to get this trial started. I ran back that way to check on things."

"Has Saidie arrived?" I asked, not taking my eyes off Luther.

"She came in late last night and is waiting for us in the courtroom. She wants to be sure she sees Luther get put away." Oliver looked down at Luther. "It won't look good on you for trying to escape."

Luther grunted as we got him to his feet. "Let's go." We then started back to the courthouse. Luther was in no shape to walk on his own, and he certainly had no way of running off like this.

When we made it back to the courthouse, Rhett, Ashley, and Mathew, who was seemingly back to normal, were waiting for us. They were sitting near the front desk, waiting for us to go into the courtroom.

Rhett looked at me, puzzled. "And what happened to Luther?" He looked Luther up and down, eyeing his leg and the ripped pants.

"He tried to run and was attacked by a dog. Fate, I guess." I pushed Luther towards Ashley, who stood up and took him down the long hallway.

"How are you, Mathew?" I was feeling concerned for his health.

"Better, I'm not entirely sure what happened, but it did." He leaned on his left leg and put his hand on the chair after standing up.

I patted his shoulder. "Let's get in there and get this over with already. We don't need to keep Saidie waiting."

Rhett had agreed, so we all went inside the courtroom. There inside, I saw Saidie sitting in the stand, and with her was Roxann. It gave me comfort knowing Roxann was staying with her and helping. I looked back to the doors, feeling Joseph behind me. He was standing back there, along with Zeke. I moved to sit at the table, and then Ashley and Mathew sat down next to me. In the seats behind us, Oliver took his place. He already knew what he had to say when Rhett called him up to the stand. Ashley patted Mathew's hand. They smiled at one another, and I knew they were both nervous; they probably didn't do this often.

"This isn't your first courtroom, is it, Big City?" Ashley poked my arm.

I shook my head, watching as our judge entered the courtroom. "No, it is not."

Ashley let out a smile. "Then you should know that Mathew and I have had to sit here in court maybe two or three other times. This isn't our first, but it certainly isn't something we have done frequently enough." She looked forward to the judge. "Here we go."

Rhett hushed her and then stood along with Luther's lawyer to start.

Chapter 20

Rhett called Luther to the stand first because we were convicting him of Elizabeth's murder. Rhett started with a few questions that would lead us into Ashley and Oliver and finally me at the end.

"Where were you the night Elizabeth Keaton was murdered?" He looked Luther in the eyes. Rhett stood so still that I figured it had something to do with his own abilities.

"This is the part where you want me to confess so that this case can be closed, isn't it Suez?" Luther sat back in the stand as if this was a joke. He wasn't going to take this seriously, was he?

"Answer the question, Mr. Emsworth. This is not a game; please take this seriously." The judge seemed bored and displeased all at once.

Luther rolled his eyes. "Alright, so maybe I did, why don't we just play it out then?" He paused as if he was waiting for someone else to comment, and when no one did, he proceeded. "That night, Beth and I went out for some drinks as friends, nothing more. We decided to take the long way home, and that was when she fell to her death."

Rhett sighed, we were getting nowhere with this, I wanted to get Luther off the stand and move on, but we had to start with his side of the story. "And how did she fall?"

"She went over the railing on the bridge in town." He had sat back in his seat. He was mocking us; he didn't care about Elizabeth, not one bit.

"And what town would that be?" Rhett proceeded anyway, ignoring Luther's movements.

"You know what town it is Rhett, don't play with me." Luther shook his head.

"Tell the jury anyway." Rhett demanded; his patients were running thin.

"Golden Loch." Luther gave an uncaring shrug.

"And what was your job position?" Rhett continued asking his questions.

"Captain, on the police force." He motioned to Ashley and Mathew. "Those two are my subordinates."

"Did you kill Elizabeth Keaton?" Rhett asked finally.

"Is that relevant?" Luther leaned forward and glared at Rhett.

"Yes, it is." Rhett didn't move. He was waiting for Luther's reply.

"I don't have to answer that." Luther stood. "Are we done?" Rhett sighed and waved Luther to go. "I'm calling upon Ashley Aequitas next."

Ashley stood out of her chair as it squeaked against the hard floor. She moved to the stand and took her place there.

"Ms. Aequitas, tell us what you know and have found about this case." Rhett said to her.

"Well, for starters, when we first arrived on the scene, Lieutenant Mathew Reames and I, we found Elizabeth's blood on the rail, her backpack in the water, and some of her hair in the river as well. However, there wasn't a body, nor were their fingerprints."

"And how did you come to the conclusion it was Mr. Emsworth?" Rhett tilted his head slightly. This was what would make the case. She had a hunch, but she had to explain it with reason.

"That was my question. What made me know it was him? At first, I wasn't quite entirely sure, but as we brought in Detective Frankie Dawson, he started becoming more and more suspicious. Luther wouldn't allow us to go to the scene, but we had to get there anyway. He didn't want us to see Saidie Keaton either." She looked towards Luther. "But he would change his mind almost instantly and let us go to where we needed until he chose to shut us down."

"And who is Saidie to Elizabeth?" Rhett got Ashley's attention back to him.

"Saidie is Elizabeth's little sister." Ashley informed Rhett. "Our eyewitness, Oliver Verda, has seen the whole scene play out, and we have a confession by Luther as well."

"Then why don't we watch?" Rhett turned to the TV on the wall and played the video of Luther confessing that he was the one who killed Elizabeth as Mathew walked into the office.

"Objection!" Luther's lawyer yelled out. "How do we know that he was not forced to say that?"

"You can clearly see he is sitting there with his own free will." Ashley interjected.

"Proceed, Mr. Suez." The judge told Rhett.

"Why don't we bring Oliver Verda onto the stand then?" Rhett spoke to Ashley.

Ashley agreed and stepped down, letting Oliver take her place.

"Oliver, why don't you tell us what you saw the night Elizabeth Keaton was murdered?" Rhett asked him. We all knew he saw nothing, but his nose picked up the entire scene and all he had to do was say he was there, and we were in the clear.

"I saw Luther push Elizabeth to her death. Then, he took her body and ran. She is buried somewhere. Oliver looked at Luther, disgusted. "Luther killed poor Elizabeth." He then pointed at Luther.

Rhett gave him a nod. "You witnessed them together up until he pushed her over the edge."

Oliver sighed and nodded. I could see him holding back his anger towards Luther and let out a low growl.

"Thank you, Mr. Verda. That is all." Oliver got up. That meant it was my turn. Rhett then called me up into the stand. "Mr.

Frankie Dawson, tell us what you know and how you helped Detective Aequitas bring down Luther."

I looked towards Joseph; he was smiling. He knew we were going to be fine. "I was hired by Ashley to help her solve the murder of Elizabeth Keaton. When I came in, it had already been a week since Elizabeth's murder. Coming from Miami, I knew better than to trust everyone. You take the case one step at a time. I looked everything over more than once for myself, and when Oliver told us what he knew, my theory came to light. There are signs that you look for when someone is guilty, and Luther fit them all. Ashley and I discussed our next moves, and Luther then admitted to his fault. It wasn't easy, but we got it done." I was hoping that would be enough for Rhett.

Rhett smiled and patted the call stand. "Thank you, Mr. Dawson. That will be all from us." He then sat down.

"Alright. Mr. Nickols, the room is yours." The judge asked Luther's lawyer to take center stage. "I would like to keep Mr. Dawson here for the moment." I saw the smile on his face. Axel must have said something to him. "Mr. Dawson, why did you move here?"

"I came here from Miami soon after my wife's death." I told him.

"She died of cancer, no?" He wanted to get under my skin, and it was working. Why did he have that information?

"She did." Luther knew I did not enjoy speaking about my wife. Somehow they found out about Layla.

"Then you know that family is important. Yet you uprooted yours and moved far away." He shook his head. "And then you come here, putting the blame on Golden Loch's best."

"He had killed Elizabeth." I replied. "Pushing her to her death."

"Are you sure she didn't just fall?" He looked at me.

"She did fall, but it wasn't by accident. She had been pushed over the edge." I bit my lip. He was trying to get us to change the story. "We have shown the proof."

"There is no proof at the scene that she was pushed over the edge, Detective Dawson." Nickols told me. "And, you were not there, you were still in Miami. You don't know a thing about the people of Golden Loch."

"That is right. I was in Miami, but we have both the eyewitness and a video of Luther admitting." I answered. "Ashley was there, as was Oliver."

"This is about you, not them." Nickols rolled his eyes. "And you cannot claim something that you know nothing about."

"Objection!" I heard Rhett come to my rescue.

"Mr. Suez is right. Please get to the point, Mr. Nickols." The judge wasn't happy about Nickols stalling.

"My point is, a detective from a large city such as Miami won't have a clue about what goes on in a small town." Nickols looked as if he was ready to throw the case out the window. "That is all." He turned around and looked at Luther, making his way back to the desk.

There was a long silence between Nickols taking a seat and then myself following before the judge spoke out about what was next to come. Of course, I already knew what was going to happen. First, the jury would go into the back room and talk about the case; we would them come back in after a half hour or so, and then they would tell us what they thought. Beforehand, both Suez and Nickols would tell them what they believe should happen and why their side is right. I had a feeling we would be alright, that Luther would get what he deserved. Finally, the judge sent out the jury while we waited here quietly. I leaned over to Saidie to see how she was doing. "How are you feeling?"

"Do you think Luther will go away for good?" Saidie asked me. She almost seemed as if she was begging me to do it myself.

"Don't you worry, the jury will do what they must. They are usually on the side of the police." I gave her a sympathetic smile. "You just give them a chance to come to that conclusion. There is no need to think too much about it." I looked at Roxann. "Thank you."

Roxann smiled and shrugged. "Oh, it's nothing. I do it because I know it makes others happy. I like helping others." I knew she was referring to Ruby, but I let her have the moment. It had made Saidie smile. That was what she needed right now, reassurance. Roxann was going to be her friend.

Ashley took my arm. "Take a walk with me." She motioned for me to follow her out the side door of the courtroom and down the sidewalk. "We need to talk about Mat." She shook her head, her hands going into her pockets. "He is here, but I feel as if his mind isn't."

"Do you think it has something to do with Luther biting him?" I asked her. I had a feeling it did.

She pulled me off to the side and down an alleyway away from the public. "If you haven't noticed, Mathew isn't exactly himself right now." She looked around. I looked too, thinking she saw someone. "Frankie, I didn't want to say this in front of anyone else, but once we get Luther put away, we will need to convince Axel to help Mathew."

I wasn't sure what to say to her. The man bound me in a dark room and then left me there alone for days before coming to speak with me. "How do you expect him to do that? He isn't exactly someone we should be trusting, Ash."

She crossed her arms; I knew she was thinking of what to say to me.

"I am aware of everything going on. You don't need to keep it a secret any longer."

"Remember when we got Luther to tell us that he killed Elizabeth?" She looked guilty like it was her own doing.

"What about it?" I wasn't sure what she did to Luther had anything to do with Mathew.

"Well, that is sort of my ability." She bit her lip. "I can get people to tell me the truth by looking them in the eyes."

"Oh, Ashley." She looked disappointed in herself. Maybe she wanted Luther to tell us himself. "Don't hate yourself. You did what you had to."

She shook her head. "That is the problem. I never know when it is appropriate to do so."

I patted her shoulder. "You want to convince Axel to help Mathew." I led her back to the courthouse. "Why don't we see where this goes with him first. Maybe you won't need to, and Mathew will be okay."

"You don't just recover from a Vampire bite." She opened the door to the courthouse. We crossed the lobby together and made it to the doors of the courtroom. "It haunts you for the rest of your life, and you have no idea what happened. PTSD without knowing your fear." She opened the door and let me in first. We then sat down at our table.

The judge came back only minutes later with the jury. Both Rhett and Luther's lawyer Nickols, gave their speeches to the jury explaining what they think the final verdict should be. Nickols was known for talking to one person for only minutes, and it has won him many cases. This, however, wasn't just some case. We believed in Rhett Suez because he knew how to smooth talk to people. His voice so smooth with every word coming out of his mouth, I wasn't sure if that was the lawyer in him or the god. I smiled as he finished up, and the jury smiled. Now they had to leave for a second time. Rhett sat down with us. "Don't you worry. I have a strong feeling that we are going to win this."

"For Beth." Ashley nodded. "And Saidie." She reached back to hold the girl's hand.

A few minutes later, the jury came back. One of the jurors stood up and spoke to everyone on their choice, which had won us the case. There we go. Luther was done for.

"Luther Emsworth, you are sentenced to prison for third-degree murder." The judge spoke out after the juror sat back down in his seat. Two city cops came down the walkway, who had grabbed him and took him away. He gave us glares on the way out. It was finally over; we had won. I let out a deep sigh. "We did it." We were finally released from the room, and we went right into Rhett's office in another part of the building.

"Good job in there, everyone." Rhett shook Ashley's hand and then Mathew's. "It was nice to meet you, Detective Dawson." He shook my hand last. "You have two good officers working by your side."

I thanked him. We had then left his office and made our way outside. Oliver was waiting for us, along with Roxann and Saidie.

"Thank you!" Saidie hugged Ashley. "Thank you for helping Beth."

Ashley hugged the teen girl back. "You are very welcome, Saidie. Now, why don't we all get the hell out of this city?"

I drove back with Oliver while Ashley took Roxann, Saidie, and Mathew. "I'm worried about locking up a Vampire like that."

"Oh, trust me, he will be back. There is no way Axel is letting one of his own stay in there." Oliver pulled down the ramp and onto the road that would lead us back into Golden Loch. "Axel is going to be biding his time until he can get Luther out of there."

I sat back in my seat. "We can all get some real sleep now." I drifted off into a nap.

I felt a shoulder pushing me to wake. "Hey." A woman's voice. I rubbed my eyes; I was lying on my chair by the fire. "Ruby." I jolted awake, standing immediately.

"Hey, calm yourself." She handed me a cup of tea. "Everything is okay. Luther is gone and Oliver brought you in, not wanting to disturb your sleep."

I breathed and sat myself down. Everything had suddenly come back to me. I realized that we had finally ended things and that this case was over.

Joseph was standing by the fire with Keiko. He turned to me and nodded. "Good job in there, Frankie. You did good."

"Is Jacquelynn here or with Bailey and Jean?" I wanted to know that my daughter was okay.

"She is with Mr. and Mrs. Wilson." Ruby informed me. "I figured it would be for the best tonight."

"She is okay then." I glanced down at my tea.

"Why wouldn't she be?" Ruby asked. "If this is about Mathew, you don't need to worry. Ashley is taking care of it. She wants you to rest a bit. Let her take over from here."

I finally took a sip of my tea. "Tomorrow, I will see her, then." I got up and handed Ruby the cup. "I should go to bed and get some real rest." I went down the hallway and got settled in bed. Luther was gone for now. Knowing this, I closed my eyes, but that did not mean he wouldn't be back.

Chapter 21

I woke up, feeling rested. This was the day I was going to spend with Jacquelynn. I wanted to take her to breakfast, and then we would go into Detroit to get Ruby signed over to me so she can finally have a family. I was also planning on fixing the steps to the front porch as well before someone fell through and got hurt. My main concern was Jacquelynn, but anyone could fall through. I got out of bed and put on some casual clothing. I peeked into the bedroom to where Ruby was sleeping and saw Keiko in a chair next to the bedside. She waved to me, and I waved back. I put my finger to my mouth, telling her not to say anything. I walked into the bathroom to comb my hair and then trim my face. My beard was starting to get long as I had not kept up with it since we had moved here, so I decided to clean myself up now. I cleared out the sink, shut the light out, and walked down the hallway. Joseph was standing outside against a porch post, so I grabbed my jacket and walked out to him. "What are you doing?"

"Waiting for you." He looked at me. "You slept late."

"What?" I looked at the time on my phone. "It's only nine. That is not very late." I then remembered I don't have a car. I let out a deep sigh, and as if on cue, Oliver pulled in with my SUV. He got out and handed me the keys. "Addi apologizes for what happened. She feels bad, but she had a good reason."

I shook my head, patted Oliver on the shoulder, and went to the SUV. "I plan on spending the day with my daughter, so thank you for fixing it up."

Oliver followed me to the car. "No issue at all, Detective. Oh, and here." He handed me a box.

"What is it?" I asked.

"Just open it, and you will see." He started down the path to the road. "See you later." He disappeared behind the trees.

I looked up at Joseph. "Let me know when Ruby wakes. Today is the day."

Joseph had a huge smile on his face. "You are really going forward with your plans."

I got into the SUV and stared at the box that Oliver had given me. I hesitated before I opened it and found a whistle with the symbol of beta on it. I opened the glove box, putting it inside. I was not really sure what I would need with something like that. I shut the glove box, leaving it in there. I then drove down the gravel path and onto the road. I was starting to enjoy the scenery of trees. This was the best part of having this lake house. I was in isolation and surrounded by trees everywhere.

I turned down the road towards Wilson's farm. Once I reached their house, I drove up to the front door, careful not to hit any livestock. I turned the SUV off, ready to get out, but heard someone come outside. There she was, my daughter. I smiled as she came running to the SUV. She opened the door to the car and got into the back seat. "Hi, Daddy."

"Hey, Pumpkin. How was your day with Snow?" I asked her.

"We had a whole sleepover!" She put her seatbelt on. "And I think he is starting to really like me."

Bailey and Jean walked up to the car. I rolled the window down. "Thank you for everything. You have both been a huge help."

Bailey waved to Jacquelynn. "It is no problem, Jacquelynn can come by anytime she wants."

Jean agreed, taking her husband's arm. "It is nice to have an excited kid around here again."

I reached into my pocket, getting out my wallet. "Please, let me give you something."

Bailey rejected my offer. "Really, it is not a problem. Please keep your money."

Jean agreed with him. "Let us know when you need to drop her off again. She is very pleasant to have and well behaved."

I turned to Jacquelynn in the backseat. "Alright, Pumpkin, let's get breakfast." I waved to Bailey and Jean as we backed away from the house and made our way down the road. "How's school been?"

She glanced out the window. "I like it."

I saw the way she looked out that window. She made that face when she wasn't happy. Her eyebrows bushed together, but her mouth formed a smile. "What is wrong?"

She shook her head.

"Pumpkin…" I pulled over to the side of the road. I climbed into the backseat, sitting next to her. "What is it?"

She gripped at her shirt. "The other kids don't like me because you are a police officer." She leaned into my side. "They said that I should go back to Miami."

I wrapped my arm around her. "You don't let them bother you."

"I know, but you are working so hard." She looked up at me; tears were rolling down her face. "You are a hero, Daddy."

I held her tight while we sat there in silence for a few minutes. My heart was breaking for her, she needed me emotionally, and I had not been there.

She shifted and wiped her eyes. "Food now?"

I gave her a nod, pushing her hair behind her ear. "We will get something good. Malcolm is letting us come back."

She sat in her seat. "Then, we go to his diner."

She was like her mother that way. Always ready to spill everything and then turn around as if it didn't happen. It always hurt me, knowing they were feeling broken inside. I got back into the drivers' seat. "Then we go and get something to eat." I was going to do everything to make her happy again, no matter what.

We walked into the diner, and it seemed to be pretty busy this morning. Payton immediately greeted us at the door. "Good morning, Detective." She grabbed two menus. "This way." She led us down the aisle and sat us in a booth. "What can I start you off with to drink?"

"Coffee, black. Thank you." I saw Jacquelynn looking over the menu drinks. "Apple juice." She then chose.

Payton wrote them down. "A few minutes, then?" She walked away and into the back.

"Did you catch the killer?" Jacquelynn asked me.

I raised my hands. "We did, he is gone." I looked up when Payton handed us our drinks. "I will be back in a moment to see what you would like." She went away again.

"That means the good guys won again." Jacquelynn's shoulders went up. She seemed happier than ten minutes ago. "And you are the good guy."

I sipped my coffee. "That I am." I motioned Payton over, and we both ordered pancakes with extra syrup.

"Just like when Mommy was here." She shifted in her seat. "Pancakes for breakfast."

"Just like how Mommy would want them." I patted her head. "She would be setting up for the extra syrup if she were here right now." I started putting down napkins.

"More, Daddy." Jacquelynn giggled. "Mommy made sure the table was covered."

I let her put more napkins down on the table. She was happy when she thought about her mother, and that was all I wanted for her. Her mother was supposed to be a good memory.

Payton came back minutes later with our food and put it on the table. "Looks like you are ready to go, Jacquelynn." She knelt towards Jacquelynn.

My daughter's head bobbed up and down so fast. "Mommy is watching us. She will probably want some too."

Payton looked at me and smiled. "Enjoy, guys." She then stood to leave.

"Mommy says to enjoy the good food." Jacquelynn said to me as I picked up my fork.

"I am sure she is sitting here with us right now." I cut into Jacquelynn's pancakes. "Now, here is the syrup." I let her pour it over herself.

"This is the best part." She watched it go onto the pancakes. "We should have invited Ruby."

"Ruby was busy late last night. We will bring some home for her."

She started eating as did I. Jacquelynn talked of Snow and how she was getting better at riding him. She talked of how she loved the farm and that Sarah and Gage were always helpful to her. She spoke of how she brushed Snow every single day. She couldn't wait to climb on top of the saddle and ride him when she was there, and she wanted to make sure he was always happy.

After breakfast, we bought an extra set of pancakes. We drove back to the house to leave them on the kitchen table so Ruby would have them when she woke. After, I took Jacquelynn with me into Detroit. When we arrived, she seemed excited to be in a city again.

"It isn't like Miami." She looked at me, disappointed.

"It really isn't." We were at the city's government office. "Detroit and Miami are very different from one another." I led her inside the brick building. "Hold my hand, Pumpkin." The ceiling, floor, desk, chairs, and walls were all made of stained oak. The teen boy at the desk asked us what we needed.

"We need to speak to a judge about adopting this young woman." I put the paperwork onto the desk. "Her name is Ruby."

He grabbed the paperwork and then typed it on the computer. "Sign here." He printed a form. "And here." I signed in both places before he led us into a private room. The door shut behind us, and I let my daughter have the only chair in front of the desk. This room was also made up of stained oak ask well.

"Ruby is going to be so happy." Jacquelynn bounced in her chair. "And I get a sister."

A man walked in. He was wearing a suit, but I figured he was a judge. He looked at the forms. "You are serious about adopting this young woman?"

I nodded. "I am."

"You are a Detective from Miami." He read aloud. "I will have to do a background check." He made some phone calls. I hushed Jacquelynn, making sure she wasn't going to start talking.

After about what seemed like forever, but was probably only twenty minutes, he signed off on the paperwork. I pulled out my wallet.

"Do you have a check?" He asked me for an amount.

I wrote down the amount on the check that he had asked me for and handed it over.

"Then Ruby is now a Dawson." He declared. "Give me a minute to get you a copy of the paperwork." He left the room to find a copier.

"I have a sister now!" Jacquelynn jumped up out of the chair and hugged me. "Ruby is going to be happy."

I got a phone call. "It's Ashley." I told Jacquelynn to quiet her down. "Hey, Ash." I answered the phone. She told me she had a lead on where Elizabeth might be. "You do?" She then told me that she wanted me to meet her as soon as I could. We were going to do a search with Oliver. Mathew wasn't coming this time as he was resting. I agreed with her. "I have to go. I'm in the middle of an adoption." I then hung up before she could answer.

The judge came back in and handed me the paperwork. "Congratulations Mr. Dawson, you are now the father of Ruby."

I thanked him before taking Jacquelynn back outside. "Let's get home then. Ruby will like this."

We pulled up to the house and found Ruby sitting outside with Keiko and Joseph.

"Sorry, I didn't call." Joseph said to me. "I figured it was better that way, to leave you be."

I shrugged, he was here with Keiko and Ruby, so it was fine. "You'll have to heat up your pancakes, but we figured not leaving you out of this family endeavor. We left them on the counter for you."

She looked at me oddly. "Thanks?" She stood up and went inside. Jacquelynn followed her. She promised to keep it a secret for now.

"Well?" Joseph asked me. "Did you do it?"

I showed him the folder. "Of course. I will show it to her later. Right now, I have to meet Ashley and Oliver at Ash's home. They have a lead on where Elizabeth might be."

"You go find her then." Joseph seemed to be happy with that. I walked back to my SUV and hid the folder under my seat. I was going to show her, but not yet.

Chapter 22

Arriving at Ashley's house, Oliver was standing out front. I wasn't sure what had his attention, but it wasn't me. I got out and walked up to him. "Smell something?"

He waved me to go inside, not answering my question. I shrugged, pushing the front door open. "Ash?"

"In here!" She called to me from the living room. I heard Bruce grunting, and I looked to see if Joseph was here, but he wasn't. When I went into the living room, I saw her crating Bruce. "Bruce doesn't like Oliver very much."

"He smells like a wolf." I answered.

"Right, and this old dog is territorial." She led me back to the kitchen.

Oliver had come in. "I am not going to get in a fight with your dog." He fell into a chair at the kitchen table. "What's our plan of attack?"

"I figured you turn into a wolf, and we follow your nose." Ashley told him. She made her way to the sink, clearing it out and putting a few dishes into the dishwasher. "We have an idea of where she might be."

"Who called?" I then asked them.

"Anonymous call." Ashley, she had shut the dishwasher and turned it on. "Could be anyone."

"Did you trace the call?" She must have.

"Yes, which is where we are going first. It came from the cabin." She seemed sure about that. "Then we go down to Luther's. The caller said she was there."

"So, we know she is definitely around." Oliver admitted. "There is no way she is dead. I saw her, and someone has seen her too. That can't be a coincidence."

"That much seems to be true." Now we just had to track her down. It sounded much easier than it was going to be. She could be anywhere in town by now.

Ashley touched my arm and then leaned towards Oliver. "Let's get out there and find her then, boys. We are wasting time hanging around my house." She led us both out the front door and into her Ferrari. "Time to find Beth." She started up her car and backed out of the driveway and into the street. We didn't talk much during the drive down to the bridge. I was thinking of what I was going to say when we met her. Ashley and Oliver knew her well enough, but seeing a new face probably wasn't on her list of ideas she wanted to do. Was she okay? No. Elizabeth had been pushed to her death.

I followed Ashley down the dirt path and into the woods. Oliver was in his wolf form, leading the way to the cabin. The girl Diana was not there, and the cat was sleeping on the floor. Oliver sniffed around, looking for anything that he could. He grunted at us. Ashley and I looked at one another with no idea what that meant. He ran down the hallway and into the bathroom. He sniffed around and growled before running outside. In seconds he was gone, before Ashley and I could follow him out.

"Hold on. I think he is turning back so he can chat with us." Ashley stopped me before I could follow him into the woods. Oliver then came back moments later.

"She was here. It was very recent, but she is gone now." Oliver sighed. "It is almost like they wanted us to come here." He turned around to head back into the woods.

"They as in the Vampires, or as in Luther?" I asked. I started to follow him, with Ashley behind me.

"They as in the Vampires. I don't smell anyone else. The last person here was Diana and Luther, but that was days ago when we stopped by." Oliver explained. "They are probably keeping her somewhere." That was good to know. Luther wasn't here, and he hadn't gotten out of prison.

"We head to Luther's home then." Ashley motioned deeper into the woods.

"That castle, you mean." I stopped walking.

"Don't freeze up on me, Frankie." She grabbed my arm and pulled me forward. "We need you. Send Joseph inside."

I called Joseph to us. "Frankie."

"Do you mind poking around in the castle? We need to make sure Elizabeth isn't there." I asked.

"Will do, my friend." He disappeared.

"He is going inside to poke around. We will wait out here then." I looked at Ashley. "If you wanted Joseph to take a look, why didn't you just ask me to have him come here while we looked in the cabin?"

"I wasn't sure how far Joseph could get from you." She shrugged. "We are here now, so when he comes back with information, we can go up to the doors."

"They dragged me across the floor and forced me into a dark room, remember? You are crazy if you think I will go in there." I was not prepared to go back inside the house of a bunch of maniacs.

"I am going to go through the backside." Oliver told me. "You will stay out here. If someone sees you, you let Ashley know."

I let out a sigh of relief. "I won't have to go in then."

Joseph came back. "She isn't here."

I looked at Ashley and gave a nod. "He says that she isn't here."

"Then, they have nothing to hide." Ashley made her way towards the castle.

Oliver followed her. "Stay here, Frankie." He ran towards the back.

"They do know what happened to you, right?" Joseph leaned on a tree. "Torture."

I sat down in the grass. "Oh, I reminded them, but Ash is a Half-Demon, and Oliver is a Werewolf. They have abilities that they can use to save themselves."

Joseph let the silence drag out after that. I knew he wasn't upset. He thought that talking to the dead was way better than turning into some wolf or even having a demon as a father. "Look, Frankie, don't pity yourself like that. You and I are great together. We have done so much good. Just because you can't go up against a Vampire does not make you any less than them."

I looked up to him. "I can't even talk to my own wife." I know I shouldn't beat myself up over it, but that didn't make it hurt any less. I barely took my time to grieve for her. I got out of Miami the first chance I could.

Joseph sat down in the grass next to me. "We are going to find her one day, and you and I will talk to her. I promised you that."

We both sat in silence after that. From the moment we found out Layla was sick and up until her death, we had made the most of every moment. The very last time she was hospitalized, I took Jacquelynn to see her every day. I wanted her to remember her mom as much as she could. I did not want her to think that her mom was leaving her on purpose. I explained why her mother was never coming home again. I told her that one day, she would be able to talk to her. I didn't go into detail about necromancy, but I did let her know that her mother was watching her. I was sure that Layla was around; she was just not reachable right now, and Joseph couldn't see her.

Ashley came running out to me with Oliver behind her. Oliver had already turned back, and they both explained that Elizabeth was here not too long ago. That meant she was still in town, and there was still a chance we could find her. It was, however, getting late. We needed to head back before the sun went down, and Axel sent his Vampires after us.

"You look drained." Ashley spoke to me from the front seat of the car. I was sitting in the back behind Oliver.

"It has been quite a day." I reminded her. "We just need to try again tomorrow."

Oliver shifted in his seat. "We may never get the closure we want." He bit his lip, shaking his head. "I hate saying that, but wherever she is, she is probably okay."

Ashley turned hard on the corner of her street. "Stay the night." She told us both. "That way, we can get started first thing." We were about to get out of the car when Ashley's phone rang.

She let the person on the other end speak. "Okay. Thank you so much." She hung her phone up. "Guess who is your new Captain."

Oliver and I both congratulated her at the same time. "You deserve this." I told her. "Really."

"We celebrate then." Oliver got out of the car. "I will drive since I probably have a better tolerance level then the two of you combined."

Once at the bar, we sat at a table talking about how Ashley has done such a great job. She was the best this town had, and we were going to have a celebration along with a toast to that. We called Mathew to come out to join us. In addition to being a celebration of her promotion, we were celebrating the closing of the case. Ashley and Mathew had thanked me for helping them put Luther away. I told them that I was going to be pulling the folder out of Ashley's new desk and working on solving those cases that never got a chance once things returned to our town's normal. She was okay with me doing so as she wanted to empty that folder as much as I did. Not much happens here, as they have said, at least on the surface. Humans around here were not aware of what really went on in this town. It made me feel sad for Mathew. He was going to work with me now on solving crimes, and I had to work as if I was also human. This was nothing new, but I was just starting to get used to the idea of being able to solve a crime in this town with Joseph. We talked about how Mathew was feeling, and he said he was doing so much better. Ashley wouldn't tell me what she did to help remedy his bite, so that was something we could talk about at a later date. I checked the time and stood up. "I really need to get back. Jacquelynn and Ruby are waiting."

Oliver took my arm. "Then, we go." He led me out the front door. "How long has it been since you went to a bar, Frankie?"

"Last time was before Jacquelynn was born." I answered. We got in the truck and started to leave. We made it about ten minutes down the road. We were just about to pull into the gravel drive of my home when Ashley called me.

"Hey, I know you are probably just about home, but turn around and get back here." She told me. "You will not guess who just walked into the bar."

I hung up. "Ashley says we need to go back. She said she ran into someone at the bar. I have a feeling that this is important."

Oliver grunted. "If you say so." He turned around quickly and made his way back.

We had got back to the bar and found Ashley standing outside with a woman with sandy brown hair and white highlights who was wearing a beanie hat on her head along with a white t-shirt and jeans. The woman's boot heels clicked on the sidewalk as Ashley led her towards us. "Frankie, meet Elizabeth."

I swallowed hard, was this true? She looked like nothing ever happened to her. Her green eyes told a whole different story, though. "Hello."

"Beth, this is Detective Frankie Dawson. He came here to- well you know." Ashley looked at Oliver. Mathew started walking across the parking lot to us.

"I'll see you tomorrow, Ash." Mat patted her shoulder. He was a bit intoxicated. Oliver shoved him into his truck. "You are not walking home, friend." He then drove off with Mathew.

"You can say it, Ash. I know I died." She admitted. "It is okay. I am not afraid of talking about it. However, you may want to talk to Mat tomorrow about this."

"He is so out of it, he won't remember." Ashley assured her. "Tell Frankie what you told me."

Elizabeth looked me up and down. "You were the one who got rid of Luther then." She looked up into the starry sky. "Have you ever loved someone so much that you would do whatever it takes to be with them forever?"

I gave a sympathetic smile. "I do understand that. My wife was my everything. I would have loved to be with her for the rest of my life."

"Then, you understand why I did what I did." Her eyes came back to mine. "I was not expecting it to be Luther. I was hoping Felix would have taken the leap himself." She shrugged. "He didn't want to bestow that fate on me, though."

"Oliver said the one who bites, then kills you, and brings you back is your sire." I was sure that was how it worked.

"He is right. That is why Felix wouldn't do it. He respected me, and my free will too much. He didn't want to take it away. However, Luther found out about it, and we were friends…until he pushed me over." She rubbed her arm. "And now I am dead, and I can never see my sister again. I didn't think it would be like this."

Ashley put her arm around Elizabeth. "Just know that Luther cannot bother you ever again."

She tried to smile at Ashley but was struggling. "Thanks, Ash. I still feel his energy pulling me in. I cannot escape him."

Ashley comforted her some more. There was nothing we were going to say or do that would make her feel perfectly one-hundred-percent okay.

"I think I will be okay." She looked at the bar. "I have to get to work." She pointed to the bar. "It is the perfect way to make money without coming out during the day."

Ashley and I let her go into the bar. "She is going to be fine." She took my arm.

I agreed. "I think so too."

Ashley and I walked back to her house. This case was now closed, and there was nothing left for us to do except know that Luther is away, and Elizabeth is fine. She was going to move on with her life, even if that wasn't what Saidie or any of us wanted, but it is the best that she can do for herself. She had to make a new name for herself, and Saidie couldn't be a part of that. As much as I regret it, Ashley told me that was how things had to go. We could never tell the humans what we were, and we stuck to that rule.

Chapter 23

After getting to Ashley's house, I called Ruby and explained that I would be home tomorrow. I had fallen asleep on Ashley's couch that night. The very next morning, after waking up, she brought me coffee, and we sat on the couch, discussing how we were going to tell Saidie. What were we to say? We had to tell her that we found her sister's body, but we couldn't take her to see her. Saidie had to accept that she was never going to see Elizabeth again.

"We can't talk on the matter after this." Ashley told me. "Especially with Mat around the office." She put her cup down on her side table. "I also need to tell you something."

"What is that?" I asked.

"I knew since the day you walked into the office." She told me. "I knew who you were, and I knew what you were capable of doing. I knew you were a Necromancer. However, you didn't seem to know about me, so I let it go."

"Why didn't you tell me then?" My eyes hit my coffee cup.

"Because if I said, 'Hi Frankie, my name is Ashley, and I'm a Half-Demon.' I am almost certain you would not have taken me seriously. You weren't ready."

"And why did Oliver think I was?" I looked her in the eyes. "Was it because I ran into the Elves trap?"

She shrugged. "You were opening up about yourself, and I guess Oliver thought he wanted to help you. He wanted to tell you what he knew, and since you were already part of this world, he must have figured telling you about himself would make the case come into the light." She stood up. "I'm sorry."

I sighed. "It is fine, Ash. Just no more secrets, okay?"

She agreed, walking to the closet. "Okay. We should probably visit Saidie then." She handed me my jacket. "Come on."

We had knocked on the door when we got to Saidie's home. The kitchen light turned on, and Saidie answered the door. "Hey."

"Good news, Saidie." Ashley told her.

"What is that?" Saidie asked, her eyes lit up.

"We found your sister." I figured that Ashley and I would tell Saidie together.

Saidie's eyes filled with tears. "Let me see her." She hugged Ashley.

"We can't." I saw how upset Ashley looked when she hugged Saidie back.

"Why?" She looked up at Ashley. "Please."

"It's best if you didn't. You should remember her for who she was." Ashley assured Saidie. "It is better this way."

Saidie looked at me. "Do you think so, Detective Dawson?"

"She is right, Saidie." I put my hand out. "Your sister is going to be fine."

Saidie wiped her tears. "Thank you for telling me."

Ashley smiled sympathetically. "Why don't we talk?" She looked at me. "Chat later."

I took that as a signal to see my family. I'm sure they would be happy to have me back home for a little while.

When I entered the house, I found Ruby sitting on the couch while Jacquelynn was doodling in a book on the rug. "Ruby." I sat down in my chair.

Jacquelynn sat up and watched as I handed Ruby the folder. "I want you to have this."

She looked at the folder. "It's my folder, the one from the state. Why should I have this?"

"Open it." I encouraged her. "You never know what you will find."

She hesitated before slowly opening it up. She read it to herself a few times before she jumped out of her chair. "Are you serious?" She leaned forward. "Can I hug you then?"

I got up and put my arms out. "Yes."

Ruby embraced me into a hug, and Jacquelynn joined in. "We are a family, Ruby." Jacquelynn had told her.

"I guess you are right." She put a hand on her new little sister's head.

"Alright, family, who wants to help me fix up the steps out front?" I asked.

Jacquelynn raised her hand. "Me!" She looked at Ruby. "Raise your hand!"

Ruby laughed, raising her hand. "Family, then."

Jacquelynn ran out of the room quickly and then went out the front door.

"Ruby Dawson has a ring to it." I put my hand on her back. "Come on, before Jacquelynn comes back and drags us out there.

Epilogue

I promise you my story isn't over; it can't be. Life goes on as usual. I have a new family. If my wife saw my daughter and I now, she would probably smile at us. She would say that Ruby was meant to be here with us. Fate had put Jacquelynn and me here. I was here for the last few weeks so I could help Ruby, Ashley, Elizabeth, and everyone else. Miami used to be home, but Golden Loch is starting to become the new place we would call home. I had a good job, and I was very thankful for my new daughter. We did everything as three from that day forward. Whenever we did housework, we did it as a team. I guess, in a way, this was the course that my life was to take. You can't control every aspect, but you can choose what you do with it.

About the Author

Dana Macellaro lives in the suburbs of Philadelphia, Pennsylvania. She lives in a house with her two cats, Cosmo and Chaka. She works full time in a bakery and writes part time. Her dream is to become successful enough to write full time and visit conventions with her books. She draws her inspiration from authors Michael Connelly (Author of the Harry Bosch series), Kelley Armstrong (Author of the Otherworld series), and Karen Charlton (Author of the Detective Lavender series).

The Disappearance of Elizabeth Keaton is the first book of this series and there is hope for at least a few more books to come. If you enjoyed this book, please leave a positive review on Amazon or GoodReads. Look for book 2, Fate of the Dragon to be released in the new year.

Follow on Facebook: Dana Macellaro – Author

About the Book

Frankie Dawson and his daughter Jacquelynn have moved from Miami, Florida to Golden Loch, Michigan for work. There he is greeted by his partner Ashley Aequitas and Lieutenant Mathew Reames. They work together on solving the murder of Elizabeth Keaton, who has been pushed to her death. Frankie, who is a Necromancer, works to uncover what happened to Elizabeth and while doing so he uncovers the secrets that the town is holding. Along the way, he makes friends with Oliver Verda and Ruby who both help him come to his conclusion.